Bruce
and
Albany

In Memoriam:
JAMES P. NAPIER

"We clam the hill thegither
And monie a cantie day, Jim
We've had wi' one anither."
after BURNS

Alistair Macnab

Bruce and Albany

A Public Relations Venture in
14th Century Scotland.

Alistair Macnab

Printed in the United States of America

ISBN 979-8-89114-027-1 (sc)
ISBN 979-8-89114-029-5 (hc)

Library of Congress Control Number: 2023922573

2024.08.28

MainSpring Books
5901 W. Century Blvd
Suite 750
Los Angeles, CA, US, 90045

www.mainspringbooks.com

AUTHOR'S NOTES

The Kingdom of Scotland was a tumultuous place in the 13th and 14th century. After King Alexander III (1249-1286) there was no clear succession to the throne and, in fact, there was no single Ruler until all the pretenders had had a shot at trying to be Monarch, among whom were Robert the Bruce, John Baliol and Queen Margaret (Alexander III's granddaughter from Norway). The Interregnum lasted from 1286 to Bruce's accession in 1306.

Even so, after Bruce and his immediate heirs had ruled the land, between 1306 and 1420 the country was sometimes in the hands of the Regent, the Duke of Albany, and during David II's reign, no other than Edward Baliol (John's son) made life difficult for the young David by challenging him for the crown six times between 1332 and 1346.

Needless to say, the general populace was reasonably unaffected by these dynastic maneuverings largely engineered by the English Kings, Edwards I and II. It is true that there was a serf and servant class in Scotland but the comparatively large number of feu-holding, freemen farmers was significant in the country and artisans, artists, clergy, academics, and merchants in the towns, had created the beginnings of a *middle class* of freemen when compared with other countries in Western Europe.

This book, it must be admitted at the very beginning, is a work of *Historical Fiction*. It has its genesis on the curious and frequent creation and dissolving of the noble title of the Duke of Albany. It has historically been created six times since the 14th Century and at most junctures there were unfortunate circumstances that brought the Dukedom to an end. Always in the gift of the reigning Scottish, then British Monarchs, it was usually bestowed on a close member of the King's family and because there is no estate assigned but a generous annual stipend attached to the title, we can surmise that the entire exercise was designed to remove a troublesome family element from Court without loss of face.

By troublesome, we mean rivalry for the Monarch's throne or perhaps a winning personality that attracts other magnates and subjects to the detriment of the King's exercise of power and may readily cause mischief in times ahead. Then, there is the question of religion. Scotland was to move to a form of Calvinism away from Catholicism. The Stewards/Stewarts/Stuarts who were directly descended from and immediately gained the crown from the Bruces through marriage, remained solidly Catholic which was a strong factor in their falling out of general popularity after Bonny Prince Charlie. Such an exalted title as Albany seemed naturally to go to the head of its bearer and give him thoughts above his station. In most cases the *second son syndrome, or "spare"* often applied.

Each termination of the Dukedom had a history of scandal and included three deaths whilst in the office among whom was Lord Darnley, Queen Mary of Scotland's husband who was blown up at Kirk O' Field in Edinburgh, and an infant who died when only one month old. Two Dukedoms merged with the Crown to the detriment of the existing holders, and the others were either deprived of their status by attaintment, forfeiture, or deprivation owing to grievous circumstances usually associated with espousing regicide, real or imagined.

One of the more recent Dukes of Albany, Prince Leopold of Saxe Coburg Gotha, (Queen Victoria's grandson) lost his title and his sinecure by being a German at the wrong time during the First World War in the 20th century. Today, the title of the Duke of Albany is in the hands of the present monarch of the United Kingdom, King Charles III. Historically it should go to Prince Harry as the King's second son, or even a grandson.

The idea that the concept of the Dukedom of Albany ennobled by King Robert I was tried out first by Murdoch Stewart (1) and is a fabrication of your author which seemed to fit nicely into the story. The reality is that a high position of a Duke who could take the blame for a King's misdemeanours and if not invented in 1307 when the King ennobled our fictitious protagonist, the actual official creation in 1340 was a tacit approval that the idea was a good one. Note also that another Murdoch Stewart (2) followed on 1362 as a Duke of Albany. He was not a blood relative of our fictitious Murdoch but a real-life Stewart and a Bruce in-law.

Your author toyed with the idea that there would be only one Murdoch Stewart but the first Murdoch would have been 75 years old on assuming the title instead of his namesake and in the 14th century there were not too many people who attained that age and anyway, the monarch at the time was the anglophile King David II whose tenure had been tumultuous and forever challenged by the Baliol family, that recruiting a septuagenarian for assistance was unlikely to yield positive results.

So, you see, that I visited most of the angles before setting on the narrative that drives our story forward. Otherwise, the persons are real; the described events are real; only the dates have been adjusted for my own convenience. Even the Murdoch of good fortune is real except for his unexpected ennoblement and subsequent death. His accession to the Lordship of Cumloden, however, is real, and was bestowed for services to King Robert. This honour is in existence to this day.

Times and dates are telescoped or elongated to suit the narrative but as far as research is reliable, all persons surrounding our protagonist are real but, of course, what they say are from this writer's imagination.

As customary, I must admit to reading a great deal whilst researching this subject. So, from the far distant place of Brooklyn New York, I have shamelessly devoured Wikipedia and available books from the Brooklyn Library Association on topics about Scottish royalty, farming, Scottish wars and skirmishes, ocean and coastal shipping, as well as Norwegian influences in Scotland during the Viking period and beyond. I am also indebted to the British Ordinance Survey maps of Galloway and Ayrshire which resurrected treks on foot when I was a teenager over the same ground. Not much has changed as far as the hills, glens, rivers, and lochs are concerned but many small hamlets in the 14th century are thriving towns and villages today. The extraction of limestone, lead, and coal industrial encroachments are now nearly all gone although there was tremendous desecration of the landscape between the second industrial revolution and mid-twentieth century. These commercial depredations arose from their small beginning in the 14th century. Perhaps, we are all the better for the changes. There is a natural wonder and majesty to the Carrick landscape that has no equal although certain places in India and South Africa come close.

With the exception of the weather, of course. Even at the height of summer a cold bleak southwest storm sweeps across the escarpments impregnating the wet mosses and dubs with more moisture to make walking even more tiring. Most of the castles mentioned are nowadays only heaps of stone. Just two have been capably restored to their ruined form when Loch Doon Castle was removed from its island in the middle of Loch Doon and rebuilt on the nearby shore, and Dundonald Castle has been reconditioned to make it more accessible and safe for tourists, I suspect, however, that a visit to a heap of rubble distinguishable with difficulty from the rocky cliff face at Turnberry Castle is hardly worth an interrupted golf round at Mister Trump's palatial Turnberry Golf Resort which is close by.

Lastly, the language spoken by all participants in this book is certainly not as presented on paper. It has been beyond my capabilities to devote time in trying to record social speech as spoken that I decided to write as if the action and the conversations were made today. I apologise for modern solecisms!

I have a guilty feeling about this as my grandparents were some of the last local people to speak in the pure Ancient Scottish Tongue in their daily lives. This fact has imbued me with a passion and understanding of this lilting and expressive language now sadly subsumed by common city and vulgar euphenisms.

Alistair Macnab,
Brooklyn, New York.
Spring 2024

P.S. Please, do not overlook my paper on Scottish poetry and sagas at the end of the book which were the means of broadcasting news to the overall population in the Middle Ages. Sometimes it was scurrilous, sexual, and libellous and often very funny. It is surprising how the popular press has remained largely unchanged through the centuries but that it has and is obviously related to giving the *lumpen proletariat* what they want. Also, stories of patriotism and past heroic deeds are standard fare.

TABLE OF CONTENTS

The Frontispiece is the work of Patrick Bucoy who has perfectly captured the Spirit of 14th Century Scotland.

CHAPTER I

ESCAPE FROM SCOTLAND TO IRELAND

*I would not want it to get around that I used to be self-*conscious about my red hair and being over six feet tall with vivid blue eyes. It was awkward that the ladies tended to favour my ruddy good looks and men always found an unfortunate nickname that disparaged my appearance, but by the end of my teen years I had become inured to it all. There was no doubt that I looked like a foreigner on this small wind-swept excuse for a human habitation.

This piece of bare rock off the north coast of Ulster is called Rathlin Island once occupied by the short, dark, and nomadic Scots who were on their way by boat from Ireland to make a life further north after the Great Ice Sheet had sufficiently receded.

This newly exposed land would eventually take its name after them. It would be called Scotland, but the building of the nation would not be easy. This mountainous space which had already been partly occupied by the Celts, and

Picts in the ice-free areas, and with Angles and Saxons moving overland up the east coast from England, presented an enormous task for any new emigrants.

In fact, many centuries were to pass before just out of my time and a free man, I have been hired by no less than King Robert the Bruce who arrived at Erik's Boatyard in Loch Ryan in Galloway the other day together with his small group of supporters on the way to Ireland. There seemed to be some sort of haste with the entire episode. A suitable new boat, designed in the Viking-manner, was readily available but no seafarers to man her. The King was not pleased.

Erik was apologetic but sending runners to neighbouring villages produced no results for everyone seemed to know that the King and his few followers were trying to flee ahead of a strong band of English troops headed by one of his arch enemies who was bent on revenge after the murder of John Cormyn in Dumfries.

John Cormyn had been appointed by yet another temporary Scottish Assembly as one of **Scotland's Guardians** along with Robert Bruce. Both were rivals for the throne which had been empty for twenty years and disliked each other intensely. But as Guardians imbued no doubt by the popular and patriotic reputation of their predecessor, Sir William Wallace, they carried out their duties. But Wallace had subsequently been betrayed, captured by the English, and barbarically executed in London.

Cormyn and Bruce never really reconciled their personal differences and at a private meeting between the two held in a Dumfries Monastery, Bruce had rejected his role as co-guardian and they had come to blows. and Bruce had left Cormyn fallen and bleeding, but still alive in front of the altar.

On narrating his story of the argument to friends afterwards, one of the King's young knights vowed to complete the deed. He sought out Cormyn and killed him. Thereafter, King Robert was blamed for the murder by King Edward I of England and excommunicated by the Pope in Rome at Edward of England's request.

All this back story was getting around and it seemed that Robert had few sympathizers willing to be associated with him at this stage. The avengers were closing in and no more than a day away when I had a meeting with the King.

"What is your name, young man?" asked the King. "I see you working around the boatyard and sailing in the loch. You seem to be an experienced sailor, are you?"

"Your Majesty," I humbly replied, "My name is Muireadhach."

"Ah! A fellow Gael!"

"Not really, Sire. My mother liked the name. Here in Galloway we have a powerful Norse-Gaelic culture and Gaelic names are quite common."

"You are tall and blue eyed. I can see the Northman in you."

"Thank you, Majesty."

"In fact, that red hair of yours must get you into a lot of trouble!" added the King.

"I would hope not, Sir, but I have often been taken for a Viking."

"Some of my best subjects are formerly Viking warriors. They were great sailors as well. How about you? I have noted you on the loch expertly handling Erik's boats. What do you say?"

"In addition to just completing my five-year boat-building apprenticeship with Erik I have sailed around Loch Ryan and out into the broad Firth, to and back from Ailsa Craig and Holy Island off Arran."

"Have you ever crossed the open sea to Ireland?"

Sensing where this conversation was heading, I replied:

"No Sire, but I'd like to. Is that where you are going? over the years we have sold many boats to gentlemen and merchants desirous of making the crossing to Ulster and I have longed to go with them."

"What is your family name, Muireadhach?"

"I only have one name. We are a little backward in our part of the wild Merrick Plateau, but I am a free man. My mother is a wee bit landholder at Craigencallie, Loch Dee in the Wigtown District." I added, "And I'm free of my Apprenticeship to Erik. Please ask him!"

"I am talking to you. Muireadhach, will you join me and sail my boat to Ireland?"

"Yes Sire!" I enthusiastically responded.

"We'll need some sort of title for you. How about King's Boatmaster?" Robert raised his eyebrows and looked me straight in the eyes. For the first time I noted his eyes were blue and his hair was long and yellow. There was obviously a trace of Viking in the past of King Robert the Bruce. "When you are not engaged with boats you shall be the King's Page. How about it?"

For a moment I was speechless but quickly recovered.

"Your Majesty commands and I am at your service, Sire."

So here I am, on Rathlin Island having brought the King of Scotland and his small band of followers away from Scotland and out of the reach of his enemies. We had originally set sail for my Lord Coleraine's domain at the mouth of the river Lagan, but currents and tide had directed our course towards Rathlin Island, somewhat shy of our intended landing.

The King seemed unworried about the change in plans and as he said, *'I have cousins in the Bissett family'* which was the name of the family that occupied the only castle on the island. The other occupants of our boat were glad to have a shortened trip in the open sea, for just as soon as we had cleared Southend at the Mull of Kintyre the choppy nature of the ocean had caused our stout boat to rise and fall as a series of Atlantic swells and a fresh breeze continually beset us. There was not one sailor among them!

Approaching the rocky inlet that was just below the castle I could see that it was going to be a tricky manoeuvre. I managed with difficulty to bring our boat in just off the stone pier and was wondering how I would ever bring us alongside when a lone old man on the dock shouted to me that this berth was treacherous and unsafe but there was a good, safe dock in the next inlet. I managed to make a complete turn-around and headed back out just almost striking the jagged rocks on the lee side.

The next inlet was an altogether wider and sheltered bay. Having rounded the rocky headland that separated the two bays we immediately sighted a substantial pier populated by workers engaged in removing cargo from a ketch berthed alongside the dock. Compared to steering in the unruly sea outside, the berthing alongside the jetty was extremely easy. We tied up astern of the ketch heading outwards and were all secure to the jetty in no time at all.

A functionary of Lord Bissett greeted us and learning who was on board requested that we delay our landing for one hour so that the family could prepare a more formal welcome. On learning this, King Robert dismissed the idea and declared that we would proceed to the castle at once.

Accordingly, our welcome was a subdued one. Lord Bissett himself met King Robert at the postern gate of the castle with a warm salute. We were then ushered into a large reception room located just off the main hall. Here, a fire was in the process of being set in the huge fireplace and the magnificent tapestries that hung around the walls were damp and frayed. A large four-poster bed was located in the middle of the floor and some small chairs and divans were scattered here and there around the room's perimeter.

Bruce and Bissett went off to have a private discussion and the rest of us were left to fend for ourselves. Fortunately, the castle steward soon arrived along with several servants bearing refreshments, so we settled down comfortably, mostly on the worn, carpeted floor to await developments. I was just deciding to take advantage of the last of the daylight to go back to our boat and tidy her up when the King returned with the news that My Lord Bissett was going to throw a magnificent banquet tomorrow evening in honour of the King to which we were all invited to meet many of the Ulster gentry who had been invited as well. In the meantime, we would be free to wander about the castle and to use its facilities.

The senior gentlemen of our group included our Sovereign's two brothers, Sir Thomas and Sir Alexander naturally co-opted the bed while the lesser nobility seized the divans close to the fire which had caught and was now blazing finely. The rest of us were in the process of finding a less-draughty location on the carpet when Sir Thomas said to me that I was to sleep in the hallway outside the chamber door to act as a guard when we had retired for the night.

So much for a royal appointment which represented a stone floor in a draughty hallway!

Next morning saw me down at the boat to finish the job of making her tidy and ready for whatever the King had in mind for me. I was working on a mast fitting in the bottom of the boat below the bulwark and out of sight from the dock when I overheard two men talking.

"She's a fine craft" said one to the other.

"I'll say," replied the other, "Looks new as well. I bet she's built at Cairn Ryan by the look of her Norwegian style" he added knowingly

"Where did she come from?" enquired speaker A.

"From Scotland, I bet" was the answer. "They say the King of Scotland has arrived here to recruit an invasion force to conquer his kingdom."

"Hell. No! We have enough problems here in Ireland. We don't need to be fighting for anyone else!" The reply was fierce.

"What can we do?" enquired speaker A.

"I know. Let us get the brothers together and attack them all as they are drunkenly sleeping after the banquet tonight. We can do it! There are at least one hundred of our boyos would welcome such action!"

"Do you think so?" Speaker A was clearly doubtful.

"Of course, we can ...and should" was the reply. "Go off to the mainland right away. catch the boat from the Island Harbour. Instruct them that they are to come over in small groups looking like merchants. I'll be waiting at the pier, and we'll plan our course of attack. The King of Scotland! Won't that be a splendid prize, Dead or Alive. Think of the ransom!"

After going into some more detail, Speaker B hastened away. I did not dare to put my head above the gunwale in case they would see me, so I did not budge until they were clearly away.

Asking around on the dock if anyone had seen or identified the plotters, no one seemed to have been observant or even care. I hastened to the King with my news.

The King quickly assembled his advisers with the intention of addressing this new problem. The outcome was that we would attend the Banquet then sail immediately in the dark back to Scotland far away from Galloway and seek shelter somewhere on the Western Islands. On enquiring if I were comfortable with night-time sailing, I replied that a good full moon was all that I needed and a fair wind from the west.

The King said: "It will be well into daylight by the time we get anywhere even with a following wind. I propose we make for Holy Isle in Lamlash Bay on Arran."

He looked at me directly, and I recalled that I had mentioned that very place when boasting of my sailing prowess.

This arrangement was acceptable to all. Thus, was it arranged that by being cautious with the whisky and inclining only to the beer, we would all be in good shape to sneak out of the castle at midnight or so and embark on our night-time sailing adventure.

That afternoon Lord Bissett had arranged for some sporting games to entertain us. I particularly enjoyed the bow-and-arrow contest because for some reason I have a good eye and a natural skill for archery. I was winning in the contest against the King's lords and some archers from the castle security team when one of the Irish men came to me and enquired where I had been taught to be such a great marksman with the long bow? I replied that it was simply a natural talent. He was impressed.

"You must thank God for the gift." He spoke.

"I do." I replied, "but I have little use for such a gift except for playing in games."

"You will never know when you will need your prowess in more serious circumstances. How old are you, Boy?" the gentleman added.

"I am going to be twenty next week." I volunteered.

"Then you have a brilliant future ahead of you. I see the King favours you."

And with that we continued the archery contest. I was to find out later that this gentleman was the Bishop of Armagh who was a brother-in law of Lord Bissett.

I was the winner in archery but since I never participated in any of the other games my victory was largely overlooked at the end of the day. It was becoming dark when we ceased playing and went back to our quarters to prepare for the banquet.

I had never been present at such a distinguished gathering as My Lord Bissett's banquet in honour of King Robert of Scotland. Most of the barons and other landowners from Ulster were present and I would never have been in attendance as a mere sailor except that His Majesty has apparently taken further interest in my presence and declared that when I was not practicing my seamanship, I was to be a Page Boy and Body Servant to his Majesty. While I was completely honoured by this sudden good fortune, I soon found that my job was mainly to be ready with a bucket every time the King desired to relieve himself which was quite often during the lengthy banquet. There were many toasts in recognition of the great Lords who were present. All this quaffing meant that my piss-bucket duties were in great demand.

I had been given a fine costume from some source. It was made of green velvet with cap to match. Knee britches and silk stockings completed the outfit although my working shoes were not entirely appropriate, I soon found myself standing by the Lords and Ladies but within earshot of my Master yet just out of sight with four other young men who were engaged on similar duties as was I but for their own Masters.

As the banquet progressed, I found myself with the other pages who were like me, to attend to their Masters' personal matters. Two of my new companions were sons of courtiers and the other two were actually Knights' Squires in training. But what surprised me was their casual gossip of their Masters' sexual activities. In many respects, they were worse than common labourers with the coarseness of their language, I refrained from participating in this type of conversation eventually my companions noted that I was silent.

We then got to talking among ourselves on other topics. The others were most intrigued that I was in the King's service and wanted to know more. As it happened, I was quite ignorant of any protocols or duties that had just been bestowed upon me but perhaps the paucity of my answers only laid the ground for a reputation of discretion. I was quite the tallest red-headed boy in our little group, and it suddenly struck me that I was also a person of some rank even as a piss bucket carrier by Royal Appointment to the King of Scotland. Servants automatically took on the rank of their Master and my Master outranked them all.

The Supper was over, and the grand speeches all made. It came as a shock to some of my own Scottish party and me to discover that the Northern Irish were the original Scots and it was they who had settled Scotland and begun the steady progress to civilization. Scottish Christianity had been brought to our land from Ireland that signalled the eventual decline of the earlier non-Christian Pictish settlers.

Many of the younger men present then settled down to steady and copious drinking. I must confess that I drifted off to slumber several times but always managed to hear my Lord call whenever he needed me. Other Lords noticed me and beckoned to avail themselves of my services as their own bucket service young men seemed to have disappeared. I was pleased to do their bidding for I often was awarded a small payment. Many seemed to be of the opinion that peeing in the Scottish King's bucket was an honour in itself. Who was I to resist such service especially as some useful pocket money was the result?

At last, the King made his departure. Accompanied by his two brothers and closest Lords with me trailing along, we soon found ourselves in the bed chamber where everyone settled down for the night. I was told to stay on the outside of the chamber door as previously instructed and to raise an alarm should anyone approach. Finding some discarded cloaks and cushions in a hall closet, I made a bed for myself in front of the door and promptly fell asleep. The first day in the service of My Lord, King Robert Bruce, Sovereign of Scotland had finally ended. But not for long. In a matter of hours, we would be setting out to sea in the dark and I would be responsible for the safety of the King!

Lord Bissett had been appraised of our plan and had alerted his private guard to assist us and to make sure that any intruders to the castle or the docks were apprehended and disposed of in a manner befitting armed raiders.

What a day it had been! Starting off the day as a mere Apprentice Boatwright and ending up as a Personal Servant to the King of Scotland.! Little did I know what would eventually become of me but as a young man just out of his teen years, I was forever optimistic at this stage and fell into a deep sleep at once.

CHAPTER II

HOLY ISLE, ARRAN; THE VOICE OF REASON

In what seemed like no time at all, the castle captain of the night watch awakened me and suggested it was time for us all to be up and moving towards our boat that would take us away from Rathlin Island and on our way back to Scotland. Calling softly, I entered the chamber where my sleeping passengers were quartered only to find that all of them were already up dressed and armed in readiness to go.

Lord Bissett was on hand to bid us farewell. He had with him, his Steward who explained that he had arranged to supply our boat with food and drink for the trip and that even now the servants should have completed their tasks. It was a magnificent gesture and I noted that the King shook the Butler's hand, delivering his thanks in a more remunerative form as he did so.

The path to the dock and the dock itself were in complete darkness as we boarded and cast off. The moon was shining on the water which greatly assisted me in navigating the inlet entrance. Soon we were outside and sailing north in a gentle but persistent wind. I was particularly pleased with myself. I was fully awake whereas most of the others had settled down and were dozing.

As we passed the castle headland, however, an alarm gong was sounded and there were all sorts of shouts and loud yells as intruders were discovered and put down, Torches were lit and we could see men running about in the glare of these lighting sources. We had escaped just in time, and we could see that the castle guard were fully in charge of the situation.

The King came aft to thank me for having saved us from peril. He seemed to want to linger and talk, I was unprepared for his topic.

"You know, Muireadhach, that in times gone by the Vikings ruled these lands. They were hard men, quite ruthless, but were unable to effectively rule their conquered land except in the Far North and Western Islands where they are still present. Mind you, they were never interested in founding colonies and much more interested in obtaining farmland and wives."

"I do not think my father was one of these," I said "It was only twenty years ago. Apparently, he got lost from his friends and eventually found my mother's house during a Winter storm. Our house is quite isolated in the middle of the Glen Trool Forest in Galloway and we do not see many visitors. My mother is a widow, and she was obviously taken by this handsome fellow.... Here I am!"

"I can see that." replied King Robert. "Big fellow, red hair, blue eyes, you have all the markings of a Norwegian and Viking background."

"Well do you know, my mother got me an Apprenticeship with Erik the Boatbuilder down at Loch Ryan, Sire, and you know by my record that I helped to build this boat. It is the largest boat we have ever built at Loch Ryan. Erik is a Master Boatbuilder, and I am glad to have had the benefit of his skills. His own apprenticeship was in Norway."

"All this shows in the workmanship. This is a fine craft constructed in the Viking manner. I think you have a calling for higher service." And with that accolade still ringing in my head my Sovereign Earl left.

The voyage across the North Sound was rougher than previously and it was just before noon when we were off Sanda Isle at the Southend of Kintyre. Several mentions were made of spending the rest of the day in Campbeltown Bay, but My Lord the King was anxious to press on and consulted me regarding that feasibility. Since there was to be a full moon that night and I could already see Pladda Island at the foot of the Isle of Arran to my right, I replied that I could navigate onwards without encountering any peril by adhering to our present course and even if nighttime came the early rising of the moon would give adequate light.

The King agreed so we kept on sailing and as we came under the lee of the Mull of Kintyre, the seas were calmer, and we made good progress towards our selected landfall.

And where was that landfall expected to be? Only the King knew, and he was not about to share this information even with me. *'Scotland'* was all of us knew where we were going and that now we were in the mouth of the Clyde Estuary, Ayrshire, possibly Turnberry Castle on the Mainland might be the destination? He had mentioned Holy Isle last night but that seemed to be a directional thought rather than an actual landing place.

But as usual. it was impossible to second guess the King's intentions. After passing Pladda he directed me to make for Holy Isle in Lamlash Bay. I knew this small island to have a very steep shoreline where I did not know of any landing places. I had sailed around this rocky outcrop several times when practicing seamanship from Loch Ryan and I understood it to be uninhabited since the Vikings had plundered the small monastery a century or so ago. An altogether peculiar destination choice for our larger boat, especially as it was now getting dark.

King Robert had been there before and knew of a small gravel strand on the southeast corner which was just as well as navigation was becoming more difficult as the daylight faded. Approaching the shore, I was having my doubts when I finally saw what he had described to me. A steep shingle bay with heavy rocky outcrops at either end. We slid in on the smooth stones that made up the seabed and found it necessary for all aboard to jump into the waist- high water to pull the boat up onto the shore. Even so, the stern of the boat was still afloat, but it could not be helped as there was no more room on the small strand.

Disguising the boat as best we could with the sail, we scrambled up the steep side of the island to where the King positively declared we would find a rocky ledge suitable to make an encampment for the rest of the night. By now, everyone was tired and wet and most anxious to get some sleep and to dry out, to argue with the King's directions and sure enough, we found the ledge which again was sheltered from view from the Lamlash shoreline and just large enough for everyone to find a spot to thankfully lie down on what turned out to be hard rock covered with a light sheet of moss. The cooks who were with us passed around some bread and cold pieces of cooked chicken but by the time the meal was offered, most of the Lords had fallen asleep wrapped up in their heavy cloaks.

I myself, sank into a fitful half-sleep still thinking of the voyage I had captained from Rathlin Island. It had been a great experience for me, and it had improved my confidence as a sailor. Up until now I had been largely conducting my experience as a sailor on what I had witnessed real sailors in performing their craft. That I had largely faked my stated sailoring capabilities, now I was becoming surer of my boat handling skills. I had a fulfilling sense of achievement.

When the King silently came over to me, I was alert to his orders. Bidding me to remain silent and not to disturb our soundly sleeping comrades he bid me to follow him We carefully made our way towards the left outcrop which I had previously viewed as a solid, sheer granite barrier to scaling or bypassing and when the king started running his hands over the smooth surface I was mystified by his actions.

True, there were the odd veins and the occasional small rough patch but nothing that might help us to scale or bypass this old, solid outcrop of hard and weathered rock Then I noticed that he had found what he was looking for. In a whiteish vein that was running more or less horizontal he was busy scooping out some of the loose material that had gathered until something like a handhold had been revealed.

"Good." The King said to himself before tackling a new location just above this indentation. The result of all this scratching and gouging was the revelation of a series of shallow handholds and footholds progressing ever upwards into the dark. As this access went higher up the rock face, the disguised pathway became less concealed and most of the indentations in the higher reaches were readily identifiable and clear of loose material.

At about 200 feet upwards the basic granite rock levelled out to a small shoulder shelf where I caught up with my Leader. We were both out of breath so paused for fifteen minutes or so before proceeding. I dare not look down because I was afraid of heights. The King was whispering to me as in the still of the night, our voices would carry far, and the King had no intention of awakening our comrades.

A sort-of horizontal pathway to the right seemed the only way forward so proceeding along this narrow path with a very erect posture to keep our personal centre of gravity as close to the sheer stone wall to our left, we ventured along this route. I dared not look to my right as our way took us back over the location of the camp immediately below and we were almost at the other rocky outcrop that protected the other end of the inlet that the King had found for us. Suddenly, the pathway we were on began to narrow until it was no longer wide enough to take a full foothold. I was now walking on the side of my boots.

I was fully frightened by now and had visions of me plunging headlong down the cliff past the camp to be dashed to pieces on the narrow, stony tidewater line between the island and the ocean.

It was at that moment when I could feel my heart thumping against my breast that the King spoke.

''Ah! Here it is! Thank goodness as I think that this ledge is going to disappear into the face of the cliff not many feet from here.'' He was holding on to a small outcrop of the rock between us both when he suddenly disappeared.

For a horrible moment I thought he had fallen down the rock face to a certain death but on the other hand he had never shouted out in alarm. I inched forward by this time my feet were barely sideways onto the narrowing ledge and cautiously manoeuvred my body around the outcrop. Where two quartz seams were running parallel down the cliff face, they parted company as they approached our ledge and between them there was an empty space.

A cave entrance? Indeed, it was, and the King was just standing at the entrance and beckoning to me to come on.

"I knew it would be here!"

He turned to me:

"Boy! I have not been here since I was your age, and the experience changed my life. Keep by me as we enter this cave and do not say a word!"

On his hands and knees, he squeezed into the low narrow gap and disappeared from sight. I followed as best I could. Because of my greater height I probably had more difficulty than my Sovereign but once inside I bumped into the fully standing figure of the King who helped me to my feet. There was an eerie silence but if one listened closely the outside sounds of the sea and wind emanating from the entrance provided a ghostly background that seemed to be nowhere and everywhere at the same time. The sound resembled that of a softly singing distant choir in a vast cathedral but by now my mind was playing me all sorts of tricks.

"After the small entrance, the pathway becomes taller even although it is still very narrow." The King spoke softly yet it sounded as if it had a hundred echoes. He put a finger to his lips to signify that we had better not talk." His *Sheessh* was no sooner out of his lips that it reverberated and bounced all the way down the invisible passage losing volume but just as imperative as it went.

Signalling me to follow him we must have gone inside this opening for about a good one hundred feet when I realized that I could now see the outline of the King up ahead. It was as if my eyes were getting used to the darkness but then I realized that the cave was still devoid of any light other than through the small opening and twisted passage that we had already traversed which might have let in the starlight but was extremely unlikely to have penetrated so deep into the cavern.

I knew that natural granite could be made to sparkle when polished but surely the effect of light emission was a reflection rather than from any interior source? The King stopped. I was not imagining the eery grey penumbra. There must be an additional opening to the sky up ahead I surmised, otherwise the rock that surrounded us would be black in the absence of light. But my musing was interrupted.

In his loudest voice the King called out:

"Master! Are you there?" The question reverberated all around us in echoes of echoes. There seemed to be an internal wind that suddenly rose more as a sound than as a movement of air in the confined space of the tunnel.

To my astonishment that made my blood run cold a ghostly voice responded, not so much as loud but which nevertheless seemed to come from all over the walls, floor, and roof as multiple echoes not quite in synchronisation with each other:

"I am, Robert. I have been expecting you."

King Robert went down on his knees, and I did the same.

"Master, I have made recent mistakes and am distressed that I am not fulfilling my Destiny. You said I would be King and now I am, but all is not well in my land."

"You bring another with you? It is written that you would. Is it Muireadhach the Sailor?"

"It is."

"It is also written that he will be of great help to you. Guard him well and he will do the same for you."

I began to tremble at the use of the Anglo-Gaelic version of my name. It was never used except by my mother in intimate moments. How could this ghostly voice know all these things?

"Robert! I said you would be King. Do you doubt me now?" The voice was stronger now with a slight tone of reproach.

"No! No! Master. But what can I do? I am wandering aimlessly about getting nowhere?" The King postulated.

"You must keep on trying and you shall succeed!" The voice enjoined.

This last piece of instruction was now fading away and diminished to silence over the next three words:

"SUCCEED…Succeed…*Succeed…"*

as the iridescent glow from the granite tunnel was diminishing. We were left on our knees in total darkness. We remained like this for several minutes in contemplation of what we had just learned.

"You will have to lead us out, Murdoch. This tunnel is too narrow for me to get past you."

And with that statement we made our way back to the tunnel entrance with me leading. My legs were still trembling over this experience, and I banged my head several times on the tunnel roof as it again began lowering towards the entrance cleft. It was with welcome relief when I could see the outside again but then I realized that the King was not behind me.

Bending down, I called softly:

"Are you there, Sire? I thought you were just behind me?"

The King answered:

"I am just inside the entrance. I am going to take a rest to recuperate. I am getting too old for this spiritual experience. Come back inside and we shall keep each other warm until daylight comes."

Coming back inside the cave mouth I squeezed past the King who was now sitting on the tunnel floor facing the entrance. Sitting down behind him so that our backs were supporting each other I settled myself to do some thinking. Had my apprenticeship with Erik at Loch Ryan and the King's journey to Ireland been pre-ordained? However, was I going to be able to guard the King when I had no military training? And he to guard me? These were imponderables. Was a circumstance like that ever to occur? It was a puzzle. Then the King again spoke.

"It is getting light now and I am watching a spider trying to spin her web across the entrance. She has tried to establish the first strand twice whilst I have been watching. There she goes. Look! Suddenly, the feeble, ghostly voice that we had heard before came booming down the tunnel:

LOOK TO THE SPIDER

IF AT FIRST YOU DO NOT SUCCEED

TRY, TRY, TRY AGAIN ."

It was still too dark to note that any colour had been drained from our faces but the shivers that ran down our backs revealed the strong emotions that were engulfing Robert, King of Scotland and his very humble and frightened servant.

CHAPTER III

REVEREND PADRAIG
AND THE EARL OF MAR
AT TURNBERRY

Slipping and sliding down the precipice, we arrived in the camp where there was utter confusion. The King's absence had been noted although no one had yet commented on my absence. The King's brothers wanted to know where he had been and was he all right? The King's explanation was simple:

"You know how restless I become when I have a big decision on my mind? Well last night when I could not sleep, I decided to explore the Rock to ensure that we were alone. I took Muireadhach with me for company. The poor boy must be longing for sleep since I have deprived him of a night of rest. Being young he will recover soon enough."

Breakfast on last night's leftovers was served then the King called for a meeting of the Lords. The object was to plan for a return to the Mainland, Turnberry Castle in fact. But since he had been forced to leave the family stronghold on the information that John Cormyn's supporters together with an English presence were gathering in Ayr to come and capture him, it remained a question if Turnberry was now safe?

This information was re-enforced by the fact that Ayr Castle was only a day away from Turnberry. True, we had spies and supporters at Ayr and Turnberry but how to contact them to get intelligence that would guide our forward strategy?

In the end it was decided that I would sail across to the Ayrshire coast along with two other strong servants rather than any Lords since they could be readily recognised. I would say that I had just come up the coast from Loch Ryan and would like to rest before sailing back. This seemed to be a reasonable ruse, so young and strong servants, Connel and Fergus, embarked with me on our venture.

The Lords helped us to push off from the gravel and soon we were sailing southward, I wanted to reach the coast further down from Turnberry so that on coming towards the castle from the South it would look like I really was coming from Loch Ryan. The three of us had some difficulty in handling the big boat but with the sail up and a steady breeze from the west I headed for Ailsa Craig before turning towards the actual coastline. Here we were hindered more by tidal conditions, so it was necessary to keep well offshore until we saw Turnberry Castle on its rocky outcrop jutting out into the Firth.

Landing just south of the castle we were having some difficulty in pulling our boat up onto the beach when a sturdy fisherman came along the strand and assisted us.

He was very friendly and seem satisfied with our story of taking an unofficial sail from the boatyard where we were employed. He invited us into his shack which was above the highwater mark and just inside the line of trees that formed the back of the beach.

His comely maid servant bid us welcome and started preparing a hot meal on the open fire. We sat around a table constructed of driftwood but so constructed as to appear of the finest workmanship.

"What a marvellous table," I said. "You must be a fine craftsman in wood as well as a fisherman. Oh! By the way, I am called Muireadhach. What do you call yourself?"

"My name is Padraig. Yes, it is my own work. I was apprenticed to a furniture-maker in my youth before I was a fisherman. This table and the chairs are all made from driftwood picked up along the tide line."

"We sure could use someone of your skill at Erik's boatyard." I said.

"It's too far away and I have a good trade providing fish to the Castle. It is a job for every three days and so far, the fish have been most obliging."

"Ah! So, you go regularly to the Castle?"

"As a matter of fact, I shall be going this evening. The demand for fresh fish has been cut back as the English military have gone. Did you hear of Lord Cormyn's murder in a church in front of the altar?"

"Who could possibly be the murderer?"

The fisherman lowered his voice.

"They say that My Lord King Robert is to blame. All this happened in Dumfries. But I am not convinced. This version of the incident has been circulated by Cormyn's men."

"Indeed, that is a sorrowful tale. How do you know of this?"

"Some, of my Lord Cormyn's men still are billeted at Turnberry. They ride out every day looking for any trace of the King as he is rumoured to be hiding out somewhere on his estate or in the wild lands just beyond."

"These are, indeed, wild lands beyond Glen Trool, I have heard it said." I remarked thinking of my own youth spent in such places.

"They think that he will come back to Turnberry soon if only to see his young daughter Marjorie who has the same name as her grandmother, our late lamented Countess of Carrick," said the Fisherman.

"Lord Robert was heartbroken when his first wife, Lady Isabella, died shortly after Marjorie's birth. They were seen to be very much in love."

"You seem to know a great deal about the gentry" I ventured "Perhaps you were not always a Fisherman?"

"How observant you are! Yes, I was formerly in holy orders at Whithorn. We were a very poor abbey because many years ago a band of roving Vikings from the Isle of Man sacked our establishment, and we never recovered our hereditaments."

"Is that where you acquired your carpentry skills?" I enquired.

"We acquired all the practical skills in order to keep our community alive. But in the end, it was no use and we had to undergo dissolution. It was very sad."

"How came you here?"

"Our Abbott, Father Ninian who now lives in a cave here to the South of Wigtown in the Machars, suggested that I throw myself on the Earl of Carrick's charity, so I came north only to find that he was absent. But on being introduced to the late Lady Isabella of Mar she promised me the education of her yet unborn child."

"And yet you fish?"

"I started fishing at night when my teaching tasks were done and found I was good at it. When another tutor was sent from the Mar household after Lady Isabella died, to ensure that the Mar family would maintain an interest in young Marjorie in the event that the King remarried which was very likely, I was by-passed, and here I am!"

"My Goodness!" I exclaimed.

"Now that My Lord Robert is King, young Marjorie is a Princess and at the moment heir to the throne of Scotland!"

"Now that's something for in-laws to be thinking about."

"The machinations of our Ruling Classes!" added Padraig.

Just then, the slight jingle of harness followed by the sunlight now being shut out from the open door by several aggressive men with drawn swords who forced their way into Padraig's cottage. We stood up in alarm and Connel and Fergus drew their daggers.

"Fisherman! Who are your visitors?" spoke the leader who was first into the room. He pointed his sword at Padraig who in the meantime had moved away from the table to stand between the girl and the invaders.

"Why My Lord, they are merely travellers from the Boatbuilders at Loch Ryan who have sailed further than they intended and who landed this morning and who return tomorrow morning." Replied Padraig in a soft voice. "Will you join us in a bite of food?

The invader spoke to the two soldiers who were immediately behind him also with swords drawn.

"Disarm these two!" said he, indicating Connel and Fergus. He then turned his attention to me.

"What is your name, boy?"

"I am Muireadhach, apprentice to Erik the Boatbuilder at Loch Ryan. You can see I am unarmed and mean no harm. My men were only acting in response to your sudden arrival."

'Then that is your boat outside?"

"It is a boat that I built but which does not have an owner yet. In purely legal terms the boat is still Erik's."

"You stole it then?" The question was not couched in a pleasant manner.

"Let us just say we were taking the boat for a trial run. Erik instructed me to take her for a sail to work through all the securing system placements and leads. It is a fine craft. Would you like to buy it?"

"Do not be insolent, young man or I shall run you through!"

"I just thought that a man of your authority and standing might need a boat to enhance his position. It will make an excellent war boat. She is called a dragon boat. Do you see the fierce dragon's head carved on the prow?"

"We Mars are not in need of a war boat" but for the first time the point of his sword wavered. As a matter of fact," he added, "we Mars are the Lord High Admirals of the Royal Fleet."

"Murdoch," interrupted Padraig, "You need to know that the distinguished gentleman you are conversing with is Gartnait, 7th Earl of Mar and betrothed suitor of the Lady Christina, our Lord King Robert's sister."

"My Lord!" I knelt down on one knee and lowered my head in submission.

Gartnait sheathed his sword and signalled to his soldiers to do the same.

"You are welcome, stranger," he said, "I see that our good and faithful servant Padraig the Fisherman is looking after you."

"Padraig is indeed a good ambassador." I replied.

Gartnait came forward and vigorously shook my hand.

"Since you will be gone tomorrow, I shall consider it a favour if you will show me over your boat today before darkness descends."

So, for a couple of hours we climbed all over the boat examining the several woods that were employed in specific settings, the shape of the hull, and the fittings that were placed to secure military shields in times of battle.

"She is very much of the Viking style" noted Gartnait.

"It is because Erik the Boatbuilder's family line came from Normandy at the time of Duke William's incursion into England. He is clearly descended from the Northmen."

"And so, are you, Muireadhach?"

"It is so, My Lord" I replied. "I share the same family name as my deceased father, Craigencallie." This of course, was a deliberate misrepresentation of my name which I thought was prudent given the circumstances.

"Our Lord, King Robert had a foster brother of much the same name" observed Padraig who had accompanied us on our boat inspection. "Such a Norman-Gaelic construction is often translated as Murdoch. But his family name is Craigencallie."

The Earl looked sharply at me. He suddenly looked less cordial.

"But that family name is a Galloway name and not Norwegian. On second thoughts, I believe you should sail this afternoon and not wait until the morrow." He said very slowly and almost menacingly.

"It would not do if we were to find some kinship. The relationships between the Houses of Mar and Bruce are delicate and the male succession to the Kingdom of Scotland is by no means settled." Mar allowed himself a moment of self-promotion. "In fact, I am a contender for the throne myself."

"I wish you well, My Lord. I have no intention or reason to become involved in such a momentous decision." I responded with feeling.

"Whether or not you are a Craigencallie or a Muireadhach!" and he gave me a piercing look. "I'll say Farewell, Craigencallie! Go in Peace!"

"Your servant, My Lord."

As the 7th Earl of Mar rode away, Padraig commented:

"That was a close encounter. I have never been so nervous in all my life! Earl Mar is noted for having a very short temper. It is said that there are more than a few dead men who had no argument with the gentleman but were dispatched with no discernible reason other than my Lord's misunderstanding."

"Good heavens," I involuntarily expressed, "In that case, we had better take His Lordship at his word and prepare at once to get underway".

"Especially, if he puts together your name and the King's. It might remind him of the story of your father and Lord Robert. I saw him working it over in his mind."

''Oh? And what story is that?" I enquired.

"The King owes his life to Muireadhach and everyone knows it."

"I have never heard that. Do you know more than you are telling me, Padraig?" My curiosity was thoroughly aroused.

"It is only a story that went around many years ago. A Viking called Muireadhach was separated from a hunting party and was lost in the highlands and forests of Glen Trool. He was still in his youthful years when he came upon the gravely wounded Robert at the bottom of a narrow glen who had been thrown from his horse. Although the Norwegian did not know where he was or which was the correct direction for help, he picked up Robert and put him over his shoulder and between them they eventually found a young widow's dwelling who took them in and nursed Robert back to good health. What is more, she eventually got word to one of the Bruce castles that Robert had been found alive and could be collected which is what happened. He and his saviour went back to Turnberry and Robert made him his foster brother.

"Now, if that was your father" continued Padraig, "then you are the King's nephew and a threat to the Mars. Once Garnait not to mention the King work out that you are Muireadhach's son, who can tell what will happen next? And in the present case if Garnait puts two and two together and you are still here, then your future is certain!" He made a symbolic motion to represent a murderous sweep of a dagger across his throat.

CHAPTER IV

THE GLEN TROOL MASSACRE; CRAIGENCALLIE

We are at sea, and half-way across the Firth of Clyde between Turnberry and Holy Isle off the Arran Coast in Lamlash Bay. It was a hurried departure but given the circumstances, the quickest that could be achieved. Padraig had insisted on providing us with fish and water which we had gratefully accepted. Darkness had fallen and I was entirely dependent upon keeping a pre-sunset visual course. This was to say a very risky means of navigation because the currents and tides in the Firth of Clyde were extremely variable, and we really had no idea where or when we would reach the western side of the Firth.

Luck was on our side, however, for we came across a fishing boat just after midnight which told us that we were heading for Whiting Bay and that if we altered our course by only a point to the right, we should be in line to enter Lamlash Bay. Not wanting to search for our hidden berth on the south-east corner of Holy Isle in the dark I decided to navigate in a big circle off the Arran coast until daylight.

It was six in the morning when I considered it feasible to proceed towards land and I was pleased to see that the outline of the landscape was familiar to me and gave me confidence that I would not inadvertently run our boat ashore.

Finding Holy Isle was one thing but finding our little harbour was something else. Scouting along the south-east corner failed to detect our destination and we were obliged to circumnavigate the small isle with Connel and Fergus on the oars and me on the steering tiller.

Second time around, Fergus espied several crates and barrels that had been left on the strand as being too heavy to lug up to the camp site. These were the only markers we had to go on as the two headlands that we were looking for were only apparent once we had come much closer. The natural concealment of the cove had been much better than I had thought I mused ruefully as I brought our boat into the little bay.

Fortunately, we had been seen by our comrades on the shore so there were several hands to help us pull up to the gravel and disembark. Climbing up to the camp terrace, I handed a full cran of fish that Padraig had sent with us to the cook before approaching the King.

His Majesty was eager to obtain our news although clearly disappointed that we had not gained access to the Castle. But by the time I had completed all the information that had been gleaned from Padraig and the Earl of Mar he congratulated us for a job well done under the circumstances. The next move was to plan what we were going to do? He called his brothers, Sir Thomas and Sir Alexander and bid me stay for the discussion.

"This King is desirous of campaigning on the mainland of his realm" Robert announced in a formal manner, when all were gathered out of earshot of the others. There was no disagreement on that point. But how and where? These were the points that needed to be defined.

From our position on Holy Island, the nearest Mainland was located in Ayrshire . There was no need to consider Turnberry as its occupation by the Mar Clan was too dangerous.

Perhaps somewhere between Turnberry and Loch Ryan might be suitable, but it would need to offer a clear way inland to quickly get away from the Coast where north-south movement of our enemies could be quickly mounted.

In the end a position south of the fishing village of Girvan was selected near the mouth of the river Stincher with progress inland until we reached the head waters of the Cree. Reaching the confluence of the Cree with the Water of Trool we would then be comparatively on safe ground on the edge of the Wild Lands beyond Glen Trool and in an area I knew well.

What's more, we might reduce the size of our party by sending the boat down the Coast to Erik the Boatbuilder's yard manned by the men we are not taking with us. The boat can be safely stored there at Loch Ryan and her presence will give no clue of our landing spot and inland route. we planned to take.

The decision once made, however, had an unexpected outcome especially to me as I was unaware of the jealousies that existed between and among the King's Lords. All at once a clamour arose as to who would accompany the King and the identity of those who would take the boat to Eric's. Everyone wanted to be in the King's party, and no one wanted to be left behind. The Lords were all mindful of their special position to the Monarch and the loss of position would be a serious blow to their prestige and possible benefits in the form of land and titles. I also discovered for the first time that I was a figure of suspicion being so close to the King and not being from a noble family. All the Lords to a man, disliked me intensely and would fain see me reduced to a servant's position.

And so, the drama continued until the King said:

"Enough!"

"I did not know I had a bunch of childish, self-serving parasites in my personal suite! You may carp and complain but if there is one or more of you who does not want to take the King's orders, let him or them depart right now!"

No one moved. The King continued:

"As for the presence of Muireadhach, He has the King's favour and you will harm him at your peril. He serves the interests of us all. He is a sailor, and he also understands and knows the Wild Lands to which we are going.

"As a matter of fact, I am placing my two Brothers, Thomas and Alexander, to take the boat down to Loch Ryan to await orders from me for the introduction of Phase Two of our venture. We shall miss them, but they hold in their hands the future of King Robert's Scotland."

At that, the murmuring died out and one by one each Lord came to the King and vowed personal loyalty. I was by-passed in this demonstration of humility which worried me not at the time.

The pride of the Lords in Attendance having been resolved for the moment, we set about making the boat ready for its part in the venture. It was decided that there was nothing to gain by sailing in the dark so early on the morrow when the boat set sail into the great waters of the Firth of Clyde. We viewed the approaches to the Ayrshire Coast looking for landmarks as we now ventured south-east, and by the afternoon of the same day, we who were to be left on the shore viewed the approaching Ayrshire coast.

The shore party incorporating King Robert, myself, and eight Lords with their Squires and staff were soon on hard ground along with their accoutrements to watch the fine boat that had featured so prominently in our wanderings continue her passage back to her birthplace at Erik the Boatbuilder's Yard. I was sorry to see her go; she had been so much that was good and honourable to me. But we were headed to my home ground after five years and I must confess to a touch of excitement when I thought of my mother and two brothers at home in our remote shieling among the mountains and lochs.

Keeping the Polmaddie Ridge as our landmark up ahead as we made our passage upstream along the line of the river Stincher, sometimes making good progress where the undergrowth had been cleared and at other times when being forced to walk in the rocky stream itself where footing was limited by rocks and boulders.

The River Stincher ran bright and brisk coming down to the Firth in a short run off the higher land which was its source. This was the south-west edge of the great plateau. We noted many salmon and caught a few for our meal. The fish were all very fat and carried plentiful roes which made good eating.

We stopped for the night on the southside of the Polmaddie Range just where one of the River Cree tributaries rises for its long and twisted route to Wigtown Bay. The hillside was comparatively open, but we found a fold in between two grassy crests where we could be sheltered from observation. Sleeping on deep moss and reeds would be a pleasant change from hard boat thwarts or rocky island stone.

It was at this location that my position within the royal community was firmly established. Some of us were passing the time with our bows by shooting our arrows at the plentiful number of ravens which had been following us all day and killing them one at a time. This was good sport but imagine my good fortune and good luck in *killing two birds with one arrow.* By happenstance, one bird was just flying abreast of another and happened to be in line when my speeding arrow pierced the head of the first bird and travelled on to catch the second bird also in the head with both birds falling to the ground still attached to each other by my arrow! I considered the event to be a fluke but the gentlemen and professional archers who had been part of our shooting party were overjoyed that they had witnessed one of their own performing a miracle shot. I was overwhelmed by congratulations. Even the King shouted out what he called *'my excellent feat'* to those who had missed the event.

We slept soundly that night until a passing shepherd awoke us with the news that the Earl of Mar had gone down the coast from Turnberry all the way to Loch Ryan where he and his troops had encountered a landing party of the King's men and slaughtered all of them. Two of the raiders were said to be brothers of the King who were tortured before they died and admitted that the King and an army were intent on pacifying Galloway. As a matter of fact, the military were moving ahead this morning and heading towards this direction!

This news alarmed us, and the King was much aggrieved at the thought of his brothers being tortured and killed. What was even worse, however, was the fact that Mar and his troops were not as far away as Turnberry but were actually in this area, a much closer threat. Mustering our group, we therefore proceeded at some speed on our journey.

Continuing down the Cree Valley was no longer an option as it was in effect, going towards the enemy, so we decided to shorten our journey to Glen Trool by heading east to the

Waters of Minnoch and descending that stream to join with the Water of Trool many miles away. This was a long day of skirting the Merrick's foothills and rocky ridges. We were all exhausted on reaching the Black Linn Waterfall in Glen Trool Forest by nightfall.

It was there that we were obliged to rest for the night. At least the trees were somewhat of a protection although on the contrary they could also conceal the approach of an enemy party.

Our lookout aroused us at daybreak, and we moved quickly along the Trool Valley and loch side until the path became so narrow at the top end of the loch that we were obliged to ascend the steep hill that was on the right-hand side. On reaching the crest with much effort, the King ordered us to stop rest, and partake of our food and water which we had earlier missed in our hasty departure from last night's stop.

At that point the King came up with the idea to trap the following military as they entered the narrows. By carrying and pushing as many of the loose rocks that were all around, we lined the crest of the hill with a veritable wall of stone in preparation. Already, we had seen the glint of the sun on steel armour at the foot of the loch and were now confident that our enemy followers would come up the loch side path in pursuit.

At first the soldiers marched side-by-side four abreast with military precision until the path became a bit narrower between the cold dark, and deep waters of the loch and the high overhanging steep hill. We saw them reducing their ranks to three-abreast then to two-abreast and finally, they were obliged to march, or rather walk, in single-file as the path came to its narrowest at the loch head. All this we noted from our observation post above on the cliff crest while making sure that we were not observed ourselves.

At the right moment when most of the platoon was on target, we started pushing the heavier stones over the crest. The largest boulders, crashed down on the troops below and were immediately followed up by the lesser rocks to create a veritable rain of deadly stone down on the unsuspecting soldiers.

The result was mayhem with some soldiers being crushed to death by direct strikes from falling rocks and others struck down and driven over the side of the path into the loch waters. The few remaining troops who were not yet in the target area took fright and anyway, they were unable to proceed as the narrow pathway was now obstructed by rocks and dying or dead bodies. The cries from the drowning men in the cold, deep water were horrendous to hear and there was great confusion.

Altogether, we counted about fifty casualties but there may have been more. All-in-all, it was a tremendous victory for the King as the soldiers kept running back down the loch side path and, we hoped, were anxious to get back to their mothers. We did not see any obvious leading officer and concluded that the soldiers were only loosely organized. This brilliant action has been called *The Glen Trool Massacre* and was one of the first of King Robert the Bruce's victories in this new campaign.

It was an easy days walk to my mother's house skirting the southern foothills and rugged ridges of the Merrick Hill in Southern Scotland. The steep cliffs provided a mystery to the landscape unlike any other topography in all of Scotland. Small lochs, often called lochans, alternated with rushing burns often meant leaping from one mossy outcrop to another and avoiding swampy land where rushes grew but on average the vast plateau from which the dramatic hills and high passes abound, was reasonably flat which accounted for the numerous lochans and comparatively short stream courses. Eventually, we approached the small pool of water called Loch Dee.

Our house, called *Craigencallie* not readily identifiable from a distance as it was fitted into a fold in the ground and was built of local stone. With a roof of rushes, it gave the appearance of a marshy depression, and it was only on close approach and perhaps the presence of domestic animals and hens that indicated habitation. There were not many visitors in the course of a year and most found us after having been lost on the plateau, hills and forests.

We all stopped in what could be called the front yard and I took the King into the house to meet my mother. As customary, she was working at the large, scrubbed table on preparing a meal. She was of medium height and graying hair done up in a bun at her neck Her bright, quick blue eyes and her smooth brow seemed to bely her physical age for they were indications of intelligence and searching as if nothing passed her by that she did not assess it for its worth.

She wore a cotton gown right up to her neck and down to the floor. It was a modest grey in colour and scrupulously clean. she abandoned what she had been doing and rushed to me:

"Muireadhach, my son. How lovely to see you!"

She threw her arms around my neck and gave me a strong hug: "Lovely! Lovely!" she was saying her bright eyes temporarily clouded by tears of joy.

"And your friend...?"

"Mother, I'd like to introduce you to King Robert Bruce of Scotland.

Without a break in her effusion, she curtsied very low and welcomed him into her house.

"Your servant, My Lord. Welcome to my House. I am much honoured to have you under my roof."

The King formally stretched out his right hand and my Mother kissed it, bowing as she did so.

The King spoke. "How kind you are. Your son has taken the liberty of bringing me hence and I can immediately see why he is such a fine man. Do you know he is quite a keen shot with bow and arrow and displayed such prowess last evening and put my own professional archers to shame! But I believe you have two other boys?"

"Aye, Your Majesty. Muireadhach is the eldest and the other two are as yet not out of their teen years."

I started to tell my story to her, but she bid me be silent.

"The main item is that you are home in good spirits and in one piece and if I can be so bold, in good company!" She glanced up at the King and I swear she was flirting!

The King laughed.

"I suppose I am accepted as a worthy visitor?"

"By all means, Your Majesty Your presence brings honour and distinction to this house as I have said before."

In fits and starts I got my story told. Even although it was not continuous, I was sure she understood the spoken details and the underlying implications as soon as I spoke of them, perhaps even before I spoke of them with regards to the dynastic inferences.

Just then my brothers, Mackie and Macclurg came into the house. There were welcomes again and appropriate formality when the King was introduced. Mackie was like me in that he was tall, but whereas Mackie was fair, Macclurg was dark in complexion and only of medium height. After a while we all sat down at the big table and conversation became more relaxed. As befits any young person on being first introduced to an older man, especially a King, both boys were initially quite reticent but soon warmed to the easy and relaxed style of our Monarch.

The peat fire was burning red hot and practically smokeless.

The large single room was sparely furnished with numerous chairs and cushions and the odd small table or two. Several hanging presses and chiffoniers were against the long window-less wall at the back and daylight was obtained through two square openings with heavy canvas curtains and the one top-half open Dutch door, all on the other side of the room which faced the front yard.

As a continuation of the single-storey house to the south was the animal byre served by a double door on the front and no other opening. Within the attic of this space were sleeping places for the family accessible from the main room next door by a ladder pitched against the gable wall in which the fireplace was situated. In all there were three gable walls one at each end of the structure and an intervening one between the living space and the animal byre.

To Muireadhach it was the home he had left five years ago to work for Erik the Boatbuilder. In that time and recently, he had learned the arts of sailing and boatbuilding, services to the King of Scotland, and diplomatic missions of high importance. He had even faced certain death several times yet here he was, back at home in the company and love of his mother.

To add to the pleasure and contentment, the sight of my now grown brothers helping their mother; Mackie and Macclurg had caught eight rabbits. Throwing their catch on the table Mackie related the story of how they had nearly caught a fat capercailzie concealed in the heather and ready to flee but she had got the better of them and managed to get away afore they could get their slings ready.

"A nice fat bird would be a welcome feast!" said Mackie known to his family and friends as *Kye*.

"I must say I am getting sick of rabbit stew." chimed in Maclurg who was also deprived of the first part of his given name and was called *Lurg* to friends and family.

"Well, boys," said their mother, 'Tonight is a special night. Go out and take five hens from the yard and hang them up to drain. We have a special guest as well as your brother. A King is obviously a 'special' guest."

Being instructed to cull the hen population was indeed a sign of something 'special'. They went back out to do their mother's bidding and selected the fattest hens.

It was decided that the Lords and their Squires would spend the sleeping hours in the living room when the principals had ascended to the sleeping space. They would eat with the family or utilize the animal shelter whichever was their preference during the day but as Kye and Lurg immediately set about organising entertainment for the visitors there was not much time for hanging around doing nothing.

The feast of grilled hen was enjoyed by all accompanied by a potent and early type of whisky which had been fermented from wild barley. But once the light from the setting sun was not fully replaced by the embers from the burning peat even although some wood had been thrown on top to brighten the fire, everyone was ready for sleep, and some had already done so.

My Mother and I talked far into the night even after the fire died down. There was a lot of catching up to be made and Mother was very interested in the family connections of the Lords and Ladies I had encountered. She wondered aloud whether Lurg's father had come from Ireland? Somehow it fitted in with her remembered details.

She told me that my Father had been born in Norway and was attracted to the Viking way of life and that his Father had been descended from the Vikings that had raided Scotland when King William of England came from Normandy and had disestablished the church properties. He was a sailor, and as she had thought at the time, he may have been a kinsman of Eric the Boatbuilder down at Loch Ryan. She had in fact used that supposition when she had negotiated with Eric all these years ago for my Apprenticeship. Apparently, Eric had never contradicted her guesswork.

Now, both boys usually answered to Kye and Lurg. It was explained again that the young men were named after their separate fathers who had visited my mother for a short while after being lost in Glen Trool Forest. It was a story she told without any hint of embarrassment. She had been made a widow quite young when her husband had been killed by an English raiding party. Then she had been a young bride abandoned in the back of beyond and forced to fend for herself.

On the following morning Lurg organised a bathing party in Loch Dee with a splendid breakfast to follow. Next a race to the top of Merrick was suggested with all the young fellows going off to see who could first find a way to the crest of the highest hill in Southern Scotland. They set off in groups of four after arguing which group would get Kye and which would get Lurg as guides.

On yet another occasion we had a competitive bow-and-arrow contest which I won. It was a craft I had never been taught. It seemed that I had a great eye and could discern and calculate a bow's strength and the distance to the target. I hit the greatest number of bullseyes on the targets and the visiting Knights began to accept me for the second time and were gradually becoming less antagonistic of my closeness to the King. But it was my shooting of two ravens with one arrow when we were camped at Glen Trool that really impressed all the onlookers. Admittedly it was a fluke and a feat I have tried to duplicate without success in following years. Nevertheless, apparently my reputation as an eagle archer was made at that instant and has supported my reputation forever.

Several days passed by in such a manner and not much thought was put into what should be next done to progress the King's plan for pacifying the whole of Scotland and getting the Lairds to acknowledge One King. As it was there were still several competing interests to the position, all blood relatives or in-laws of King Robert but by his calculation and by ours he was the rightful Monarch. Time, however, was not on our side and if we tarried too long King Robert would be forgotten and all the rival enmities would be rekindled.

On one of the last evenings at Craigencallie, we were gathered around the big table availing ourselves of a sumptuous meal prepared by my mother who rustled up meals for a table of twenty-one hungry men as if she had been doing such catering all her life.

Settling in to a post-prandial sip of whisky, the King observed:

"Your Boys all have interesting names" observed the King.

"These are the names of their Fathers" Mother said. "I did not marry any of them How could I get an Ecclesiastical Official out here to the back of beyond?"

"I was particularly interested in my good friend. Muireadhach is an unusual name construction these days. The Norman Scots equivalent is Murdoch"

"That's what he was called. I just changed it to the Gaelic-Viking version because he was a big red-haired giant of a man with sparkling blue eyes like the seas on which he was fond of sailing."

"How came he here?

"He was hunting with his party over the moors when stormy weather and the low cloud covered everything. He got separated from his party, wandered about, and caught a fever. He finally struggled in here, a very ill fellow. I nursed him back to health and he eventually left us to find his way back to his friend's castle."

"Do you remember what castle?" asked the King.

"Let me see. It was somewhere between Girvan and Ayr. Greenan, Dunure, Maidens, Culzean, or Turnberry Castle; One of these, I seem to think."

"My Lord of Carrick's seat is at Turnberry?",. The King added with rising excitement.

"I think so, 'YES!" replied the old woman.

Replied the King:

"Muireadhach might be the son of my foster brother, Murdoch sailor. What a coincidence I remember him telling me a similar story when he eventually turned up after being missing for two weeks! We all thought it was just a fabrication to cover the fact that he had found a Bothy somewhere and enjoyed a merry time with some wench. Pardon me Madam. I did not mean to offend!"

The King continued:

"Murdoch, you are very likely my Foster Nephew! Your Mother has filled in what has been missing from the narrative up until now and she fell for Murdoch in a very special way. Such was his charm that we adopted him as my foster brother!"

The King suddenly embraced me and everybody started shouting and yelling all at once! I sat dumbfounded. It was truly amazing.

As the night wore on, King Robert and my mother were intent on some private conversation in which we three Boys did not take part. Imagine our surprise when the King announced that he had awarded some of his Carrick land to our family to be divided equally among mother's three sons. The land was the stretch of hills between the two rivers which were south of the House, the Rivers Palnure and Penkiln. There were three important hills, White Hill, Bennan Hill, and Strone Hill one for each son, and I was to be called *Murdoch of Cumloden* which is at the south end of the property. Kye will be *Mackie of Larg,* and Lurg will be called the *Maclurg of Kirouchtrie* all within Carrick Estate of the King and within the Minnigaff barony. You may imagine my surprise and delight to be a man of property!

But His Majesty's campaign needed to press on. On reviewing resting points for our party on the way north, The King recalled that he had a sister who was married to Lord Seton at Loch Doon Castle. This would be our first stop. Recruitment of additional forces could take place at the various villages along the Doon Valley in progress towards Dumbarton where he planned for a full-force confrontation with the opposing gentry of Dalriada.

The most direct route to Loch Doon was by the river courses of the Cooran Lane, the Brishie Burn and finally the Gala Lane that runs into the Head of Loch Doon. It is almost due North throughout the length of the march with some tremendous cliffs to the left that delimit the eastern foothills of The Merrick. Since the lands to the East are lined by the Rhinns of Kells range that is equally dramatic in its appearance but of lesser height, the chosen route was something of a marshy elongated valley which made progress slower than one would maintain on firmer ground.

Nevertheless, our group set off at the first glint of dawn. Kye and Lurg elected to stay on with our mother and who could blame them? As young men in their late teens it was their duty to look after their mother. They did promise, however, that should any information come their way that would impact the King's Party, one of them would follow and catch up with whatever intelligence they had.

It was a mild bright day when we set off from Craigencallie but in what is typical of the weather in this high plateau, the sky progressively darkened from the West and soon it was lashing with rain. It was not until much later as they were descending the Gala Lane watercourse that the sun eventually glinted out from the southwest although its effect was diminished by the long shadow cast by the bulk of The Merrick by this time to our South-West.

It was an absolute pleasure to be finally trekking along the stony shore of Loch Doon.

They could see the outline of the Castle on its island near the western shore of the Loch so the pace was quickened at the sight of our destination. Only the King and I had seen Loch Doon Castle before, so we were not as disappointed as were some of the others. As it is surrounded by the waters of the largest fresh water loch in the area it had retained an air of impregnability over the years to be considered an occupied landmark from long before the coming of the Norman Lairds.

There was no sign of a boat landing stage, and the Castle was too far offshore for a shout to travel. To emphasize our presence on shore, the King caused a fire to be lighted to attract the Castle's attention. Soon a boat was seen coming from behind the Castle. Passing around the North-end of the fortifications and coming towards us on the Western shore. There were six men in the boat, and it did not look like we were going to be invited to stay as it was a small craft.

The boatmen stopped rowing about 30 feet off the shore and one of its occupants called out:

"Who calls on My Lord?"

"His Lord and King! Brother of His Lordship's spouse, My Lady Christina. The King stood up next to the fire and instructed his followers to kneel so that he could be easily seen. The enquiry from the boat was not couched in the friendliness of terms and it could be seen that the speaker was fully armed as were the others in the boat. Another night on the hard ground, were my thoughts, as I was convinced that there was no possibility tonight of sleeping in front of a fire in a secure chamber. I looked longingly at the outline of Loch Doon Castle now fading into the further shore of the Loch as the Western light gradually sunk behind the mountain ridge of Arran across the Firth of Clyde: The Arran Ridges resembling a 'Sleeping Warrior' in silhouette against the setting sun.

"Your Majesty! My Lord! "Shouted the man in the boat. "I go in haste to advise My Lord Seaton of your presence." And with that he gave instructions to return to the island castle. The boat, however, was not long out of sight, when a much larger craft was discerned as it skirted the end of the Castle coming from the northern side. By now the fading light was nearly gone but the flapping of the exceptionally large banner which flew from the prow caught the last of the daylight in its silken-threaded design.

"Now we can all look forward to a good meal and a warm place to bed down" mused King Robert.

CHAPTER V

BOATBUILDING AT LOCH DOON CASTLE; ARRIVAL OF SCOTT BOYD

On this occasion however, the boat that came into sight from the north end of the Castle was a much larger craft and reminiscent of the Viking style of which I was very familiar. As she came closer, I could discern My Lord Seaton standing near the bow. He was dressed in his Norman-style Court dress now somewhat out-of-date but likely his most formal garb.

He shouted as the boat came closer:

"My Lord, Your Liege and Servant!" Then clambering over the side, he waded in the shallow water adjacent to the shore and approached his King Robert who incidentally was also his Earl Superior and the Feudal Landowner of Loch Doon Castle, the Loch itself and all the many surrounding acres of land not to mention his brother-in-law.

Medieval chivalric laws kept feuds running for generations. Even close family blood relations or those which were acquired through marriage were suspect but there was nothing else to go on. It was very necessary to keep guard.

"Keep your Friends Close and your Enemies Closer".

It did appear that the relationship between the King and me was close enough, and good enough for us both. It had raised jealousies and enmity in many directions that would only be assuaged by the death of one or both of us. Lord Seaton, however, was a friend to both of us so at least on this occasion we were on friendly territory. But I did wonder, in my head, that My Lord Seaton had a darkness of complexion that was closely akin to Kie's which suggested a Norman rather than an Irish or Norwegian background.

On the other hand, we in Galloway probably owed more to Welsh blood than antecedents from distant lands so who knew? Personal alliances and friendships *earned* were perhaps in the long run the only really trustworthy relationships upon which to place undying loyalty. But betrayal was always just around the corner. Real or imagined.

The meeting of My Lords Robert I and Seaton on the shores of Loch Doon was a momentous one. The two Principals exchanged family lore and news until well into the night when the moon came up. It was then decided that the boat would take the King's men in two passages twixt shore and the castle. I was very pleased to be on the first trip along with the King and Seaton.

Approaching the Castle, I was able to see that the North side which opened up to the length of the Loch now stretching out into the darkness between the heavily wooded banks just like an open road. Not for the first time I thought that the loch itself offered a quick and unencumbered path to the north and the well-populated Doon Valley. It was a pity that between the loch and the valley below there was a steep landfall of about 300 feet off the Merrick Plateau over a short distance of less than one mile to the meandering water meadows through which only the River Doon connected by the rocky and treacherous Ness Glen that passed through the private Berbeth Estate and was outwith the King's lands of Carrick.

But there was more to these revelations and thoughts. The Loch Doon Castle although not imposing from either shore presented a commodious stone archway that faced the entire loch to the north within which and under the castle itself an array of mooring posts and docks were located. Here and there were some elderly boat remains well past their prime, Large and small, these craft occupied less than half of the docking space. Some were afloat but the majority were submerged or half-submerged but nevertheless constituted Lord Seaton's Navy.

Next morning saw the King, Seaton, Seaton's Boatmaster and me, down in the boat area to examine what was left and useable from the detritus that lay before us.

"My goodness," I remarked," what a waste of wood. I would like to see some attempts be made to salvage perfectly serviceable parts."

"And so, you shall, Muireadhach." Said the King, "I am appointing you and Lord Seaton's Boatmaster to re-build the boats and put the docking areas into good shape. Lord Seaton will command the military actions. The gentleman next to me is Halfdan, Lord Seaton's Boatmaster You must get to know each other."

It was a splendid plan, and I was immensely proud of the part I was to play in it. All the negative feelings I had had over the King's apparent injustice at putting the blame on us to cover his own shortcoming by neglecting to share his thoughts with us were now dispelled and I looked forward to whatever lay ahead. I was not sure that Lord Seaton shared my optimistic view. Several questions immediately jumped into my mind, one of which was: *'Where were the money and the new materials going to come from when we started to build or rebuild the boats?'*

"I shall prepare a budget for the boats and boatyard" offered Seaton seeing how he had to say something to please the king. It was as if he had read my thoughts and knew that treasure would be a crucial factor in the entire operation. "My Boatmaster, Halfdan, shall help me with the technical details. There is no one who knows the intricacies of the harbour and the boats more than he."

King Robert immediately looked on this remark with favour.

"Thank you". simply stated His Highness. "It is very kind of you to volunteer and I shall match whatever amount you allocate to the plan from your personal fortune as I have no doubt that the Estate finances are in bad shape".

It was a heavy hint if ever I heard one!

"I am sure we shall have sufficient material salvaged from the damaged boats to build two or three war boats and prepare the ribs for the skin boats." Chimed in the Boat Master finally summoning sufficient courage to speak in this formal setting. He had had no problem on speaking with the Monarch surrounded by his own comfortable working space, but his courage had deserted him when meeting the King in a more formal setting. Turning to me:

"I look forward to working with you, My Lord."

"Even if you both are King's sons where your fathers come from in Norway but here in Scotland you are merely skilled artisans and freemen with a splendid background in Norwegian boat building and sailing and will serve your Scottish King to the best of your ability and personal honour as His subjects."

> *"It is a well-known fact that men who are blessed with descendance from great men often share the same noble characteristics of their great ancestors."*

The King's wry remarks did not go over our heads

There seemed to be nothing to do but go down on one knee and bow our heads. After what seemed like several minutes but was merely a brief second or two, My Lord Seaton followed suit.

The King graciously acknowledged our fealty.

"This effort will require much attention to detail and forward momentum," said the King "so you really must *pull and push* all the people that you call upon to help you and keep up the pressure We can do it! We must do it! I will accept no excuse for failure. The Scandinavian folks who settled here and were originally the Viking Raiders have settled in well; the Scots from Ireland; the English from Northumbria; those subjects that were originally from Wales; and above all our Gaelic-speaking compatriots from above the Highland Line, all deserve a united kingdom and with historic bloodlines from all of these sectors we can and will provide leadership to form the united kingdom of King Robert the First, Robert the Bruce, Earl Robert of Annandale."

"Have you not neglected your Norman heritage?" I asked.

King Robert frowned in my direction. "Our Norman roots were originally Scandinavian roots. Your own ancestors came over to England and on to Scotland from Normandy in Northern France yet you and the Boat Master are of Norwegian origin. I can see that you, Murdoch, and you, Halfdan, will work well together as you both have the same roots and expertise from Norway. No Frenchman was or is capable of building the superb boats which will spearhead the opening of our crusade.

"You, Lord Seaton are undoubtedly of French extraction. I leave it to you to find your Scottish roots as soon as possible! *This action has not to be taken for another Norman conquest! Ours is a purely Scottish enterprise for the unification of our land! Be sure to mention that at every opportunity!"*

With that broadside we were dismissed to think about our future roles in the completion of King Robert I's kingdom, the Kingdom of Scotland, united and indivisible. The unification of such disparate social strands that stretched originally from India, Central Europe, the Baltic States, Scandinavia, Normandy, Brittany, Cornwall, Wales, Ireland and England herself, not to mention the native Gaels and Picts, constituted a major task. Religion too, was to play an important part of the effort. It was true that Christianity was winning the day but there were numerous pagan strands of worship still out there. Nevertheless, the gospel of the Trinity and the story of Jesus' life on earth were compelling and were increasingly accepted. The policy of removing church land from Royal protection and its redistribution to lay subjects was a clever idea as far as the existing ruling class was concerned although the lowest class of serf, servant, or vassal was yet to find any benefit from any religion.

Clearing the under-castle harbour system of all the wrecked boats that had been abandoned after the last invasion of the English who had tried to capture Loch Doon Castle for their Scottish allies, was a long and tedious job. We had found quite a few reusable parts of boats, especially the form fitments like oak jointing angles, ash frames and hull oak strakes that we had upped our estimate of being able to produce three war boats instead of two.

The framing of several skin boats (larger versions of the Pictish 'coracles') was moving ahead and Lord Seaton now knew that a skin boat was a smaller craft that could carry up to six armed men that consisted of ash frames covered with preserved animal hides rendered waterproof by tanning and tight sewing with animal sinews forced into the seams to make a watertight outer shell that would float in fresh water with a draught of no more than one foot.

These double-ended, nearly circular boats could float practically anywhere. They would be very useful for the final approach to a target location without detection and when not required for military purposes several could be carried aboard a 24-oar war boat.

King Robert at first came down every day but as he began to notice our significant progress, he declared satisfaction and more or less left us to our own devices. The clearance of the harbour area was executed by a group of castle workers who had no immediate jobs and we had managed to attract a couple of woodworkers from Dalmellington, and one of the nearby villages to help with the technical jobs. A young man, named Macnab, from further up the Gala Lane valley was also hired. Lord Seaton liked him as he was the nephew of one of his tenants.

It transpired that Halfdan had been sent to Norway and trained in boat building at the same principal boat yard in Norway as Erik at Loch Ryan and that their Apprenticeships had overlapped by two years with Halfdan the junior. This was most acceptable to the project as he and I had the same or similar skill sets. Of course, I was the younger man in the present partnership and Halfdan had not practiced his craft for several years due to Lord Seaton's disinterest in all things maritime. He was now extremely excited to be useful again and it was wonderful to see his enthusiasm although age had certainly slowed him down.

Today we were fashioning a long steam box to dry out and shape the recovered hull planks. Between jobs, and in the evening after work was finished for the day, Halfdan was engaged in carving the prow head pieces for the boats. He had decided that the true Vikings had favoured dragon figureheads as they were long considered despoilers as dragons were reputed to be, when the Vikings first landed although they had quickly settled down into model tenants and farmers as time passed and when marrying Galloway girls, they had been tamed as far as their own community was concerned. Their larger physique, fair or red hair and blue eyes still made them something to fear in the outland communities and that would be a good thing when we finally went to pacify these more distant population centres.

Halfdan had resolved to make the figureheads in the likenesses of him and me on these first two boats but on discussion with me we had reached the conclusion that it would be impolitic to so do and that it was better to create an emblem of 'Scottishness'- something that could be interpreted as a Scottish Monarch and to do the same on both boats. Two of the three projected large boats were in an advanced state and the ribs' structure was already erected although that was in the amidships areas where planking was not required to be so shaped as towards and bow and stern. These difficult tasks were still before us.

I had moved in with Halfdan by the King's permission in order that we might continue in the nonworking hours to discussing the project but tonight Halfdan was busy under the light from the fire with a particular facial expression on one of his carved effigies that conversation had ceased. Not being ready to lie down to sleep I stepped out for a spell. Our cabin was at the rear of the subterranean port area with a stone stair leading up to the back of the Castle's open Concourse above, so I took that way to the fresh air and emerged into the castle courtyard but against the tower wall which was in the shadows cast by the flickering lights from the burning braziers placed around the space but not at the stairs area that I was using.

I was just standing enjoying the cooling breeze that was circulating in and around the open Castle centre when I noticed a still figure also standing in the same shadow that I had encountered when first coming out of the stairway entrance door. He was standing no more than eight feet away from me, yet I could not detect any features that would identify him.

"Enjoying the fresh night air, Your Honour?" I said in a voice with a neutral tone to cover my embarrassment at having been caught unaware of my surroundings.

"Thank you. Yes." Was the response in a rich baritone. "You have come up from the Docking Area. It might get quite stuffy in there.

"Har det Gott" the voice continued.

"Jeg har det bra, Takk" I responded before my mind realized that we were no longer speaking in English. The old-fashioned greeting and response that had been a daily occurrence at Erik's Boat Yard at Loch Ryan and had come back to me in an instant without any thought.

"You are Norwegian?" I asked in colloquial English.

"And you are of Norwegian descent" was the answer also in the same language.

At once the stranger stepped out into the light. He was of medium height and stocky of build, and his beard was jet black that matched his dark hair pulled back into a bun. His dark brown eyes were partially covered by the black bushy eyebrows. He was clothed in a grey surtout or tabard which partially concealed the glint of pieces of body armour about his person however, he was not armed and seemed to be friendly enough.

"I am called 'Jack' although that is a *'nom du guerre'* which I rather like" was his response.

"Well. They might take you for a particularly tall Frenchman or worse, an Englishman. I am called Muireadhach also known as Murdoch. How did you expect that I understood Norwegian?

"Your history and reputation precede you even although you are a young man. Actually, I came to Loch Doon Castle to meet you and to offer my services."

"Well. I am honoured." I said, "But how were you sure it was I"?

"The Norwegian greeting was a test. But what Scotsman could match your Viking height and sturdy body?"

"I was born here but it is true that my father hailed from Norway via Normandy."

We continued talking and Jack revealed that he had recently come over from Norway on a trading boat as a voluntary oarsman. He was aware of King Robert's necessity to unify Scotland and had heard of our, secret, activities here at Loch Doon Castle. So much for secrecy! The rest of the country had already made up its mind. Those who would oppose the King's venture were mostly his male relatives and the Nobility, but the peasants and tenants might very well oppose their feudal masters when there was a call to raise a conscript army of opposition.

This was good news for us as we were always curious to learn about any confirmatory attitude that might exist when we began to look for allies. To hear that we were on the right track and that the King had correctly read the pulse of the Scottish people was even more than we had hoped for.

When I afterwards told the King what Jack had reported, the King replied: "I always felt that the Scottish people would support my cause rather than any other......"

> "I must join my own people and the
> Nation in which I was born.
>
> "No man holds his flesh and blood in
> hatred. I am no exception"

As he was born at Turnberry in Ayrshire, this was a declaration that was widely quoted throughout Scotland and had a lot to do with our ultimate success. But to get from here to there was going to be a hard and difficult road. "Perhaps Jack could help us?" I put the question to my Sovereign.

"Does he have any military experience?" asked the King. "I cannot rely on My Lord Seaton as he is no longer a young man and I doubt he has the stomach for it."

"I shall ask Jack." I replied. In the meantime, may I keep him around? He can help in all sorts of ways. He has some items of body armour. Perhaps he has seen active battle?

"It will be in order for you to employ him with you and Halfdan provided Halfdan has no problem with the arrangement. He can stay with you both. I shall want to meet with him casually without the customary protocol This way I shall assess this man for myself."

"As you command, Your Majesty. We shall be completing the stern hull structure on the first of the boats. This might be a good time to come down for an inspection."

And it was arranged that the King would casually meet with Jack to assess whether or not he would be a suitable addition to our team.

In the meantime, and after the noon hour, I took Jack down to our apartment. He and Halfdan were most cordial to each other. Our cabin at once began to take on the ambience of a "Boy's Club". Jack noticed the almost completed sculpture of the first boat's bowsprit ornament and complimented Halfdan on his artistic talent. Right away he identified the head as that of the mystical Pictish king which endeared him to the old man although afterwards Jack confided to me that the carved head was undoubtedly 'Norwegian' in its treatment of hair and moustache! They had chatted in conversational Norwegian, and I was forced to ask them that they confine their talk to the Old Norse-Gallic tongue which was then prevalent in Galloway. I could understand the modern Norwegian language, but I did not want them to know that.

I knew I had made a good choice when Jack proved his worth in the bending of the hull planks as we were trying to fit them on to the frames. His strength matched mine and was greatly superior to Halfdan's and bending and securing hull planks especially at the ends of a boat where the shape of the hull was more extreme needed a great deal of pushing and manipulating to conform to the required shape. Halfdan could be allocated the watertightness part of the planking process with no loss of prestige.

Heavy, narrow strands of woollen plank stuffing intertwined with animal sinews which had been prepared beforehand were forced between the planks with a flat chisel-like implement and a wooden mallet into the horizontal seams. The fitting and securing of a wooden Roman-style helmet at the very top of the stern planking where it swept up to a short level platform about two feet above the bulwark which had been carved by Halfdan as a finishing touch.

We all stood back to view and admire our handiwork at this time and were just complimenting each other when the King arrived.

"Very nice!" He commented, "but without a bow, this boat is going nowhere!"

He came forward. "Who is this fellow?" he asked, looking at Jack.

I hastened to address the King:

"He came looking for some work. I mentioned it at the time that he brought good news about the general feeling in the country was positive about you and your plans to seize the reins of proficient government, My Lord."

"Ah! Yes!" replied King Robert then turning to Jack, "Tell me where you come from and who are your family"?

"I am of Norwegian descent although I was born in your Kingdom, My Lord. My father came over to Scotland with King Haakon to oppose the late Scottish King Alexander's attempts to take back the lands on the mainland originally won by the Norwegian Vikings. My Father as the nephew of Walter the High Steward of Scotland, was married into the Boyd family of Kilmarnock and you will know that he was a strong supporter of you and your cause, My Lord. It is unfortunate that the Chief of Clan Boyd at that time lost his life at the Battle of Largs. We came over to England with King William from Normandy when the family had the name of de Morville."

"You are most welcome to join us here" the King said simply. My Lord Murdoch of Cumloden and the honest Boat Man Halfdan of Lord Seaton shall be your mentors. Although Largs was a great victory for Scotland. The stormy weather was in our favour on land and against the Vikings on the water. I really think that Largs will prove to be the end of Viking invasions. We lost some fine men including many other local Boyds and Montgomeries. At this time, we shall welcome any support that is available to us as we progress towards the unification of Alba into the Kingdom of Scotland."

This was going even better than I had hoped. *Lord Murdoch of Cumloden*'? was the first time the King had recognised me with my land title. Of course, I was not a 'lord' in the real sense, and the King was using the honorific to emphasize my leadership role,

"I do not wish to speak of you as 'Jack'. You are a Christian I suppose. All your family were. What was your baptismal name? The King was getting down to the business in hand.

Jack provided the finishing touch.

"Robert. In honour of You, My Lord."

"Oh well! We cannot have two 'Roberts' Do you have a middle name?

"Stewart".

"Goodness Gracious! we are getting nowhere that is not a stumbling block. Now I understand why you continue to employ your *nom du guerre*. You will make fewer enemies by calling yourself 'Jack' Let me re-christen you as 'Scott'.

The King drew his sword. Jack knelt down and Jack became Scott. Scott Boyd.

"You are now officially subject Number one" the King smiled. Now let me look closely at this half-completed boat!

The inspection of the boat continued.

Whilst examining the caulking of the hull seams, Halfdan remarked to the King that we had developed a new form of creating watertightness which we were also using for the skin boats. lt was the combination of woollen strands intertwined with animal sinews.

"Whose idea was this?" asked the King.

"We both came up with the idea after work whilst taking our meal in the cabin." Halfdan spoke and I nodded in assent.

"Very good!" We did not often get compliments from the King. Then, turning to Scott: "You do see that project requires thinking as well as brawn? Do you anticipate that you will fit in and be a contributor to the success of the enterprise?"

"My Lord, I shall give all my effort to the project, so help me God!"

"Good! Your allegiance is accepted, and you have given your word."

With all this additional encouragement from the King we renewed our enthusiasm and hard work and three weeks later we had completed the first boat and four skin boats. On reporting this ground-breaking event I suggested to him that we might want to highlight the occasion by creating a formal launching and naming ceremony with all the members of the Castle compliment in attendance.

"What a good idea." His reaction was very positive. "I'll request that Lady Seaton do the honours and we shall have a formal reception afterwards at which I shall make a policy speech. We shall also request that the boat be named, and the Lady Seaton do the honours. Shall we ask Her Ladyship to suggest a name or will be give her a list of acceptable ones?"

"The latter option is by far the better strategy," I said. "That way we may be assured of an appropriate name that should reflect the glory of your reign and the eminence of your Kingship."

"If that ridiculous form of flattery you use means that you are going to include my name on the list of boat names then let me warn you in advance, I do not want it! In fact, I positively forbid it! It is my opinion that boats are customarily female. No male names or male-sounding names, please!"

I was a little taken aback by the King's strong conviction. "I was thinking of your noble sisters' names, Your Highness." I even astonished myself by my quick thinking that seemed to have saved me from a ridiculous embarrassment.

"Ah! Yes!" was the response, "Yes! That will do nicely'"

I signalled to Halfdan and Scott that we should get back to work so with short bows in the King's direction we went back to our workplaces to resume what we had been doing earlier.

I hoped that the blushing of my face had not revealed my original thought but being red headed it was a natural reaction to an embarrassment and I could not control it. The King's mind was already elsewhere but I observed Scott's recognition of my condition. He looked like he had read my thoughts and perhaps would recall my affliction and take advantage at some future occasion. I would have to watch myself when in Scott's presence.

It was now the mid-day mealtime. I sat on my own contemplating the harbour and how it might be defended. Halfdan and Scott sat together on a stack of restored hull planks some distance away. I finished my repast quickly and moved off without saying anything to the others. Walking from one piece of jetty to another and occasionally having to hop aboard what was left of a boat I gradually reached the outer line of the connecting link by means of sunken boat, wrecked jetty, or optimistic dangerous leap that outlined what poor defences had previously been set up to deter raiders.

I was rather enjoying my ability to complete the progression along the front line despite its many gaps. Extending my view from time to time, I was observing the dark blue waters of the Loch which merged into a dark green as it reflected the mirrored green of the hillside trees.

But what was that?

Something was moving over the water not more than three miles away. It was obviously a boat, and it was keeping close to shore on the shaded side of the loch. The loch was choppy in response to the stiff breeze that was coming from the north-west. 'It would be a bad day to make passage to Ireland' I mused to myself. I passed by one of the guards who was stationed along the outside line of jetties which were immediately just in line with the outside Castle wall overhead. The highest clearance was at the mid-point of the elongated arch which constituted the entrance to the docking area. For the first time I wondered if the mast height of our new boats would permit them to actually sail out of the Castle harbour rather than be rowed. This might be a critical factor in the future but what about right now?

Who could it be? Spies, no doubt. With the wind behind them as it was, the boat would be near to the Castle in much less than an hour. They must be intercepted and examined! I shouted to the guard that I had just passed. Would he run and report the incursion to My Lord Seaton and rouse the Castle Defence Team? He rushed off to do my bidding and I made my way back to the boat-building area to where Halfdan and Scott were back at the skeleton of the second boat which was coming along quite well, probably a little speedier than the first boat at the same state. That is experience for you. The job gets easier with more experience and less time is wasted when thinking of what to do next and how to do it.

"Men!" I shouted, "strangers approaching by boat!"

Right away and just as we had planned and practiced, the emergency boat that was lying afloat nearer to the archway with an unobstructed, direct access to the loch waters was readied and Halfan and Scott pushed off from the jetty with four of the sturdiest castle workers bearing cutlasses and daggers. It was quite a fierce-looking group although unpractised and untested in actual aggressive action.

I was making my way to the north-side curtain wall when I encountered Lord Seaton. We both headed in the direction of the nearby watchtower that marked the north-east end of the rampart. By now, the warning gong was summoning the Castle occupants who had defence duties to their posts. In all fairness to Lord Seaton, it looked like he had organised this drill and the participants very well.

The King joined us in the tower and looking around at the signs of readiness to repel attackers, expressed his approval to My Lord Seaton.

"Very good, my Lord! I can see that you have been well trained and are experienced in the art of defence!" He turned his attention to the pending drama taking place further down the Loch. "Now let us see what these interlopers are up to."

By now, our boat was better than half-way towards the strangers. Sailing and rowing into the wind was difficult for our crew and making much of any headway was problematical. The strangers were clearly at an advantage with the wind behind them and they were getting close to the Castle.

We watched through our spy glasses. This created a few anxious moments as we on the Castle rampart wondered and worried what the strategy could possibly be? Seaton declared his anxiety by putting his head between his hands in an expression of despair. I looked at the King. He was stoically accepting what he saw and recognising that we still had no idea what was likely to happen and the time for reckoning was not yet to hand.

When our boat reached the other boat, we noticed that it went completely alongside with ropes to secure the two boats as one. Then, surprisingly, we saw Halfdan and Scott climb over the bulwarks and board the interlopers' boat. We all let out an involuntary gasp at this unexpected movement of our principal emissaries. There seemed to be no movement that might suggest hostility and we had to accept the premise that our men had considered safety when they changed boats so quickly and seemingly without hesitation.

The King spoke to me: "This sort of negotiation should be over in a few minutes. The longer it extends; the better it is for us. I have seen similar examples of negotiations like this. You see, we have no part in the situation and that could create anxiety as if our input at this stage and with the short notice that was provided could be miraculously altered.

> "Worry about the things you can change and do not waste your time over things you do not control."

We must trust the instincts and native skills of our representatives."

After about fifteen minutes: "Our men are getting back aboard our boat" interjected my Lord Seaton with a note of optimism in his voice. He was nevertheless trembling, and he was having difficulty in seeing anything through his spyglass with his shaking hands.

King Robert agreed and signalled to me that I had no need to worry. Actually, I could see unaided that our boat was now running before the wind and heading towards the Castle with all six participants safely aboard. All that remained was to see what the other boat was going to do and to hear from our own team how the deed to dissuade them from coming any nearer the Castle had been accomplished.

The visitors' boat was now turned around and heading back down the Loch away from our castle. But would it stay away? It very much depended on what had been agreed to.

CHAPTER VI

BOAT DIPLOMACY; INFORMAL PLANNING; ERRIF OPERATION; RIVER DOON; DALMELLINGTON

"Do not speak at the same time!" said the King. "Who is going to speak first? Let us do it with seniority. Halfdan-- you first."

*O*ur two emissaries had been talking over each other in their excitement. But being told by their Monarch to speak one at a time and that Halfdan should speak first, some semblance of order was achieved.

Halfdan spoke:

"My Lord. We had decided on the way out to intercept the intruders that we would pass ourselves off as Norwegians to throw them off the trail that you, Sire, were involved with what was going on in the Loch Doon Castle. So, when we came alongside their boat, Scott and I were talking in

Norwegian and our four crewmen from the Castle were told to keep their mouths shut.

"On coming alongside their craft, we noticed that they were not from this area but spoke to each other in a patois which we took for how they communicate in Northumbria. Scott suggested to me that we should speak with them on a face-to-face basis so when we were secure to their boat, we boarded them without opposition. I asked in Old English might we speak with the Leader and a very tall fellow came forward and admitted that he was in charge. I asked him what he was doing sailing on the Loch?"

Scott then spoke:

"He said that they were visitors to the area and had noticed the Castle on its own island which looked deserted. Then we came out from under the Castle, and they realised that it was not unoccupied. 'What were we doing at the Castle?' he enquired. I answered that we were a division of Norwegian military who had been separated from the main raiding party at Whithorn and were moving north-east towards the east coast of Alba on the way back to Norway. Like you, we had seen this deserted Castle and taken hold of it from the few elderly locals who had taken possession before us and were glad to see us as they were short of food and not very successful at fishing in the Loch waters. Could we help?"

"Not only could we help but several of our troop were actually fishermen when not in the employ of our feudal superiors as we had been at on the Isle of Man. A bargain was soon reached. Fish for accommodation. But that was several years ago, and we had come to appreciate our accommodation. Especially with the earlier local squatters dying off or going back to their villages and their women. The Castle is now wholly ours by eminent domain and we do not want to give it up although when we move on, it will be free for the taking but we will have to talk the situation over with the 300 of our confederates before reaching any agreement".

Halfdan broke in:

"This was my idea and Scott thought up the 300 number. Small enough to be realistic and large enough to indicate that a battle would ensue should any effort made to take over the Castle. The Leader looked around at the eight of his fellow would-be refugees and probably mentally counted those of his group that he had left at his camp wherever that was and decided that an aggressive take-over was not possible. He conveyed to us that now that he knew the circumstances, he would tell his colleagues that the Castle was not available for occupancy. He would return to his group now with this information."

"Scott asked where their camp was?"

"And he told me without hesitation. When we commence our operations, Your Majesty, we should probably start there to clear out any future problem. It is on the Eriff Peninsula near the foot of the Loch."

This last remark from Scott.

The King was stroking his beard. "Hmmmmm" he mused. Lord Seaton added:

"This gives us time to get our clearance troops assembled and trained. How clever of you both to come up with a strategy that provided the majority of what we wanted. Time to finish our preparations; No attack but the possibility of retaliation by our own men; The indication that they were perhaps not a large group; and a plausible explanation of why we were occupying the Castle with no mention or hint of the King's intentions."

Again, he added:

"There was no indication of myself or my family and nothing about the Carrick Estate and its vast hinterland all the way to the Solway? These details will not be overlooked when your campaign gets under way, Your Majesty."

Our Monarch looked strangely at My Lord Seaton. At last, he spoke:

"First of all, I want to thank you all for carrying out this great and effective action. You will not find my gratefulness wanting when you come to accept your next reward." The four boatmen who had accompanied Halfdan and Scott knelt at the King's feet and he in turn lightly touched their heads.

Halfdan and Scott remained standing unsure whether the King was including them. Apparently, he was not, for he turned to walk away indicating that he wanted those that remained to follow him.

On the way back to Halfdan's hut the King was talking.

"I hope you have something palatable to quench our thirst, Halfdan. I am dried out after all the emotion this afternoon". Lord Seaton was hanging back just a little. I saw him attract the attention of one of the harbour workers and telling him something after which he re-joined our group.

Eventually seated around the large table in Halfdan's single room cabin we all began to relax. Halfdan retrieved several bottles of beer and an assortment of drinking vessels, one for each of us. But before we had taken a mouthful, Seaton's steward arrived with a couple of flagons of liquid and placed them on the table in front of the King who acknowledged the steward and the liquid which turned out to be a superior brew of beer which none of us had ever tasted. Halfdan's beer went down dry gullets in haste to get to the good stuff.

"No toasts!" the King said. "Let us drink to a very incisive and successful action to us all. Each in his own way contributed in his best manner to the adventure. We may take a collective bow. I salute you all!"

The beer flowed and the conversation grew louder, and we all relaxed and drank and talked like old friends. I shall always remember the informality of this occasion. It may have been the last time the King was surrounded by friends rather than courtiers.

As for the newcomers to the Loch we never heard tell or sighted them until we banished them from Carrick and the surrounding areas.

This last statement is written many months later with the help of hindsight. There was a lot of work still to do to get to the point where action began, and planning and exercises had been completed to our satisfaction. Every day we laboured on the boats and at last completed three full-size and fully equipped war-boats and eighteen skin boats. As agreed, the three larger boats were named after the King's female family: *lsabella; Marjorie*; and *Elizabeth* and the skin boats*: I, M*, and *E* followed by a number to represent the fighting boat they were attached to and identified by the initial. We had decided that there would be six 'skins' attached to each war boat.

Under normal circumstances they would be towed behind the larger boat but on long passages they could be lifted on board and stowed on both sides of the mast with three boats on each side. For portage, the skin boats would be carried overland by their crews; the larger and heavier war boats would have to be given portage also by their crews in two or three shifts. Manning consisted of six men to each skin boat and the war boats were built for 24 rowers. Altogether a projected assault fleet would consist of two big boats and twelve coracles with the remaining craft and crews held in reserve and kept back from the initial frontal assault.

Practical exercises were held on the south-side of the castle where there was a terminal build-up of flotsam and sediment where the small burn, the Gala Lane, made entrance to Loch

Doon. This feature would be readily utilised for practicing portage. It would also not be visible from further down the Loch from prying eyes where views of the practice area were hindered by the Castle itself standing and blocking the line of sight.

The next activity was the 'council of war' headed up by Lord Seaton which we eagerly awaited. It would have to be a sort of Combined Operations affair involving our waterborne initial involvement; the clearance of all negative forces from the environs of Loch Doon; Portage of the boats beyond the Ness Glen and their relaunching below the escarpment at Berbeth; descent of the River Doon to Bogton Loch; Pacification of Dalmellington Village; Continuation of the descent of the Doon River; and the riparian hamlets of Craigmark, Downieston, and Carnochan. With the element of surprise, the undertaking could be successful and not beyond our forces and capabilities.

As far as the boats were concerned, I believed that when we attacked any waterside targets, we would do so from two widely spaced points on the two sides of the target area. I had been told that the Viking raiders had preferred a full-frontal attack at the centre with several war boats tied side by side to each other to deliver a simultaneous maximum heavy and demoralising blow. I did not favour this strategy for the sort of attacks we were staging for in the first place, the opposition was unlikely to mount a united counterforce. Our attack from both flanks would be much more efficacious.

Further, we needed time to encourage defenders to join our cause from the village communities Those folks who changed sides would ride in the boats as long as there was space and weight abilities, or march on the river banks along with the balance of our fighting force and lastly, King Robert would be seen as the leader of the expedition. This last was especially important lest the entire enterprise would be considered an armed insurrection at best, or aggression by the Duke of Carrick (which it was in a way) to enlarge his estate. Our activity was already being named an **'Armed Insurrection'** by The King of England, - after the news spread about the Glen Trool Masacre as it was being called by our enemies. It was up to us to change public opinion, this, may be the first occasion in domestic aggression when public perception would be critical.

After all the plans were discussed and the boat activity integrated with the overall strategy, I began to feel that my role in the entire operation was being diminished. My Lord Seaton was to be in charge of the land forces and the attacks. Good for him. But was he capable of the responsibility? True, he will have Scott as his second-in- command. Good for him. This arrangement will be the making of Scott as he will prove to be the superior leader.

Admittedly, the boats under my command will act like the tip if the spear in the initial stages.

But what after? Or during any portage? What will be my role in that case? I can see how necessary it will be to ferry the King into any overcome community to let the people know what we are doing and to observe his presence and purpose.

After all, the entire operation is to put King Robert Bruce on the throne of Scotland and to ensure general acclaim and peace in the land.

All these thoughts were running through my head as we headed to our couches to restore energies for the morrow. Strangely enough, no one was very interested in going over the details again.

Halfdan had already thrown himself on his couch and pulled up the cover, and Scott was disrobing and washing down the day's dust from his face and body. One of the fine habits that he had learned from his Viking father was cleanliness of body. As a matter of fact, I had tended to copy this cleanliness habit.

Was I conscious of learning from Scott because I was secretly jealous of his person? It was all so complicated. He was clearly the kind of fellow who takes to the military discipline lifestyle and is inclined to think of every situation as a battle which he must win.

Reduced to a silent role I sat in the large chair that was Halfdan's favourite resting place when he was in the cabin. It was placed on one side of the fireplace and there was a handy fire iron on which to place one's feet when sprawling on the fur coverings and being almost horizontal but with the head and shoulders sufficiently raised to continually observe what was going on in the surroundings.

Scott had finished with his ablutions.

"Are you not going to sleep on your couch?" he asked, "You will have a stiff neck come the morning call."

"I do not know." I replied. "But I want to be ready when we start tomorrow."

"Please yourself." Was Scott's reply. "But it is obviously better to waken up all fresh and raring to go instead of approaching new challenges encumbered with yesterday's dust."

"Oh! A philosopher yet?" I said rather sarcastically. "Please do not attempt to lecture me at this time of night!"

"Now, Muireadhach, it is unlike you to be so disputative. You are certainly out of sorts." Scott added: "You are not worried about tomorrow, are you?"

"No, no" I responded rather quickly, sensing that I had revealed my inner feeling too much.

"Because, if you are needing some moral support, you can always count on me."

I bristled at this suggestion.

Scott, now you are insulting me! I am in no need of your assistance in any way. It is the other way around. You needed MY help which I gave freely without reservation or conditions. You go too far!"

Now Scott was irritated.

"The King says I have military talent."

"I am the King's Sailor!" I retorted.

"It is the King's Soldier that is needed now!"

Just then a querulous voice arose from the pile of skins that constituted Halfdan's couch.

"Shut up, both of you and get abed! You are both like a couple of kids quarrelling over a toy. The King needs you both. I need you both. Do not foul the King's quest over personal animosities!"

We both immediately pulled back from the aggressive posture we had assumed.

"Oh, Halfdan. I thought you were asleep. I am sorry to disturb you." I said and Scott, too, made conciliatory noises.

"You two young men have come very far, and you accept the honours and position you have been given as if you expected none less. Be happy with what you have attained, so far. Keep your long-term ambitions to yourself and gratefully accept all the favours that have been bestowed on you by our Sovereign, King Robert Bruce!

I for one was humbled and I suspect Scott was too.

The fire in the big grate was going down and our room was getting noticeably colder. Tomorrow is another day, and we must do our best for His Majesty and Scotland.

But, as I settled down to get some sleep, my thoughts were about Scott. I would need to watch him. I wonder if the King had any cognizance of our internal and personal competitiveness?

Midnight came much too early. The night watch came knocking on our door and by the time we moved down to the boats. the castle soldiery was already lined up in the platoons we had pre-designated with all three war boats having a sailing crew of six and a military crew of 24 who also performed as oarsmen when required. There were three persons in charge.

Each skinboat had a crew of six with one of the six in charge These men would also double as soldiers and oarsmen when appropriate. Thus: each force unit constituted 48 men and the total force was three times that number. The King, Seaton and I would be on the third reserve war boat and Boyd was to head the first attacking boat.

The first target area was the camp of the Northumbrians who had originally scoped out our castle. We wanted them out of the way when we turned on the villagers who by that time would have heard of our prowess in vanquishing our foes. There was a second purpose in attacking the Northumbrian location.

This was the site of our eventual landing for our portage route to the River Doon below the Ness Glen and would be a good place to establish a bridgehead. Our plan called for a landing on the Eriff Peninsula with a portage to the Muck Water which was unnavigable then down the Muck Glen past Dalpharson to the River Doon below Berbeth then by boat to the Bogton Loch.

Before the clock struck one, we were silently gliding down Loch Doon in the dark, the three war boats each towing six skin boats. At half-past three we were off the Northumberland Camp and before the sun was up the Northumbrians were routed and our cooks were preparing the breakfast for our successful troops on the vanquished adversary's fires.

A useful and a valuable hoard of silver and gold artifacts had been uncovered and some of our men had gone through the clothing and bags of the dead men. A small quantity of valuables from this source was amassed so when the King called for a meeting by mid-morning, all the booty was collected into one place and divided among our men. The larger pieces were donated to Lord Seaton's castle.

"So far, I have counted twenty bodies (*'50 bodies' shouted an anonymous voice from the audience)...*"

The King laughed. "Whatever the number, those who did not perish ran away and that is the main thing.

"But what you all must know and appreciate is that for the next month, our foes will actually be our neighbours. It is not our ambition to kill all of them lest we deplete our villages of fit men". (*laughter*) I am serious. What we want to achieve is some men with the right heart to join us in our quest and to humble and subdue the remainder so that they will never think of attacking Loch Doon Castle when we are away attacking the rest of Scotland to persuade all the inhabitants that we bring peace and order to the country under the strong but just rule of King Robert the Bruce...." *(Cheers from those present)* " AND his loyal followers who have been with him since Loch Doon." *(More cheers)*

"Our foes in the days and weeks ahead are not enemies in the truest sense but neighbours who might want to join in our crusade. When you have the opportunity to bring any of these country people to my attention you can tell them that all personal vassalage obligation will be bought out or cancelled. Housing for recruits' families will be provided as I may remind you all that as Laird of Carrick My writ is law, and what I say will be a disclosed policy from now on. And, may I add: As King your rights as my subjects will be preserved and improved, as necessary. Thank you, again. For those of you who are Christian. 'May God bless you and keep you from harm' Amen."

Scott had had a particularly good battle. He showed me two rings of gold and precious stones and a golden arm bracelet in the Roman manner which he had taken off a particularly aggressive opponent's body. He seemed to have no negative reaction to last night's argument between us. I too, was taken up with the euphoria of the moment and we sailed together on the same boat back to the castle in perfect harmony.

That evening, we consulted a map of the region and decided on our next foray. We would make our landings at the mouth of and as far up the tributary streams as we could take the war boats. If there was a community on the banks on the way we would start our pacification there but if there was no habitation, we would sail as far as the navigation allowed. The mouths of the Craiglee, Garpel, Beoch, Cullendoch, and Polmedow, were north of the castle and would be first attended to after which the tributaries south of the castle would be visited. The burns leading to Loch Recar and Loch Finlas were expected to be the most populous and develop the greatest return of our stated purposes and invitation to join with us.

For the next two weeks our campaign continued. As we had conjectured, we were most successful with the serfs who were always looking for a way out of service or another life. Younger sons of yeoman farmers and other freemen were always welcome, but we had to set the minimum age of fifteen for new recruits and forty as the maximum age of ex-military-trained individuals. One gentleman applicant from Loch Finlas had actually served with the previous Earl Carrick and had been stationed at Annan for a couple of years!

Taking a short respite at the castle on the second Sunday of the campaign we were somewhat idly planning the foray to the south of the castle to complete the pacification of the loch environs when we received notice from the King that he was convening a meeting in the evening and would expect us to attend. There was no mention of an agenda, but we could and did guess that the landing at Eriff and the portage to the river Doon would be the principal topic and perhaps what we were going to do beyond that.

"At last! We are going to do some serious campaigning." I observed.

"Tell me, Muireadhach, why will we have to carry our boats down the Gow Glen? Can we not float on the down current?" This question was from Scott.

"Scott. You overlook the fact that the Gow is like the Doon but also coming off another plateau. It is swift and rocky and not suitable for boats until it reaches all the way down and joins the Doon."

"You seem to know the landscape well".

"Yes, I do. I have the brother of my mother living at Dalpharson which I have visited many times."

"Oh! I forget that you are just a local boy when all is said and done."

Halfdan who was not really listening to our exchange nevertheless picked up the Scott's inuendo.

"Hold on, you two!" Halfdan warned. "I do not want any unpleasantness here or when we meet with the King. We should be going. We don't want to keep the King waiting should be your concern right now."

He was right. It was time we moved along to the King's room. As we were walking along the passage, we encountered my Lord Seaton. He looked like he had something on his mind and when we were in the King's presence, he revealed what was troubling him was his wife's presence in the castle when he was away doing the King's bidding.

You will recall that Lord Seaton was married to Lady Christina Bruce, the sister of King Robert the Bruce together with her Lady in Waiting, her sister-in-law, Lady Mary Bruce. It had been reported that Christina had married Gartnait, 7th Earl of Mar and when I met that gentleman at Turnberry, he had been described as 'betrothed to Lady Christina' the King's sister. This proposed union did not happen, however, because here she was, happily married to My Lord, Sir Christopher Seaton with whom she had several children.

The King was paying more attention to Sir Christopher's dilemma because of his sisters' involvement so he gave the matter his first consideration.

At first, he said to Lord Seaton:

"Do you believe our families are going to be in peril because of the successful pacification of the area around the loch? I hardly think so. Have we not been successful at all?"

"It is not the local hotheads I worry about but I fear the Earl of Mar and his roving English troops might select Loch Doon Castle to inflict a telling blow on your quest? He can come up from Ayr where he and his troops are based and besiege the castle at very short notice, and they would be here before we knew of it! With all the menfolk away and our boats otherwise occupied and not yet returned, we will be comparatively vulnerable to attack." My Lord Seaton was sincere in stating his problems and revealed a pessimistic fear level that alarmed most of his listeners who did not expect to hear such an abject personal statement from a man who was supposed to be in an executive position and already in charge of overall security.

"I must admit to not thinking too much of our rear." Said the King after pondering what Lord Seaton had just said. "My thoughts have been looking ahead first other than considering what we are leaving behind. Certainly, we had always planned to leave one of the war boats and her attendant skin boats behind as castle protection, but from what you outline, this would not be adequate. Their fresh troops from the barracks at Ayr Castle will be a difficult foe to deal with. I am aware that it is only one day's march from Ayr to Loch Doon."

Scott and I exchanged glances with the realization that the overall plan of forward action will be about to undergo a major re-working. What was Lord Seaton thinking about and how would any bolstering of this castle's defensive posture be achieved?

A silence descended upon our little group.

At last, I was forced to break the silence.

"Your Majesty," I started," since the Lord Seaton has raised the question, perhaps he has an idea of its solution?" King Robert seemed grateful for someone providing the opening gambit.

"Good idea" he said and turned to Lord Seaton. "I am sure my Lord can speak for himself. The last thing I want to see is that my team do not get along with each other."

"Thank you, your Majesty." Seaton responded as if he had his answer ready and was just waiting for the right opportunity to place it on the table for consideration. This type of mendacity always annoyed me, and Lord Seaton was always trying to get what he wanted by devious means. Perhaps he had been too long a diplomat?

"Perhaps I can take the ladies away to some safe place? I would of course, miss the main battles to come but it may be that my sovereign could manage without me?" Lord Seaton had his tentative answer ready.

The King raised an eyebrow. "So that's it. You desire to withdraw from our precarious venture? So be it. I have felt for some time that your heart was not into sitting on a barrel of gunpowder. It is true, however, that your point concerning the women is a valid one."

King Robert stood up and in his best magisterial voice intoned:

"Decision Number One: After the main fighting force has departed from Loch Doon Castle, the security and defence of the castle and its occupants shall be the responsibility of Sir Christopher Seaton with particular emphasis on the safety of all women and children in place. Your Boatman shall be your second in command and he will arrange for a small escape fleet hidden from view if required.

"Now, my Lord, you may depart from this meeting and any decisions made that can be of concern to you will be confidentially passed on to you! Halfdan will stay and report decisions to you."

The King turned his back on his brother-in-law and sat down.[8]

Seaton had perforce to immediately retire. He was not a happy man. He had been successful in withdrawing from the King's venture but had received nothing additional with which to protect the castle after the main force was withdrawn.

With Seaton now out of the way, the King spoke to those of us who remained at his side.

"I was looking for a way to get rid of him. He did us a good turn. Muireadhach, you will be my aide on the second boat and Scott, you will command the leading boat. We shall

---

1 *[There is a tragic post scriptum to this decision. Not long after the King and his forces had embarked on the mission to quell any opposition to the King being crowned, young Macnab whom you will remember joined our team at the same time as Scott turned out to be a spy for the King's opposition. Loch Doon Castle was raided and sacked by an overwhelming force of rebels made up from Strathclyde, Dalriada and England. They put everyone to the sword including My Lord Seaton, his wife, all the children in the castle, and by the time their gory work was done, all the other women were also dead. Macnab was rewarded with a piece of land in the Gala Lane on the north side of Meoul and this perfidy is locally remembered down through the centuries until today. Fortunately, The Queen and the Bruce children had left Loch Doon Castle and travelled to Dundonald Castle before the invasion and were safe from harm]*

have only two dragon boats as our spearhead, the third boat we must leave here to protect the castle. I nominate you, Halfdan, as the commander of the third boat and the protection of the castle under your lord's orders. Are any one of you unhappy with these new arrangements, speak now!"

There was no reaction or reply. Perhaps there were one or two who were sorry for Lord Seaton, but generally, any support he had was in favour of him remaining in the castle, looking after the ladies' welfare and supervised any defensive action. In this case, what was Halfdan to be doing? Other than commanding the third war boat?

In the event of an attack, it had not been decided which other part of the defence strategy he would take on. It all depended on how Seaton would handle the situation.

The King's warning against dissidence in the ranks was felt by me and by Scott. It was not that it was my preference to always irritate and be irritated by Scott because as a rule I am an even tempered individual and can easily tolerate fools gladly if it is necessary to do so. No! It was his constant superior attitude that irked me. He displayed no sign of any weakness and treated me just the same as he treated everyone else, even including the King at times. If I made an effort to accommodate him I would be succumbing to his undoubted charm and demonstrating a weakness on my part. And if I did stand up to his aggressive ways I would run the risk of displeasing the King and perhaps jeopardising the campaign.

Our eyes met. If I could read Scott properly, he seemed to be silently indicating that any disagreement was simply not worth it. He made a private gesture with his right hand which I took to read that he was going to be more neutral that previously and perhaps even conciliatory. I nodded imperceptivity to him making sure that the other occupants in the room did not notice this important exchange that was to have a significant impact on the King's eventual strategy.

In the meantime, I had some success sailing up the Whitespout Lane towards Lochs Riecawr and Gower where there was a considerable concentration of hamlets. Scott and I ended up less than two miles from each other and the overall effect was a sort of '*pincer*' movement although it was not designed for that.

Not only did we succeed in pacifying and reassuring the inhabitants, but we obtained some potential candidates for our small army. Apparently, our activities at the Castle had led the general populace to believe that some important campaign was in the offing which might provide jobs in lieu of waiting for elders to die off for younger sons of farmers, either yeomen or tenanted.

More can be written of the loch head campaign, but it was much the same outcome: small communities impressed by our superior show of force and our message that it was all about the Unification of Scotland. These two things would be good for the peasant class.

Scott had displayed considerable initiative by taking the Gala Lane stream past the portage limit of the skin boats then going overland around the foot of Craigmawhannal Hill to the Elgin Lane in order to intersect with the larger population centre that was based at Loch Macaterick.

The day finally dawned when we were about to embark on Phase Three.

I recall landing on the Eriff Peninsula. All our men were in some form of armour and shields. The archers were in good supply of arrows and the foot soldiers mostly had claymores or spears. The landing was taken as a real-time exercise complete with war cries and aggressive attacks on clumps of bracken and heather while the boats were made ready for portage.

For those of you who are not familiar with Scandinavian boats you will not realise how comparatively light these boats are. If we reckon that the boat without accoutrements would weigh less than 4.0 metric tons or no more than 8,000 pounds. With a rowing crew of 24 carrying their boat on a portage, each man would be required to lift 330 pounds. To get the weight down to 200 pounds for each portage man it would require 40 portage persons, which required the participation of all hands assigned to the craft, including sailors, servants, leaders, and purely archers.

Fortunately, there was only a brief uphill route followed by a long decline to the River Doon so the portage of less than two miles was accomplished in good time, gravity playing an important part of the calculation and roller logs cut down from the young adjacent trees for out boats to roll on. The skin boats were not a problem.

On the way, I stopped into the hunting lodge of Dalpharson to appraise my granduncle of our activity. At first, he was incredulous but when actually looking out of his window and saw the prow of a boat going past, he had to go out and see for himself. I introduced him to Scott who was impressed by my uncle's position as retired factor of the Berbeth Estate. His main occupation, however, was as Steward of the estate.

We had always planned to fleet all of our boats at the small inlet by which the Gow Burn lead into the Doon. This we did and by sunset this arduous job was completed. This bend in the Gow Burn actually was shielded from view in all directions by a new grove of young conifers and a very mature fir tree which stood tall in the middle of the group as with an air of a bishop surrounded by a veritable gaggle of acolytes.

Our men camped for the night on the forecourt of Dalpharson; the senior leaders were invited into the lodge's splendid reception room to share a drink with the occupant.

King Robert was not in our company having decided to join us at Bogton Loch on the morrow. When he left the castle, he had taken his family with him to Dalmellington to get them on their way to Dundonald by stage coach with transfer at Dalrymple to avoid Ayr. I do not customarily put much store into praying for good weather but on this occasion, I was close to begging for a sunny day if Pagan or Christian divine intervention would provide for this form of assistance, I was not beyond getting down on my knees to request such favour. As it happened, however, when the rising sun lightened up the eastern sky with the promise of a glorious day to follow, I mentally thanked whichever Deity had been on my side.

Mustering the men and crewing all the boats we proceeded out into the mainstream. In this location after the turmoil of the Ness Glen, the River Doon was flowing quite swiftly as we sculled out into where the current was at its maximum velocity and soon found ourselves cruising down the dark brown translucid water between water meadows and ornamental trees that had been artfully located by the estate gardeners to enhance the views from the manor house on the top of the hill.

Berbeth was owned by a progressive, private gentleman who valued amenity other than safety. That the main house could not be defended with its broad gables, open terraces, and large windows made for an attractive prospect as did the expensive imported Rhododendron bushes that lined the long carriageway leading from the toll road.

Rounding a bend in the river, we approached a stone single arch bridge which was actually another visual amenity as it served no great purpose. I had obtained the clearance height under the keystone and calculated that the single masts of the two boats were just a shade taller than the available height. Accordingly, I had several of the boatcrew standing by to dip the masts without unseating them which would have been altogether a heavier job, and we passed under without any problem. There was always the prospect of being seen at the Gamekeeper's House which was nearby, but at this time of the day, everyone seemed to be abed.

Floating down the bonnie banks of Doon seemed almost like a pleasure cruise. Everyone was quiet and even our campaign-hardened soldiers were reduced to a quiet smoke or to working on pieces of wood with their knives. That we were seriously bent on the establishment of a kingdom where there was presently a kingdom only in name seemed either a saga or else a fantastic tale to be related around a campfire, or in the case of Berbeth House, in front of a blazing log fire in a sumptuous drawing room.

Only the lapping of the waters provided a sound background and in less than two hours the river had broadened out into the neck of Bogton Loch just outside Dalmellington or Dame Helen's Town as it had been known when it was first established in Pictish times.

CHAPTER VII

THE BANKS AND BRAES OF BONNIE DOON ARRIVAL CASSILIS CAMP.

Our strategy was simple. We would take over the village square and our troops would go from cottage to cottage summoning all the youths and young men to come and hear what King Robert had to say. Fathers and grandfathers would be welcome too to hear the King's proposals which would be good news for the community, especially for the freemen and artisans. King Robert the Bruce had joined us at Bogton and lead our small army into the village. I had gone ahead to round up all who were afoot at that time of day and Scott had been deputised to knock on doors to rouse the occupants. We did not expect opposition but there could be some resentment at being compulsorily assembled for a meeting and, who knows? A local hothead might start some action. We had to be prepared for all eventualities.

By mid morning we had gathered a crowd of about 100 men when the King started to speak to the congregation:

"Men!" he said, "I am sure you are concerned about all these armed soldiers running about in your village. Let me assure you that they mean no harm unless there are one or more of you who are intent in causing trouble. Let me introduce myself. I am your King Robert the Bruce, also known as Robert, I, Earl of Carrick, Lord Annandale. Perhaps some of you are my tenants but this is a much bigger proposition than purely local land holding and politics.

"I was declared King by a majority of your and my feudal superiors nearly one year ago but even then, and subsequent to that time, there have been a number of rebel nobles who would not want me to be crowned as the rightful King.

Many of these noble gentlemen are actually relatives of mine! Yes! Even my brother has sworn against my rightful place in the Kingdom of Scotland sometimes called Alba depending on the local leadership and language of many parts of our nation.

You see, Scotland is divided into the likes of Northumbria, Dalriada, the Highlands of Scotia, the Norwegian-controlled Western and Northern Isles, and one or two smaller breakaway provinces which deprive you and us of the benefits of a united Scotland and the strength to stand up to England which has been trying for years to take us over and make us part of their kingdom under their own King, Edward II who is not even English but Welsh.

All of this may sound great but the question that you ask is *'What's in this for me?'* and you would be right to ask the question. Let me tell you what we plan to put in place once

I am crowned. I am aware that you villagers have a low level of national conscience but that will change once the bonds of serfdom have been severed. It is called '*freedom.*' Freedom to take on a new job more akin to your liking or skills; freedom to move to another part of our country; freedom to seek an education, to read and, to write. Patriotism is not a bad word that describes a roguish heart. Patriotism fills your heart with joy, with pride, and participation in the planning of your life and future and the life and future of your community.

"In the first place, those of you who are prepared to join us and are with us to the end of our campaign can be expected to be freed from vassalage and become freemen. Those of you that are especially recognised as being of special service will be awarded land of their own to become valuable yeomen farmers in their home district with land obtained from the church and you will be granted a family name either based on geography or of your own choice or your community. I do not mean that if your neighbours call you Harold Bignose that will become your hereditary family name! You can choose Harold Clawfin for your new land holding or Harold Craigs for the rugged escarpment that adjoins your land.

"The possibilities are endless and exciting; do you not think?

"What I am thinking is for some of you today to sign us up for service to your rightful King. We shall be going down the Doon Valley by boat to a specific point where we shall cut off and make our way across Kyle to Dundonald Castle to prepare for a full battle with the Opposition somewhere in North Ayrshire or the Irvine Valley. But that is not all.

I imagine that there is yet to come a major battle with the remnants of those Lords who still oppose us as the prelude to the crowning ceremony and the establishment of a United Scotland.

"Make your intentions known to one of my officers. I look forward to getting to know you. We shall be camped on the Common next to Chalmerston for the next three days. Come and join us even for social reasons. It is time for some of you strapping big youths to seek your independence. Do not ask your mother though. She will not want to see you go. But what is the alternative? Are you forever to wait until your father or grandfather die to take over his rank of serf? Do not tell your mother I said so! God bless!"

I have tried to keep to the main points of his speech in this report, but I may have left something out. Anyway, you will understand the tenor of his address and when I tell you that by day three, we had established a platoon of 45 new men which were already calling themselves *'The Dalmellington Yeomen'*

That night Scott and I repaired to a local hostelry to partake of a pint of their best beer. Several of the men to whom the King had addressed during the afternoon were in the same establishment for the same reason as us, so it was natural enough to start up a conversation with the local boys. They were interested in learning about the King and whether or not we were in agreement with the contents of his speech.

Both Scott and I spoke enthusiastically of the mission. Said Scott:

"But you must know my friend, Muireadhach, for he is a local man from this town?"

There was a general negative murmur from the listeners who looked at each other and seemed to draw blanks.

"But he says he's of the Cathcart Family of Dalmellington." Persisted Scott. I was in a quandary. Of course, I was the son of Muireadhach, the noble Norwegian and the Cathcart family was just a story that I had fabricated to establish my Scottish *bona fides*.

"Never heard of them" said one of the younger men taking a swig of his beer.

"Wait!" cautioned an older man. "Surely, there must have been a connection to the Cathcarts? There is a row of cottages down by the burn that is sometimes called 'Cathcart Row.' But I have no idea how it came by that name"

By now there were all looking at me for some sort of explanation. Scott had an innocent bland expression on his face well realising that he had set a trap for me. I tried to keep my anger and sense of betrayal from showing on my face. "A Mister Cathcart was once the factor of Berbeth Estate but that was thirty years ago. He was not 'of Dalmellington' as I have sometimes said, but he left his name on some of this village's cottages." I hoped my lame story would pass muster.

"Let me think" the Old Man said. "I do believe there was talk of a Factor stealing rent money from the Laird."

"AaaHaaaa!" was the collective response to this revelation. I felt my ears turning red. There was nothing to be done. I was caught in my fabrication.

"It does sound bad" I remarked airily, "I understand that the good Laird permitted Mister Cathcart to retain a percentage of the rent from his cotters in order to build new sanitary cottages by the burn. As a matter of fact, I took his name from the Game Book in the gamekeeper's house as my father was Norwegian. I felt it was important to have a Scottish 'father' as my real family are foreigners. But I have just found out that my real father is a foster brother of the King which makes me the King's foster nephew but without the Bruce name."

"Another story! Which is the better one, Cathcart or the King's nephew?" asked Scott with more than a hint of joyful cynicism in his voice.

There was general agreement that the King's nephew outranked the Cathcart's family.'

"But then he's the son of a foreigner" opined one of the Dalmellington boys.

"Rather that, than the son of a thief!" counteracted another. Scott added: "If either story is true, Muireadhach is a fraud!"

"Actually, the relevant background and true story is that I am 'Murdoch Stewart of Cumloden' down in Wigtown and that is who I am without the benefit of a father. And that's no 'fraud' story!"

I remained silent about my selection of 'Stewart' as my surname or family name preferring Murdoch as my recently chosen first name as it was identified with me when I had had only a single name. I had chosen Stewart after the married family name of Princess Marjorie when she had married Walter Stewart in 1315 with single issue, the future King.

Scott had nothing to say. He knew this statement to be true. The young man who had been doing most of the talking, looked craftily at Scott. "And what be your real name?"

"I am 'Scott Boyd'. No father. No estate."

"I think you would scour Kilmarnock in vain searching for word of Scott Boyd!" I responded straight away with a laugh. I had been irritated by Scott bringing up the topic of names and family connections. His situation was no better than mine and if one looked at the detail, I was the more exalted. Neither of us could claim any blood connection with our sponsors and that is where the situation stood with a handful of Dalmellington peasants being asked to adjudicate the merits of my background versus Scott's history.

"Well, now. Is it Scott Boyd or Murdoch Stewart that is going to buy the next round of beer?" Everybody laughed. This seemed to tidily clear up the matter.

Dalmellington had been a successful project. We left the village with the goodwill of the villagers and the local aristocracy when we sailed down the river Doon towards our next stop.

The King had settled his family on the Ayr Stagecoach as far as Dalrymple before boarding one of the war boats at Bogton Loch for what we expected to be a leisurely cruise down the River Doon. Imagine our surprise when we suddenly met some armed opposition near Dunaskin at Green Hill. The two boats were drifting along in midstream followed by their coracles. The balance of our soldiers was on the right bank, marching to keep up with the flow of the current and the drifting of the boats when, without warning, a concealed group of local men showered our boats with a host of arrows and disrupted the placid tenor of our odyssey. We on the boats immediately pulled into the bank whilst those soldiers of ours who were pacing the boats on the river bank assembled into fighting formation as we had rehearsed at Bogton,

A second volley of arrows helped us to note where the opposition was located. Scott utilised his shock troops brigade which was his group of soldiers who had already proved themselves to be brave and aggressive to charge enemy location. A small but intensive skirmish ensued and resulted in fourteen casualties among the opposition with only four casualties on our side from the original volley and some slash cuts on shoulders and arms that had taken place in hand-to-hand conflict. In the meantime, I had used my own special group which was in my boat to form a protective ring around the King and to shield him from arrows that came towards his location at the stern of the war boat with the six skinboats that had been assigned to my boat clustered around the stern of the King's boat and were prepared to repel any and all invaders.

This unexpected invasion was somewhat amateur in its execution and the enemy archers brave but not sufficiently trained except for guerrilla attack and nothing else.

Eventually in reviewing the incident we reached the conclusion that one or more of the local magnates had organised the attack and used his serfs for the purpose. We never did discover which of the several grandees in this neighbourhood was responsible, but it made not a lot of difference in our overall plan as we continued to move down the river towards our next stop.

Once the situation had returned to normal, the King came around to thank everyone of for the speedy and efficient control and protection measures that had proved the effectiveness of the training drills at Bogton. We then went alongside the other boat to permit the King to repeat his congratulatory message and at the same time instructing Scott and me to land on the river bank to impart to the foot soldiers the same message. We did not take the King's congratulatory statements at face value but considered we had been inefficient ourselves in that we had lost four good men through too casual a regard for constant vigil. It had been a learning experience!

After clearing the single high arch of the Downieston Bridge, we ambled rather than sailed down the river because of all its twists and turns that marked its route over the water meadows. For four miles of sailing, we only had traversed one mile of distance from beginning to end. It did permit the attractive sight of a high bank on the left on which ferns and primroses grew in great profusion in season, with colourful inserts of fresh greens and pinks within the light brown coloured soil and the glinting grey granite outcrops Quite picturesque.

Turning south, the river began its journey through the lands and policies of Cassilis House then turned north again alongside a particularly bosky peninsula with the Doon describing two sides of a triangle just to the south of the village of Dalrymple where we had planned to lay up all our watercraft in this secluded and private area and hide them with bull rushes and willow branches.

It was still daylight. We lifted the skin boats aboard their war boats, six 'skins' on each war boat so that there were only two boats to hide. The 'coracles' actually nested within each other; one of Halfdan's brilliant ideas. When the work was finished, we were quite pleased with ourselves.

The two boats would defy anything except a scrupulous search, and it was unlikely that anyone would set forth across the planted and extensive wooded park other than for some sort of special occasion in which case the landscape gardeners would be accused of introducing unapproved material.

We made camp just north of this crafted area which we had assumed had been planted as a recreational and ornamental space by one of the local landowners as there were several gracious and famous mansion houses in the area. In the meantime, we had actually heard that this special place was perhaps to be a heros grave site. It was certainly a peaceful and a calm sort of place reminiscent of a holy cemetery.

Setting up for the night. This time we were cautious enough to mount a guard and to keep fires to necessary jobs such as cooking and so the night passed and by dawn next day our troops were all rested and assembled in parade fashion to march down to the attractive village.

CHAPTER VIII

IDENTIFYING SUPPORTERS; DALRYMPLE; ALTRUISM AND CONSCIENCE

If only we had some musicians to spirit us more. It was a lovely morning; the sun was rising and was set fair to become a warm day. The hedgerows that delimited our route were still green with hawthorn and the birds were singing their wee hearts out as we approached our destination. The first person to see us was a stooped peasant woman carrying a bag of laundry on her back. The King saluted her with a hearty wave and a sprightly *'Good Morning, Good Woman'* which she acknowledged by stopping and turning around and waiting until our ranks had all passed by. But whether it meant anything to her, she showed no sign.

Meantime, the King had sent messengers last night to the several mansion houses in the district to announce his presence in the village and we half-expected to come across some of the nobility who would surely come to greet us. But in this expectation we were wrong, and the only indication of baronial interest was an old retainer dressed in black who said he was the representative of his master who had instructed him to bid us *'good morning'*.

After rounding up men with our summons calls to the several cottages we had collected only a small crowd to which the King addressed in front of the local hostelry at the village road junction.

(I do not want the readers to think that I only report the King's speeches, but he makes quite a lot of them. Anyway, this is a short one!)

"Men!" he started. "You must be surprised to see the King of Scotland in your midst, but the situation is of the utmost importance. You have been placed in a difficult position. Your Lairds have chosen not to be present to listen to me. I hope this is because they are all already on my side in furthering my march to **my** crowning ceremony at Easter. But if they are not then you all have a difficult choice to make. I want as many of you fine stalwart men as possible in our effort to make sure that the ***'Flower of Scotland'*** are on my side".

He went on to outline the benefits that his reign would bring to the peasant and serf class. Freedom was a tasty dish, but it needed a dash of salt to perfect it. Salt was formerly a dish enhancer that only the Gentry could afford but, in his Kingdom, it would be available for all. The address was well received and quite a few of the younger men sought out Scott or me to express their interest in joining the King's quest.

The morning flew by, and it was noon time before we were able to repair to the hostelry for refreshment. As customary, the small group around the King consisted of Scott and me as well as the three troop leaders who had been responsible for mustering our troops and setting them off for the march. Two of these were young men who had joined us in Dalmellington and the third was a stalwart supporter from Castle Doon who was already a *Cornet. Mister David Maclaren* was his name. The first piece of business was the promotion of the Dalmellington men also to Cornet as *Cornet James Newell* and *Cornet William Waugh.*

Discussion centred on how well we were doing to enhance our numbers. The general consensus that it was a great deal of effort for not a lot of result. Admittedly, the larger villages were yet to come but it was disappointing to note that the *'Men of Carrick'* were difficult to recruit even although many were ultimately tenants of the King's alter ego, the Earl of Carrick. The fact that the mansions' and castles' grandees had shown little or no interest in our quest raised the point that perhaps we should have visited these magnates before mounting our sweep for foot soldiers, but it was now too late to try this approach although the King had essayed such a strategy last evening when he had caused to be sent his representatives to the mansions of his coming to Dalrymple the next morning.

It was indicative of the King's facility to correctly strategize when his lieutenants could not, and I marvelled yet again at the King's intellect and leadership qualities. When we were all mulling over this perceived weakness in our plan of action and thinking what we could do to suggest improvements to our procedures that might enhance recruiting measures. We had emphasized clothing armour, arms, food, shoes, freedom, land ownership, status, camaraderie. It was quite a list and definitely had appeal to the lower classes. Did we need the participation of the gentry class?

The answer to this last question was 'yes'. Some had been knights on a Pilgrimage to remove the Infidels from Jerusalem or had participated in European wars as mercenaries. These would be welcome because of their military experience. But others lacked any experience in this direction but were politically powerful enough to oppose our goals should they want to do so. Up to the present, we had been short-sighted by thinking that an armed mob would ensure our success. We wanted the King to be crowned by acclamation without any meaningful under-current of political opposition. What was the apt quotation? Something like:

> *"The more things change, the*
> *more they stay the same"*

I read it somewhere and think that it is a very appropriate statement for the constant upheaval of life in general.

Suddenly, it hit me: What if we were to form a sort of second line of attack? One that would employ a true friend of the King to visit all the so-called *'friendly aristocracy'* to explain just what the King's tactics were, how they were being implemented, and asking for their help? I put the thought diffidently to our group. Right away the King thought that there would be too many of them would expect some honour or distinction for early support and he did not want to be beholden to any one or to any group when he began to assemble his cabinet.

"But you will have to bring together several great men to help you to run the country" I said. "Surely, you have a list of staunch supporters right now whom you can rely on and who are likely to support you through thick and thin, Sire?" I added

"Ye-e-s!" Robert replied but in a not very positive manner. "But these gentlemen do not need to be drawn into this preliminary action as it will only draw attention to themselves and may thwart their future participation. After all, they mostly also have estates in England as well and must consider the English King Edward II as well as their ongoing and multiple neighbour's generational differences which always **have** to be a consideration."

"Then they should not be on the primary list of supporters if you think they might get 'cold feet' when you will need them most." I replied.

"Then, on the other hand, there are probably hundreds of the gentlemen who may be happy to see our proposal right through to conclusion." Mused the King almost speaking the words that had sprung unbidden into his head.

"Especially those who had participated in a Crusade." I was warming to the idea.

There was a general murmur of approval. The new Cornets who had kept quiet until now began to participate. I could see the new light in their eyes.

"Most of us have some knowledge of the history of many of the gentry." chimed in Scott. "Even to knowing the private good and the concealed not-so-good aspects of individuals and families."

"What we will need are lists of names divided into support categories."

"Divided into two groups: those in Carrick and Kyle in one list and those in the rest of the country by shire."

"Those we have dealt with already and those still to get involved."

"Sometimes an individual's real thoughts are known to his intimates rather than to the rest of the world."

"We must interview their intimates who are often able to provide accurate background information rather than what is known to the general world."

"Let us not forget military experience."

"Don't forget participation in a Crusade."

"Existing known alliances with other families."

"Geography."

"All right. All right!" said the King. "You have convinced me. Draw up a list of ideal circumstance questions first and I shall draw up my list of individuals and families. So many opinions. We are not going to be short of ideas, that's for sure!

We all looked at each other. No one spoke but eyes eventually came round to looking at me. I was about to demur when suddenly I thought 'Why not?' Aloud I said:

"We are here for three days planning our route across Kyle. Let us plan to have our lists two days from now and meet for this particular task right here at the Inn at say, four o'clock in the afternoon." I looked at the King. He seemed quite content to let me do the leading.

It was agreed.

We then went on to talk about the progression of our campaign across Kyle that would lead us to Dundonald Castle in 120 hours. We now had about 800 followers and a dearth of officers.

"Promotions from within" was the King's counsel but he had not carried the plurality of the support that he thought he required. With resolute men like himself around him, command and leadership would take care of themselves.

It was a subdued group that broke up two hours later. We all had a great deal of thinking to do. I had set the fox among the chickens and the responsibility for a satisfactory outcome would depend upon collective advice followed by decisive action.

We had decided not to spend too much time in Dalrymple if only because it gave us the impression of a prosperous area with a minimum of peasant families around. This meant that it would be the younger sons of yeomen farmers who might be susceptible to persuasion to embark on a venture but that would be about as much as we might hope for.

This class of young manhood would be likely to be drinkers at the Pub so another of the attractions we had added was a ceilidh or musical gathering at the Kirkton Inn this evening at the King's expense with locally well-known entertainers as further enticement.

I was set the job of rounding up entertainers, so I approached the Inn proprietor for assistance in this matter. Mr. Hewitson was his name, and he was extremely helpful. He proposed a programme of community singing lead by a well-known local singer, a rhymester of renown, and a scurrilous gossiper who nevertheless exposed disrespectful but mainly true observations on the rich and famous. She too was a big draw and could be expected to engender much hilarity. This sounded like a well-balanced programme, so I left Hewitson to make the arrangements and publicize the event.

The result was even better than I had predicted. I am talking about the attendance and our troops given leave to fraternize with the local men during the afternoon and to talk up the evening's free party. This they had mostly done in the tavern and illegal drinking shebeens, so word had quickly been distributed of the forthcoming event.

Meantime, the King and I stayed behind to go over the thoughts of our top men which had been thoroughly thrashed out on the night before. The clear advice was that we should make calls on the gentry but in a modified way. Where we were likely to be well received would be our primary goal followed by the second tier of likely supporters who otherwise might have a problem with outright approval.

The rest of their class who were said to be supporters of another King candidate would be put on notice by letter which would be couched in very positive language to suggest that King Robert the Bruce was the inevitable and rightful King and he was sure to recognize those foolish enough to oppose his coronation that favours and honours would only be flowing to those gentlemen who had had the honour and patriotism to wholeheartedly support a King who would pull the disparate parts of Albany into a whole nation, thus bringing honour and good fortune to those subjects who had been in the van of bringing orderliness to our country.

We repaired to a private room in the Kirkton Arms that the King had reserved for us so that we could be private in our deliberations. Once seated in front of steaming cups of tea which had surprised us as being available in such a public country establishment since tea was a very recent imported beverage and only enjoyed by the aristocrats, I laid my thoughts before my Sovereign and waited either for banishment or rustication.

What I had to say I put down for your reading. These are not the full reporting of my remarks but hopefully convey to my readers where my thinking lay, what I thought it might be possible to achieve in the short time at our disposal given the facts that our forces would be at Dundonald Castle by the end of next week and even counting for additional recruitment, ready to march on Strathclyde and Dalriada by the end of the following week.

We did not have enough time to visit all of the gentry's castles and mansions even if we thought that that was the better route to follow. It did not matter whether we were talking of those grandees before our present location here in Dalrymple, or yet to come in Kyle or Dundonald it would still be a pitifully small number of supporters. Even counting on some being major influencers in their district it would not be sufficient cover and I said so.

King Robert took my contrary view with a glum look on his face, but he did not comment but let me continue. It was therefore with some trepidation that I continued.

"Sire", I began "It grieves me to be offering a contrary opinion to the one that was uniformly reached by your advisers. You notice that I agreed with the clear majority at the time, and you may wonder why I am suddenly espousing a contrary policy right now. I regret that this time there is no majority of opinion for I am the only espouser of my own strategy and you, My Lord, may very well be the contrarian. It is of course, up to you.

"My view is that apart from one or two ready and able supporters we should recruit as many religious, mummers, poets, and balladeers to our side then allow them to spread the good word. You heard the troops this morning marching along to songs of sexual inuendo of their betters and praising the good friars for their charity and understanding. Popular songs are on everybody's lips and Jesus Christ's admonitions covered by the Ten Commandments are ultimately what brings out the good in all citizens whether they ever thought about it or not.

"The Religious Class is already made up of those who are influenced by Christ's teachings and those who are somewhat cynical in their application to today's reality of strife, thievery and even murder. Yes, we are still a heathen race despite all the good that is out there between neighbours and friends. What is 'altruism'? Does such a generosity of spirit even exist in Scotland? And yet it does. Every day we hear of charitable deeds being performed by high and low citizens such as invaders sacking an enemy stronghold but sparing the women and children or a moneylender forgiving a portion of a debt. These acts may be counted as *'good for business'* but they also have an element of altruism within the action. What about the situation wherein a King extends a friendly hand to an implacable enemy and forgives all previous wrongs? This too, may be regarded as 'good politics' with the lesser 'good' (the cessation of war) versus the death of many citizens in battles which would be considered a 'bad' outcome. Are we always to be driven by revenge, of redeeming an historic insult, or following an urge of jealousy?

Of course, any act of altruism may be viewed by another cynical person as an act of weakness and therefore vulnerability. This is always the downside. The party extending the favoured hand must have the reputation of understanding right from wrong and for kindness where it is due. This is not a bad thing.

> ### *The Iron Fist in the Velvet Glove*

After all, as Christians, what do we fear most? The Wrath of God. When all is said and done, we do not want to die and be turned away from the Pearly Gates! It has to be said,

> ### *'Christianity is not perfect but is the best religion to come along in the meantime.'*

"The historic religious following in my own Norwegian family and I am afraid it died with them, and they never acknowledged Christ, had all these gods in Valhalla doing very human things like war, destruction, banishment, damnation and so on without any act of redemption. Our Vikings were men of action, and the human rewards were manifest. The plundering of monasteries and church riches were totally justified, and perhaps they were because *religious treasure was largely obtained by methods other than altruism.*

"The Viking raiders took over the former ecclesiastical properties and made them their own. But they largely left the land that the peasants were tilling alone. Was that altruism?

"The only thing the peasants had to fear from the Viking raids was the initial scotched earth policy of the invasion to create fear of any thoughts of retaliation or counteraction against such a formidable and wicked adversary. And the other less worrisome enemy action: the rape of their women. After all, who would turn down a Norwegian son-in-law who brought land and property to the family?"

The King gave a wry smile to that one, otherwise he was content to listen to my diatribe.

I continued:

"Let us think of our conscience. Does it speak to us when we have done something wrong? Why? And where does this unbidden voice come from? What about non-Christians or agnostics? Do they hear a conscience voice? I believe everyone does, whether Christian or non-believer. Even the most Eastern pagan. Whether we pay our conscience any attention or even listen to our own *internal* voice of conscience is a product of our conditioning as a person. *Is it all but a matter of personal choice?*

At last, the King spoke, and I could draw breath. I had really been carried away. But what of what I had said applied to the question in hand? I noticed with relief that he was not angry. If anything, he seemed somewhat puzzled by the whole thing.

"All you are telling me is quite understandable and I have no disagreement with your conclusions. But even if I were to project myself as a 'Good and Christian King' how would that have any influence at this particular time? You are a young and idealistic combination of a robust and practical Norwegian and a Celtic dreamer; admirable qualities both, but perhaps not to be relied upon in these wicked and ruthless days. I want to be crowned and accepted as the Monarch of all Scotland but I cannot see how that could be done on the basis of altruism and conscience."

"But what about others' altruism and conscience? "I queried.

"What do you mean?"

"Supposing, just supposing that the great majority of Scotsmen loved you and thought you were the best man to be their Sovereign?"

"A big supposition."

"But it would assure you of your coronation and the love of your people."

And then I added:

"Love and Freedom are not mutually exclusive. They can exist individually with separate Altruism and Conscience. For is altruism in love actually what love is about? For self-love is probably the highest love and when shared with another in an altruistic manner and is received in like manner the lifting of the souls into a higher plane of civilization is achieved.

"Any sort of freedom is to be cherished. But when freedom is attached to a clear conscience in the knowledge and understanding that such freedom has been justly achieved it is much more fitting and likely to be treasured.

"Love is the giving and receiving of unconditional unselfishness. What could be more altruistic? And true altruism opens the heart even wider to encompass a limitless love with no boundaries.

"All mankind lives and dies with these emotions rising and falling within his psyche which he either heeds or ignores."

"That is just more of what you have already said" said the King showing a little irritation at how the conversation was going. "We need to be getting on with the problem at hand. I do not want to show my impatience, but your remarks are more of an inspirational bent that something that has a chance of leading us towards a solution of how we are the best and truest candidate to maximize the opinion of the Scottish people towards my being their King. Even with the vast majority of citizens in favour of my reign, because they are good people and recognise a good person when they see one, there will still be those who oppose me and who will not give up opposing me at every opportunity.

"All that you have said only makes it likely that I shall readily forgive those who oppose me rather that seek to have them beheaded!" He added somewhat in a burst of anger that had grown out of his irritation. I felt for the first time that King Robert no longer trusted me or was prepared to listen to my advice. I visibly winced. But his Lordship was not to be put off with any play of theatricality.

"Out with it, Murdoch. Your advices grows cold with each passing minute!"

Swallowing my apprehension, I ventured:

"My humble apologies, Sire. What I have said up until now has only been the background to my proposed strategies. How foolish of me to go on so and waste my Monarch's time with concepts he knows and understands."

"Hhhmmm" was the King's reply.

What I am saying is that to bring our campaign into focus and to give it even a chance of success we must recognise that we need the goodwill of the largest number of Scotsmen and the marginalizing of the opponents into a field of poor losers."

"Yes! And…"

"We cannot obtain access but to the smallest portion of both groups when there are only two of us. You have the better chance of making converts from the opposers but even then, there is always the possibility that their conversion is a deception to cover some ambition or other. I, on the other hand, may make inroads with the younger persons but am unlikely to affect a change in the deep-rooted family dogma as dictated by a patriarch known more to you than to me." Even so, how many groups are we likely to meet in the course of a day, a week or even a month?"

"So...?"

"Let us get hold of the rhymers, the balladeers, religious, and the traveling mummers to sing your praises in courts and taverns, markets and churches. Let the whole country know of your eminence, your experience, your military prowess, your justice, your patriotism and yes, your heart driven by internal thoughts of love and freedom, altruism and conscience that you will earn the epithet Good King Robert the Bruce. We shall petition the Pope in Rome to rescind your excommunication and we shall seek your patronage of as many worth-while and holy groups as we can. These groups will be petitioning your patronage rather than us pushing for it. Selective charity donations where it will be talked about are also a noticeable strategy.

"In short, the good subjects of Albany will simply long for your coronation. After all, you are already King so your support will help the people to feel good about themselves when they do the 'right thing'. Promise them a restructuring of the nobility with emphasis on larger land areas with expanded responsibilities. Recognise craft guilds. Promote public-private enterprises such as seaports and highways. If England has the better system of trade management and banking, promote a partnership for a sovereign entity. Sign-on to a partnership with the English Navy.

"In other words, begin to act as if you were already crowned and set about *"Making Scotland Great"* and a significant part of the Island of Great Britain. Drop use of the word and geographical title 'England' and substitute *'South Britain'* instead.

"Is all this closer to the sort of advice you seek, My Lord?" I finished.

The King was laughing out loud at what I had just said.

"I must say that you have some good ideas in there. You are somewhere along the road to redemption, young man!" was his reply. "But how are you going to go about getting contact with all these free messengers?"

"Easy" I said. "We start by visiting all the ale houses in a community where sing-songs are permitted. I can identify as myself, as Murdoch of Cumloden but we will have to disguise you. How about as a knight? Say, *Sir Robert of Macrahanish* or some such Celtic name. This is a place at the end of the Mull of Kintyre and it is unlikely we would meet any fellows from that airt on mainland Scotland. We can pass ourselves off as sponsors of a music book looking for new talent with minor political ambitions. If there are no performers present when we are in any premises, we can ask for directions to catch up with such persons. I know of many work songs, both bawdy and romantic, having been an Apprentice at the Boatyard at Loch Ryan. We used to have immense pleasure in giving full throat to the more scurrilous ballads which were always the most popular. I think I could write a few, myself."

At this, the King began to look doubtful.

"By meeting up with entertainers and ministers of religion, we must position ourselves to be sympathetic to their popular works. As far as ministers are concerned, if we could persuade any priests to include the King's praises in their sermons, that would help also, we can get help from your friend, Robert Wishart, Bishop of Glasgow.

"Come on Sire! We may as well have some fun while we work on this project. We shall give all the performers we persuade to work with us a listing of words and phrases to be mentioned whenever they bring the King's name into their performances. Like: 'Here's a song (or story) I recently heard which satirises our good King Robert and his delay in being crowned. *I didn't know that being crowned was such a problem. It depends on whether you are crowned with a golden circlet, or a golden sledgehammer!*' Something funny to please and entertain the masses without loss of prestige."

"I do not think I can stand being insulted." complained the King.

"It can get worse" I countered. "How about you are interviewing arse wipers and all the applicants are arse kissers? Is this risking a loss of prestige?"

"Arghhhhh!" was the King's reaction to this suggestion.

"But think of the laughs? It is sure to be a success. The more salacious the better. It keeps your name current. Much better than *'King Who?'* A King with a sense of humour.

Self-deprecating. Prestige. Again, remember: the 'Iron Fist in the Velvet Glove'."

I added:

"But in your disguise, you must never be recognised. Remember, your voice is also associated with your persona as King. That might be more difficult to disguise. I think we have to keep you away from places where Lords sometimes gather.

"Come to think of it. It might be a useful ruse for some people to guess correctly that Sir Robert is the King in disguise who thinks that the whole operation is a huge joke. But the substitute must never be admitted."

"Where would we begin?" asked Robert. "We can hardly go back to the Doon Valley again since I showed myself openly and so often."

"Public houses in the villages off the river's path. Carsphairn, St John's Town of Dalry, Straiton, even Girvan- come to think of it we had better concentrate on the landside communities, but I think we might even try Ayr, the less sophisticated parts, that is. We can always follow our troops with our visits to Coylton, Tarbolton, and Symington. There is a lot we can do. I hope, Your Majesty, that you do not think that I have taken leave of my senses. Please do not look at me as if I have totally forgotten my place as a humble servant of Your Majesty. I who have been favoured by the Royal Person and is taking advantage of the situation. If I have offended you then I shall accept whatever punishment you may deem proper for such an egregious breach of protocol. I throw myself at your feet."

I made to do that very thing, but the King stopped me.

"Hold still, you stupid boy!" was all he said.

We sat still for a quarter of an hour with nobody uttering any speech. Looking everywhere except at each other. I moved off my own chair and knelt with both knees on the floor. The King made no comment. It was the time. Now or never! Somehow, I did not feel any fear of apprehension. I had made my best effort. My family would be disappointed at my downfall but being family, we would eventually accept the disgrace and learn to live with it.

The minutes ticked by.

"I shall need to approve of any rhymes, ballads or songs he may write", Robert mused to himself in a low voice that was difficult to make out."Machrahanish? Too rocky and remote. Do not like it.

"Arse wipe. The prerogative of a King. Arse kiss. Would they not just love it?" I ventured.

He lifted up his head and looked levelly at my face capturing the eyes.

This is it, I thought.

CHAPTER IX

ENTERTAINMENT FOR THE PEOPLE OF DALRYMPLE

King Robert spoke: "My first thought was to chastise you or even whip you myself. Then I began to think again. It is quite true that we do not have enough time to convert the national thinking to our way before the coronation, but I certainly want to be a popular King at the sacred ceremony. What happens afterwards will affect only my successor. A King must be free to impose whatever policy is in the best interest of his country. Popularity is one thing but ensuring a safe country from internal and external dangers must be a first consideration. I do not think that in the time we have before the coronation there is much to benefit by discussing our intentions in public."

"With respect Sire, the object of this campaign is to win the hearts of the public in order to tamp down any significant opposition on the grounds that the people favour you and want you to be crowned. Who would have the audacity or the foolhardiness to try and raise an army of opposition in such circumstances?" I countered. "Remember, it is not just

Galloway and Strathclyde we have to conquer but also the Highlands, Western and Northern Islands, Northumbria and Dalriada as well. It will be from those distant self-declared kingdoms that real opposition will come. What we are proposing to do is to pacify all these smaller kingdoms into recognising the one and only collective King. Our marching band of warriors storming Strathclyde will not be a hindrance to contrary forces from elsewhere in the land unless our men do well and win all the way through to Scone, our destination. By the way, where does our military campaign end? You never have said."

"Dumbarton? Arbroath? Dunfermline? Stirling? Scone? wherever a fully representative opposition army is met and decisively defeated in battle." Replied the King with more than a touch of bravado in his voice and body language.

"Spoken like a true warrior." I replied. "You see how a military solution is likely to drag on for some time and even so, the outcome might not be supportive of your goal".

"Are you suggesting that the King may not be victorious?" was his quick and fierce rebuttal. You are supposed to be on my side, Murdoch. Do I detect a hint of defeatism in your language?"

I was suddenly aware that what I said next would be very important. I hesitated for a minute.

"Why, My Lord! It is my greatest wish that you, your cause, and all the Ladies and Children be safe from any form of reprisal. It would be a terrible tragedy if we made a false step and the glorious House of Bruce was wiped out which would surely be the case!

"You recall the Seer at the Holy Island cave? He said we would be successful in our mission He said *'Keep on trying and you shall succeed'* or something like that. And what about the spider? It took her three attempts to span the opening. I was only worried that we did not have a lot of time to achieve our goal. ***'Try, Try and Try Again!'***"

"Mmmmm, you are right." Acknowledged the King. "Nothing must be left to chance if we are delayed in any way. The coronation is to be held next Spring. One battle or ten battles will take a lot of time and if they are not conclusive, where shall we be? But can we count on your 'whispering campaign' to hit its mark? I am a little wary of our plunge into unknown waters. Being a 'warrior' as you say, has not prepared me for a head-long speculative adventure into a totally unfamiliar and little understood situation such as you are recommending."

"I would try again, Sire, if I did not believe that you would tire of the effort and reject it out-of-hand." I was keeping my voice as level as I could. I did not want the King to throw away this main chance to contribute to success.

"That is very perceptive of you but since public opinion has been so allied to any military victories, I can discern the compelling reason for such coupling. You can be assured that the great military leaders of olden times never gave a moment's thought to their military activities on the collateral population!"

"Just think, My Lord! You will be the first! You see, we are not trying to conquer Scotland but to unite her!"

"That does it!" exclaimed King Robert the Bruce, Monarch of Scotland: "It has to be this way, so let us do it. Draw up a plan for me to look at tomorrow and we shall proceed!

"Thank you, Your Majesty. I shall do as you command but let us start the ball rolling by attending the public bar this evening to sharpen our strategies and take stock of the kind of men we hope, and trust will be amenable to our message! The Seer of Holy Island suggested that we should look after each other. I do not know how a great man such as yourself can be expected to be interested in a lowly servant such as myself but be assured that I shall make every effort to achieve our goals and to support the grand efforts of our troops in the field."

"What a glorious start to your reign!" I added.

It was with some trepidation that I waited on "Sir Robert" to arrive in the Tap Room of the Inn that evening. When he arrived, there was a momentous hush fell over the merry throng as at least half of those present recognised him as King Robert! So much for Rule One that recommended that the King be disguised. I did not think it would be effective for the King to canvas for his own crowning.

As I had arrived earlier, I had been scoping out those men who were likely to be gregarious enough to entertain the gathering. I let it be known to this small group of gentlemen that if there was any intention of mounting some form of general treat or amusement this evening because if so, I was available to contribute. After all, it was not every evening that a King's knight was pleased to be in their midst. He would not speak himself, but I would do the necessary communication.

But when the King entered, my offer to speak went up ten-fold and I could not fail to appreciate the interest of his subjects on what he might say. Dalrymple Village was certainly a supporter of the Monarchy. I watched the crowd grow as several fellows slipped away to spread the word. At last, the Tap Room was full to overflowing and it was still early in the evening to begin the proceedings.

I was wrong. Several fellows stood up to sing country love songs and there followed a young man who recited a poem about the river Doon. When the man I had suspected would be the organiser of the evening's entertainment tried to subdue all the clapping and talking, I recognised that my turn was about to be announced.

All at once I realized the folly of my enthusiasm. Not only was my maiden speech to be in front of a crowd with which I was unfamiliar, but the King was to be a listener as well which meant if he did not like my address it might be the first and only opportunity to try my oratory skills and the programme that was to be ratified in the morning would never see the light of day.

At our table, the King had attracted four or five local fellows. They were all talking animatedly, and Robert seemed to be in fine form. Was he playing '*King*' or '*Knight*' I could not tell? He had told me earlier that he would be 'King' tonight after he was recognised by so many people, but his bonhomie was uncharacteristic at least to me and he was clearly having a good time. I was introduced to a thumping of beer tankards on tables and shouts of approbation.

"My Lords and Gentlemen…" I began *(wild cheers)*

"…and Others" (*Boos*) Clearly this was a feisty crowd. I noticed a couple of taller men who seemed to be better dressed than everyone else move into the back ranks of standees along the walls of the room.

"Thank you for giving me an opportunity to introduce myself and my companion, Sir Robert, who goes under that name when he is clearly enjoying himself with his fellow men but is also known as King Robert Bruce, Earl of Carrick, possibly your feudal superior, when he is not having fun with his subjects." I let the short burst of subdued clapping die down before continuing…

"Robert, if he will forgive the familiarity, is a mighty warrior. He has been acclaimed our King by an assembly of the Lords and Ecclesiasticals earlier this year but has yet to be crowned in a ceremony which will give notice to all Kings in other lands that Scotland is a United Country under one strong King and now stands in the ranks of the world's Free Nations and respected leaders who have brought distinction and honour to their citizens as well as freedom from want and freedom from foreign wars.

"Many of you will have seen our small force that visited the village in the last few days. It was not here to intimidate you but to demonstrate how our just King is going on to other parts of our country to carefully persuade all citizens to acclaim his coronation and to subdue any citizens who might oppose it for one reason or another. I want all of you to rejoice in your King's crowning in the sure expectation of a United Scotland's coming of age. *(Shouts of Agreement)*

"We are a feisty race drawn from the traditional races of Celts, Scots, Picts, Gaels, and leavened with a sprinkling of Norwegians and other Northmen when they paid us a visit from the sea in their long boats. *(Boos all around)*. I am one such as you can witness. My only excuse is that my family got here just as quickly as they could, and I recently completed a five-year apprenticeship with the best boatbuilder in the land.

I was born here and carry the Gaelic name of Muireadhach which now that we have a family as well as personal names translates into Murdoch Murdoch of Cumloden in the Wigtown District. Quite a quirky name I must admit, so I added *Stewart* to my name to create something more palatable than a double Murdoch!"*(Voice from the crowd: 'How about a double Scotch'? Great laughter)*[2]

---

2 *Two Murdochs! i.e. 'Murdoch Murdoch'!*

"Our King was born at Turnberry Castle which, as you know, is on the nearby Ayrshire Coast. His loyalty to the Carrick District and to his tenants knows no boundaries. His generosity in leasing land as freehold is his commitment to the tenants who have served in some special and personal way. He has committed to the freeing of all serfs who have or will have joined the present campaign to bring goodwill. Those landless citizens who join and are with us to the end will be offered a parcel of land within their own parish as thanks for their services. (*Murmurs of approval*)

"As the King's warrant to you at this time, for the next half hour the beer from the bar will be absolutely free and the cost to the management will be borne by His Majesty.

"Now let us all be upstanding and drink a hearty and honest toast to King Robert of Scotland! Long may he live! I want all of you to sing the King's praises as you go about your daily tasks and all you clever people who write and sing your own material, I want you to compose new and noble themes that will bring honour to the House of Bruce as the successors to the House of Wallace and the greatest patriot of that ilk, William Wallace who along with good King Robert shares the accolade: **Braveheart**. (*thunderous applause and shouting*)."

It was only as the applause died away that I had the courage to look towards the King. How had he taken it? Was he angry or pleased? To my eternal relief he was smiling at me and I knew that our programme to try to persuade all dwellers in what is presently Alba and would soon be Scotland that King Robert Bruce was the rightful Monarch to be entrusted with the historic Regalia to signify his lordship of all Scotland.

The formal evening started off with fine singing by the local favourite, **Bob Eccles** who had a pleasant tenor voice and sang popular songs. Choruses that were included in several of his renditions were heartily supported by the audience and when he was finished, he received a standing ovation. This reaction encouraged me to assume that the evening was going to progress as I had planned.

How wrong I was!

"To keep the evening going, **Tam Dalziel** will honour us with his epistle written especially for tonight. As I said before, it is an honour to be entertaining in public and to have the opportunity to respectfully honour the King's name and person. Tam assures me that you will be pleased with his recitation of Dalrymple's many accomplishments and patriotism. Gentlemen. Mister Dalziel."

The good and worthy man stood up, took a swig of his beer and started to recite:

> *The King one day came by our town,*
> *With troops and Courtiers all in train.*
> *He wanted all patriotic boys and men,*
> *To hear his plans for our domaine.*

For too long, Scotland's heart was severed
From her body of stalwart men
Who had lived and died for causes parted
From goals and causes of local concern.

But Good King Bob had sought to place
The Yeoman's and the Serfs just play
Where they will receive realisation
With wisdom that will gain the day.

The King has no need to proffer
Free beer as tendered by a chiel
We all ken a dog which obeys his Maister
And takes the order:' Come to heel!'

When all's said and done red hair is family
And perhaps we know not of the tie
But blood-lines are thicker than water
And remains so until we die.'

Polite applause greeted this rhyme, and I noted one or two worried glances in my direction. The King also looked towards me but made no signal that he was either pleased or displeased with the recitation. When Tam came back to our table, the King stood up and shook his hand. If anything, the applause became louder at the gesture.

As for me, I was fretting over the suggestion that I was seen as the King's dog. Was I? When I thought more of it, the metaphor was not far off. But were not these proceedings the result of my own construction? My job was to give structure to plans approved by the King. Was this not what

I was doing? But nevertheless, the allusion upset me, I am not altogether sure why!

As for the 'family tie' because of red hair! I must admit it had crossed my mind once or twice that I might be a blood relation of King Robert whose blond hair had quite a touch of red in it. It was such a fearful conclusion that I banished it from my mind entirely, and here it was, resurrected in public! The thought must never be allowed to colour any of my dealings with my Monarch lest it become an obsession.

The public hubbub had risen to a high order as the room awaited Mistress Kennedy's participation. That she was popular there was no doubt but after what Dalziel had apparently got away with, I worried that some ghosts might emerge that would only make my life and our project more difficult?

I stood up. This time there was no need to quieten down the boisterous crowd and I sensed that there was some anticipation as to what I might say with particular comment on the *'red hair'* remark. I decided to pass it over as something of a joke. I spoke.

"Well"' I announced, "There was much to think about Mister Dalziel's remarks. I should like to draw your attention to what everyone looks like in this room. Those of you who are sitting down; Stand up! Let us all see! Why, there are one or two men over six feet here. They must be as tall as the King! Look around you! How do you do, Your Majesties!" I bowed in mock deference in their general direction.

There was a murmur then a great laugh. The tall fellows in the room looked sheepish and sat down Everyone clapped as they sat down and there was the generous sound of merriment in the room.

I had made my point. Being 75 inches tall or having red hair did not automatically make you a King. I noticed the King laughing heartily.

"Now settle down. She's not over six feet except perhaps in comeliness *(roars of laughter)* and I don't know her sufficiently well to discern whether her natural hair colour is red *(more laughter but of a ribald nature)* but Mistress Kennedy is certainly Queen of the Sharp Wit which she will no doubt exhibit to this roaring and appreciative audience. Gentlemen! I give you ***Mistress Mary Kennedy!***"

I cannot report to you exactly what she said. She spoke quickly in her country accent, so the audience had to be *'on their toes'* to catch many of her barbs. Nevertheless, here is a more-or-less report of her main points which I have rendered into standard English on the basis that many of my readers are unfamiliar with the Scottish dialect.

As mentioned, Mistress Kennedy was a buxom woman of indeterminate age with faded light-coloured hair, possibly with grey predominating, and dressed in a cotton dress of her rank as a kitchen scullion. She wore a bosom-fitting waist-cincher that exaggerated her breasts and was of generally common appearance and accent. She worked in the kitchens of one of the local gentlemen's mansion houses near the village.

"Men!' *she started,* "I usually speak with you over the kitchen door at the Big House but tonight at the invitation of no other than the King of Scots, the Earl of Carrick, whose domaines were acquired through a very profitable marriage by his father to the Lady Marjorie the Countess of Carrick, whose residence was just down the road at Turnberry Castle. I remember her well for she was a gracious and generous lady. My first job was in her kitchens when I was a girl." **(Comment from the crowd: 'Do we have to go that far back?' followed by loud guffaws!)**

"You men!" *she countered.* "Not worth a single groat, for any of you! No girl worth her salt would take any one of you for husband to share in her inheritance and I don't blame her!"

(Remarks from the crowd: 'You didn't say that to me last Sunday!')

The cut and thrust of merry banter continued for several minutes before she got around to her main points without interuption.

"My Lord the King is bound to carry Carrick's support next year when he is crowned and he can count on the full support of lairds, and vassals in this area. I have heard them talking at the Big House and the general opinion is that now that Lord Cormyn and his Baliol family have passed on; his late Lordship not having far to go seeing as *he was on the altar steps when he was assassinated. And of course, our good and patriotic Sir William Wallace brutally executed in London by that tyrant King Edward Longshanks, betrayed by an unknown so-called Scotsman! You pays your money and you makes your choice!" Do*

not shout the name out loud. It is not good manners. (She spat out these words and the audience were moved and remarked quietly among themselves.)

"Just between us ordinary folks, I always have trouble with these tall redheaded men of foreign extraction. They remind me of the stories I used to hear about the Viking invasions and how they laid waste to our fields and churches. We are urged to think of them nowadays as ordinary Scottish folk even as they take over our beloved country, through acquiring wives of historic pedigree. What can we do? Our Masters won't do anything. They'll hold their noses and follow the leader until another leader comes along. A good Christian of Gaelic and Pictish Stock with little or no taint from France or Norway would be ideal. At least, the good King Robert through his wife's family mind you, nearly fits the bill .

"There are no ladies present, but I suspect they have little regard for long fair hair and blue eyes on their men. Especially since they spend more time grooming their locks at the looking glass than their wives do!" She added. **(Subdued but guarded laughter).**

"But there's one thing that irks me more than any other is employing a mere stripling youth to try and talk us into his and his master's wishes.

Never send a boy to do a man's work.

Yes! He may be very pretty with his golden hair and blue eyes. He can be tall and slim and carry himself well, almost like a gentleman which he is not. But he's still a boy and some say, a sailor.

"Imagine a common sailor telling the good folk of Dalrymple what they should be doing? I hate to say bad things about my own craft. But the son of a sea cook is hardly an authoritative person to give advice which we should follow!"

"Now, the King is a wise man and knows how to read people. It is not for me to question his selection of a spokesperson. But a 19-year-old youth who is not even shaving is not giving his audience much respect for intelligence. Perhaps the appearance was the deciding factor. I cannot see behind his ears for his long and beautiful hair, but it looks decidedly damp in there! And we all know what a randy older man sees in a youthful companion! **(Audience reaction: Ooooh!)** *Well, the maids here in the Inn tell me that there has been no fighting off gentlemen's advances since King Robert and his pal came to stay; a usual occurrence given the attitude of noble gentlemen to serving girls.*

"Now, as I am marched off to the chopping block, remember what I have revealed to you. Do of it as you will. There is nothing wrong with this situation that a whiff of honesty would not clear up. We love our King Robert Bruce! Long may he reign! We love his pal as well in the assurance that a good woman will set him on the correct path in due course! And we wish them both well in their efforts to bring Old Scotia into the 14th century.

*"Gentlemen! Lift up your tankards filled with the King's good beer! God Bless the King and his Lords!" (**A standing ovation followed by much thumping of tankards on wooden tables and general babble.**)*

Mistress Kennedy sashayed towards her former seat next to the King. She made a gesture that asked whether she should sit down. The King extended his hand and she felt emboldened to sit. There was no rancour. Kennedy then looked at me and I took the King's lead and smiled back, crinkling my eyes that might be taken for a wink. It was up to me to conclude the evening. I stood up. There was an immediate hush.

"Well, Gentlemen" I started, "We have heard lovely singing from Bob Eccles that reminds us of the beauties of The Doon Valley and attractive villages. Indeed, how can we ever forget that we are all fortunate enough to live in the most beautiful place on earth that surely God had in mind when he laid out the Garden of Eden?

"And as for Tam Dalziel's poetic saga of the King's visit to Dalrymple, what more can be said that encourages us all to support the patriotic King's call to help him unite our wonderful and historic country.

"What can I say about Mistress Kennedy's revelations and advices? One or two points about me are undoubtedly muddle-headed. Had I been the *'son of a sea cook'* then I would not be in this ridiculous position of defending my manhood. But could aways help her at salting down a pig's arse. You know what sailors are? Any port in a storm! But sailing around Loch Ryan and building seagoing boats is hardly the place to forego my landside inclinations. But a pretty boy always has his detractors! I hope it is *jealousy* rather than anything *more serious!*

"Anyway, we have had a great night. Next time I shall wear a false beard and a helmet with ram's horns to satisfy the frivolous. Remember the message: Support the King and do not be persuaded by any other party to do otherwise, especially if they look the least bit foreign or young! **myself** excepted!"

A great round of appreciative clapping followed by shouts of *'good for you'* or *'Cumloden for ever!'*closed the evening.

----

* **FOOTNOTE,** Murdoch as a Family name as in *Jimmy Murdoch, or* Murdoch as a Given (Christian) Name as in *Murdoch Macdonald* just to name two examples gives rise to the awkward suggestion of *Murdoch Murdoch,* a construction which is seen as a duplication or a mistake .Our Murdoch of this story was always known as *Murdoch* when he had a single name and he hoped that when he took a family name in would be *Murdoch* rather than anything else. This gave rise to the *Murdoch Murdoch* name structure which he disliked although it satisfied his hope that whether formal or informal, *Murdoch* it would be. Instead, he selected **Murdoch Stewart** for the reason stated in the narrative.

CHAPTER X

DIVIDING JOBS; AYR TOWN AND AYRSHIRE COUNTY

After all the excitement in the Hotel's Tap Room, ordinary life seemed awfully dull. The King and I climbed the stairs to our rooms, and it seemed to take quite an effort. We were silent and it was only when we saw that Hewitson had set up our day room with a good fire in the grate and a bottle of excellent whisky together with two snifter glasses, that we began to settle down and relax.

At last, the King spoke:

"That was quite a demonstration of Public Relations was it not? Whatever it is called, it seems to work, and I congratulate you. Having the fortitude to persuade me to go along with your plans takes quite a degree of courage."

"Thank you, Your Majesty. There were a couple of moments when I thought the whole thing was going to crash down around our ears. We were fortunate that it did not."

The King took a mouthful of Scotch then spoke in a voice that was barely suppressing a giggle: "You realize that Mistress Kennedy was suggesting that you and I were having an unusual sexual alliance!"

I was horrified at the very thought!

"That charge had been directed towards me in several instances. I can assure, Your Majesty, that there has never been a thought further from the truth than an unholy liaison with any man!"

Oh! Do not worry, Murdoch, I never thought for a minute that that sort of thing was even in your mind! It certainly was not in mine."

"Just because I am good looking seems to bring out these charges, I am afraid."

"Do not let it concern you and as for your relatively young age, you may be sure that I value that factor in you most of all because you bring a fresh approach to old ideas. For instance, I would never have thought to organize a party with paid performers. Well done!"

"Now we should really be thinking about what we shall do next"

"What have you in mind? I am sure there is something going on in that head of yours."

I ventured a topic that I had been thinking about for several days.

"I think we should tackle the town of Ayr now that we are so close to it that we could be there in a couple of hours."

"That is a good idea but frankly, I need to be inland with my troops. We could always split the jobs. You go to Ayr and work your magic with the local entertainers, and I shall travel on to Tarbolton to catch up with the others."

"I do not like you traveling alone, Sire."

"Nonsense! What made you think that I cannot look after myself? I'll be following the path of our soldiers, and the way should be comparatively clear of footpads and assassins. I'll be armed and wearing armour. What about you?"

Oh! I shall look like a country bumpkin better still; I shall look like an out-of-work boatwright looking for a job on any boats in Ayr Harbour."

Let us sleep on the ideas and revisit them tomorrow morning. I am tired. I am going to bed. I hope Hewitson has warmed the bed covers for me. I asked him to."

What a good idea, Sire. I'll say, '*good night*' and get my head down."

And with that, we both went our separate ways for our suite had a bed chamber on both sides of the day room. I checked the outside door to see that it was securely locked and retired having waited until the King had gone to his own chamber.

On the following morning Mr. Hewitson approached us in the Dining Room downstairs where we were just completing a substantial breakfast.

"My Lord" said Hewiston, "A small group of gentlemen has just arrived to call on you and to present their compliments."

"Who are they, Hewitson?"

"They are gentlemen from the neighbourhood who wish to present their sons to you and Lord Murdoch. I have put them in the Tap Room pending your instructions."

"The Gentry is calling." The King said to me. "Tell them that we will look forward to their attending in half-an-hour in our dayroom. Hewitson, make sure the room is neat before they are shown up."

With that, we finished our breakfast and ascended to our suite where a maid was just finished tidying up our room. The King sent downstairs for a bottle of Scotch and some glasses by which we would be able to offer a drink if the need arose. With that our visitors were shown in.

Three elderly gentlemen were accompanied by two boys. It transpired that they came from their mansions nearby. The oldest man was also the tallest, he was clearly the spokesman. Having introduced himself as Lord Symington, he next drew our attention to one of the young men who was his grandson and heir. His name was **John Symington** and I took him to be about fifteen years of age. The other two gentlemen were his neighbours and each carried distinguished names. The other young man was a viscount and the son of one of the gentlemen.

The King made them all comfortable in seats. Offering them all a drink which they refused, His Highness was talking in generalities to set a relaxed atmosphere for there was quite a 'stiffness' in our visitors and we were as yet, not able to work out what the visit was about.

The King was chatting away.

"When I was on a crusade, one of my 'brothers' was a John Symington. Perhaps he is a relative?"

The elder Symington spoke up.

"That would be me, Your Majesty." He said, "We never got further than Spain as we had to deal with a strong fighting force of Moors."

"Of course, of course!" The King was full of apologies. "Symington, how stupid of me"

"It is no matter, Your Majesty. It was a long time ago. You were just a very young man."

"I recall that I learned a great deal from you, Sir. If I could say in front of your young grandson, it was you who kindled the fighting spirit in me, and it has been with me ever since."

The stiffness was melting.

"Why we are here, Sire, is to advise you that we are all very much your liegemen and you will do us great honour if you would accept our individual statements of fealty".

The King did not display his surprise but again, bowed very low in a demonstration of thanks.

"Gentlemen" he said simply, "Your kindness to this Monarch touches me deeply and I am profoundly gratified by your generous action to seek me out to express your feelings which I reciprocate.

"Lord Murdoch of Cumloden, I am sure, would wish to be associated with this ceremony." The King looked at me and I bowed low towards him and again towards our visitors.

"Gentlemen!" was all I said.

Lord Symington produced several envelopes from his clothes and presented them to the King.

"You will find our declarations of loyalty to you both signed by all five of your visitors to signify that our declarations will go to the next generation of our families."

"Did any of you attend our reception here last night?"

There was a sudden cooling of the atmosphere with a few guilty glances exchanged.

"My grandson, John, was in the Tap Room last night and reported to me what had transpired. I had forbidden him to attend but he disobeyed me. I am now glad that he did because it was thanks to his reporting that brought us here this morning.

"But we must be going. We have taken up too much of your time." Symington rose from his chair and the others did the same. Formal *'good byes'* were expressed and, on the way out the door, young John Symington took me by the arm and spoke quietly to me:

"It is a bit of a drag being in an old person's house. My father is dead, and Grandfather is my tutor. You are lucky, your principal is nearer to your own age."

I was nearly going to put my arm around his shoulder when I remembered last night's inuendo. Instead, I gripped his forearm and muttered something like *'I feel your pain'* or something equally banal.

The departure of the Gentry was giving the King something to think about.

"Well, would you believe that our *'horse-and-rider'* show had reins long enough to rope in the local gentry as well! Clearly, Murdoch, you have hit upon a winning strategy. I said last evening that we should talk about any refinements we might make on the way we are trying to refine our approach, but I see now that we should not mess with success!"

My reply was couched in an explanatory manner: "I wondered when I saw several well-dressed young men departing from the Tap Room that I just took the signal that what they thought that the gathering was for was of no interest to them. This was near the beginning of the evening, and I just thought that our programme was no use to influencing the Big Shots. I wonder what the *turning phrase* was?" Apparently, the young men had decided to go and tell their seniors that they were missing out on an important meeting.

"It certainly was not Mistress Kennedy who performed much as was expected. Looking back, I wonder if it was just your equanimity on receiving each performer after they had insulted you!"

"Do you think that was the case? I have often been told that I possess the *'common touch'* But I thought my sympathetic and approachable public persona was limited to common soldiers in the field of battle."

"I am sure that what you say is quite true, Sire, but your ability on the battlefield clearly has prepared you for dealing with the general public when called upon to do so.

"It is kind of you to say so" The King answered. "But your own contribution when you turned insults into funny situations concerning height and being of foreign lineage laid these remarks to rest."

There seemed to be no other direct correlation, so we let the discussion rest.

Early on the morrow, both King and Murdoch had a silent breakfast together in their private room before dressing in their travelling gear and going downstairs and out into the courtyard where their horses were waiting.

Much to my amazement, the King embraced me most warmly.

"Go with God's Protection" said the King simply.

"As with you" I replied.

The leaving was of two friends parting and going off into danger, one without the other. I hesitated for a moment:

"Are you sure you will be all right?" I asked. "No use analysing any longer about who has the better natural instinct for getting along with people of lower status. We shall both have to exercise tact in our separate ways."

"Now GO!" The King insisted and turning his back to me to examine his horse's harness."

"Aye, Aye, Sir" was my reply. As the King turned around in sudden amazement at the nautical salutation, Murdoch saluted his Monarch with a precision that owed not a little to his full heart of the moment when he began to understand King Robert Bruce of Scotland.

My ride into Ayr was by the firm surface Coastal Turnpike passing by the fields and policies of the local landholders that proliferate outside all large towns. Here the gentry was augmented by prosperous artisans and traders because Ayr was a successful seaport and ships arrived from and sailed to Ireland, Norway, Denmark, France, and Spain. The town had been a Royal Burgh since 1202.

I was stopped twice. Once on entering the outskirts of the town by a military guard which was monitoring all traffic to and from the town and collecting tolls for the new highways, and the second time on approaching the Sandgate in the town centre, which was just by the castle walls. Here the guard was more thorough but my cover story that I was a traveling shipwright going down to the harbour to find work was accepted and I was free to go.

Relinquishing my ride at a local stable in Newmarket Street, I proceeded on foot and crossed the low-running river by the one and only bridge within the town centre. On the Wallacetown side of the river were several inns and meeting houses that might be suitable for my first encounter with the citizens. But how to select one which would be sympathetic to King Robert? Walking along the riverside pathway I did espy one particular inn which seemed to have the right credentials. Along with a tattered Scottish Saltire on a pole hanging over the front door the establishment sported a coat of arms on a wooden shield as being under the patronage of the Provost of Newton-upon-Ayr which was a new description to me and did not signify any alliance with the late Sir William Wallace for whom the town was named.

Entering through the open door, I made my way to the Tap Room from which there was a steady hubbub of voices seemingly in friendly argument over some particular question.

Recall that I am still a youth, and some say a very attractive one at that. My height and red hair certainly ensured that I would stand out in a crowd of ethnic Scots and here was no exception. A momentary silence fell over the assembly as I entered the Tap Room. I was dressed in country garb with no armour or jewellery, only a knife in a leather sheath hanging from a belt around my waist. A wide-brimmed country hat was on my head.

I saluted the barman and the customers and ordered a draught of his best ale. It was not many minutes before one of the customers spoke.

"Do you have kin in this neighbourhood?" was the query.

"I come from Loch Ryan where I was a sailor. I am looking for work. I do not know anyone in Wallacetown." I replied.

"We do not call this town Wallacetown now. You are in Newton-upon-Ayr." This statement from yet another man standing by the fire.

"Oh. I am sorry. Please forgive me. My father told me I would find friends in Wallacetown. Anywhere named after Scotland's greatest patriot and living in a community named after Sir William will be where I would find true Scotsmen."

"That is as maybe" was the laconic rejoinder.

There was a collective rueful laugh throughout the room. The barman leaned over the counter and said to Murdoch:

"You'd better not let the English from the castle hear you saying that."

"Then this is an occupied town?" Murdoch was aghast.

"Oh, no! But we are practical folks. All my customers" and he swept his hand around the room in a broad gesture, "are honest tradesmen who do not look for any trouble from our occupiers whose main job is to hunt down and kill King Robert who is known to be in this neighbourhood with his spies!"

"Why is that?" I enquired in a naive voice.

Another of the drinkers broke into the conversation.

"King Robert is a scheming, murdering, outlaw rascal. He killed his main rival, the good Sir John Cormyn right in front of the altar in Dumfries. He betrayed Sir William Wallace to the English king. How could we stand such a wicked person to be our king?"

"My goodness! How dreadful!" I reacted. I hoped I had sounded distressed enough.

"All we get from these folks is trouble. Murder and Taxes! It's no wonder *we keeps our noses clean and goes with the tide.*" The lower-class vernacular language was noticeable.

Who is going to be crowned King, then?" Murdoch was pushing his luck.

"I could not say, and I do not care! But for sure, more taxes and more fighting."

"You seem to take an unusual interest in the Royal Succession, young man. Tell us what is your opinion of the present situation?"

Another customer spoke up: "Are you perhaps a foreigner?"

"A spy?" said an anonymous voice from the crowd.

"No, no. I was born in Wigtown" I replied. "I was only trying to make conversation."

"Well, we don't much care for strangers making mischief in our town. Wigtown. Now, was that not the place where the Northmen plundered the Abbey and killed the priests? They killed the land-holding peasants as well and stole their land!" This litany of sins was trotted out as being the truth.

"My apology for seemingly disturbing the peace!" Hastily I replied as, by now, I was an embattled young man. "I did not mean to startle you. I shall finish this excellent drink and get out of your way. I trust you will all have a pleasant evening!"

I then accomplished what I had said I would do and soon found myself back out on the street path by the river, a much wiser and chastened young man.

I was out on the narrow street. I looked to the right which was the way to the Docks; straight ahead was the bridge I had already crossed from the Ayr town centre, and to my left there appeared to be a line of buildings that looked like they petered out and gave way to open countryside. This last appeared to be the only way to go. It was not appealing because once in the countryside there would be nowhere to go except to catch up with the King and the troops already some miles away and admit defeat.

Thinking that Ayr would somehow be a good call had evaporated in my mind when I allowed myself to think what had just passed in the pub I had just left. No doubt a town made up of artisans and working people was either too cowed or so happy with the English occupation. It might be difficult to find a peasant with sons who wanted freedom or gentry that had a positive thought for King Robert.

CHAPTER XI

THE PATRIOTS OF PRESTWICK

I looked towards the tall grey and forbidding walls of Ayr Castle looming over the harbour on the other side of the river and a shiver ran down my spine. How could any true blooded Scotsmen ever give in to occupation? The English had to go! The Scottish rebels must be defeated for the good of the country! I seethed with anger. And Ayr a Royal Burgh as well!

I walked along the river front path somewhat aimlessly as my interior conflicting thoughts were churning around in my head. With hardly noticing it, I was coming to the end of the houses on my left, and I could see cultivated fields quite clearly. Trying to do any good with this community that had rejected the district name of Wallacetown and substituted it with a construction of Newton-upon-Ayr had lost all connection with patriotism and loyalty. They would certainly not support King Robert the Bruce's coronation at Scone this coming Easter!

I tried to recall the maps that we had looked at and carefully researched last night. What lay immediately ahead? I searched my brain. We had decided that neither of us would actually carry a map lest it would be seen as a tool for a spy or traitor if we were caught and searched, I remembered. But something told me that there was a dot on this road map called Whitletts just about two miles out from Wallacetown that was. So, with a new spring in my stride, I proceeded more hopefully than before.

There turned out to be no particular centre of Whitletts just a straggle of country cottages lining both sides of the road. But one particular construction looked larger than most of the others. It had an archway into a central courtyard and window boxes containing bright geraniums decorating the street-front of the building. Clearly, this was a hostelry of some character. It was across the road on the left. By now I was dishevelled and very dusty and resolved to spend the night in this place if they had accommodation for me.

Entering the Tap Room, I was greeted by a roaring fire in a broad fire ingle where local worthies had settled in for the evening. I made myself known to the innkeeper who was also serving as the barman and enquired whether he had a room for a foot-weary traveller? He at once took me towards the back of the house to show me an adequate chamber with a fireplace which he volunteered to have a fire set should I decide on occupation. I said yes and the deal was soon done as well as a meal of bread and excellent local cheese in the Tap Room to accompany a tankard of fine ale.

As I sat enjoying the first meal, I had had all day, one of the local men, clearly an agricultural worker by his garb approached me to talk.

"Good evening to you, stranger. Have you come far?" His voice was surprisingly strong and warm given the frail nature of his physical appearance.

"Good evening to you my good man" Murdoch replied equally affably. "I have come from Loch Ryan but stopped last evening in Dalrymple. Do you know it? There is a fine inn just at the crossroads."

"Indeed I do. I worked on Lord Symington's Estate for many years until my wife's family left me a small holding here at Auchencruive. Nowadays I leave all the heavy work to my two sons and enjoy the time with my friends here in this inn." He included the group sitting around the fire with a sweeping gesture.

It sounds like an excellent way to spend your senior years." I commented. "You are a very lucky man. You have a good circle of friends I see". Murdoch looked towards the fireplace where his friends were watching us and weighing me up in true Scottish fashion. I assumed without apprehension as I knew that no Scotsman would meet and respect another without first working out his pedigree or his background.

"What is your name, son? Asked the old man.

"I am Murdoch Stewart of Cumloden in Wigtownshire." Murdoch could see no harm in telling the truth in this company.

"A fine name, indeed." Replied the old man. "I still have a single name: John, but I am often called John of the Whins owing to the fact that when I was with the Symington Estate I cleared whole hillsides of whin bushes to prepare the ground for sheep."

"My goodness!" exclaimed Murdoch. "That must have been quite a task!"

"Yes. It took me several seasons." was the reply. There is a woollen blanket mill in the district so there is a ready market for fresh wool in season. It turned out that my Lord Symington owned the mill so it was a natural that he would need to have grazing for sheep as well.

"You must know the Bruce family, then." John questioned artfully.

I was taken aback but did not show it. How did this old man come up with such a question?

"What made you say that?" I queried.

"Well, the Stewarts are married into the Bruces."

"Oh! I see" I said, somewhat relieved, "I am only a Stewart because a forebear of mine chose Stewart for the family name when it became lawful. He had had a minor job with the Steward family and probably had thoughts above his station!"

John laughed. "Aye" he added. "I suppose in a generation or two it will make no difference! Stewart will be a name associated with our master's for quite a while, I suppose, but Whin with two 'N's will be forever associated with me. My boys are Whinns and their kids the same!" He sat back contentedly having made his point.

"I had not thought about names in that way." I ventured, "Your point is a very good one and you are to be congratulated, John Whinn!" Murdoch had now finished his bread and cheese and was thinking about the comfy bed that was waiting for him.

"Come on over and meet my friends" invited John.

"Do you know, John, I am very tired and would want to retire now" I protested

"Och! Come on!" urged the old man. "Come and stay for, for half an hour or so. A young man like you doesn't need much sleep!"

"Oh well. Half an hour then" and John and I walked over to the ingle where an extra chair was brought in for me.

Everyone seemed to be in some sort of an agricultural job or retired. They all welcomed **me** and then resumed their discussion which was politics. One of the group was a comparatively young man named Angus Davidson. He was an employee of a great estate while the others were free yeomen with their own smallholdings.

On eventually discussing the nearby forces of King Robert which were known to all, the discussion became how they were ravishing the countryside and looking to conscript army recruits. There were several tales of rape and pillage that had occurred only last weekend. Clearly the King's opposition was at work and spreading malicious gossip about what Murdoch knew for a fact to be untrue because he knew that Scott had placed monitors among the troops to maintain order.

Murdoch remained listening in silence but nodded his head from time to time to indicate he was hearing what was being discussed. Eventually a pause was arrived at which indicated that he was expected to speak. He began:

"When I was in Dalrymple the soldiers of King Robert had just left. I got the impression that they were well-behaved, but you know what military men are? They are sometimes difficult to manage and there will always be one or two bad apples. Both Gentry and Peasants, however, had many good things to say about this particular invasion of their normal quiet life. Several Dalrymple young men joined up with the army and the King bought several rounds of beer for the community at the pub where he organized an evening of entertainment for the people.

"Of course, all this happened before I arrived, and I only heard about it from an old codger who was rather keener on the beer that I paid for than perhaps the honest truth!"

"Perhaps he was only saying what he thought what you wanted to hear?" asked Angus sucking on his long clay pipe.

"Maybe so." Murdoch answered. "But as traveller, it is not my intention to ever get into any political question that may be locally germane. It matters not to me what King Robert's intentions are just as long as I am not involved and come to no harm."

"I think you are possibly a King's spy," observed John. "You say that you have spoken with the peasants and the gentry. What kind of visitor would have that opportunity in Dalrymple? It is just a hunch mind you and I do not much care who or what you are." Suddenly John was not the genial and benevolent old man he had appeared at the beginning.

John continued: "You had better be careful, young man. If some of the English military hear you speak and suspect the worst. They could be very dangerous for you and for anyone with whom you have spoken."

"Now, John..." warned Angus.

"Well, I would not want this attractive young man to fall foul of the English."

"Anyway, thank you all very much for your companionship." said Murdoch "Landlord! I shall go to my room now. Will you see that my good friends are taken care of with another round of your best ale!"

The innkeeper was only too anxious to do my bidding and when he was done, he said:

"Come, Sir. I shall take you to your room."

Bidding *'good night'* I followed the host out of the Tap Room. Along the way the Owner spoke to me in a lowered voice.

"I have just heard John sending word to one of his sons to alert the English at Ayr Castle of your presence here in Whitletts. He is an old rogue, but we keep him in our company to keep up with the gossip about any official activities at the garrison. You know:"

"Ah yes! What good advice!" I acknowledged.

"I'd be very careful of John if I were you" continued the publican, "In fact, the more I think of it, I would advise that you should leave the inn very early tomorrow morning. What's more, disguise your direction as you go. I'll call you at daybreak to break fast," then in a louder voice, "The fire has just settled, Sir. You should be quite comfortable here!"

It was with exhaustion that Murdoch fell into the over blanketed bedstead and was out like a light just as soon as his head hit the pillow. As far as he was concerned, sunrise came much too soon when he was summoned to breakfast at an ungodly hour. Imagine Murdoch's surprise when Angus Davidson joined him at the breakfast table to offer his services.

"I am sorry that John had marked you as a King's spy. He has already sent one of his boys into Ayr to alert the soldiers of your presence. Let me assist you in finding a way from here that will throw them off the scent."

"You are so kind, said Murdoch. "What do you suggest?"

"I suggest we cross over the Sanqher fields and come into Prestwick Toll by the back way. We shall by-pass the Toll to avoid detection and I shall take you to friends near the Prestwick Cross who can help you."

With that, we took off on foot across the pleasant farmlands until we reached the cottages that marked the edge of Prestwick at Saint Quivox Well.

Going down the boundary of the Saint Quivox estate. We reached the Well and paused for refreshment as Robert the Bruce had done during his travels as the Earl of Carrick. For that reason, the Well was now known as Bruce's Well. We then joined the turnpike into Prestwick proper, arriving at the Prestwick Cross about noon. Angus was as good as his word. Along the way we discussed the prevailing political situation of a divided Scotland and the necessity to uniting her. Angus was receptive to my goals and had in fact reached a similar conclusion.

He was very much in favour of King Robert's efforts that would unite our country and bring the several so-called kingdoms under a single control. Until that happened there would be continuous strife among the various parties and England would be the winner every time as it would play one region off against the others, just as she had done up to now. It seemed to Angus that King Robert had the best chance of achieving the goal of a United Scotland.

Angus then asked: "What is your role in this?"

I was taken aback by this direct question. In truth I had no title of job description of what I was supposed to be doing. But by *'grabbing the bull by both horns'* I decided to describe what I wanted to be doing for the King. After all, I needed something to look forward to, a goal, a definite position. Without these defined stimuli I would just drift along and the King for sure would eventually replace me.

"I am the King's Administrative Assistant" I confidently affirmed. "I also attend to Public Policy and will supervise public access to the Monarch."

"Well, I never guessed!" exclaimed Angus. He looked at me closely. "Really?, "You are not a knight or an earl or any other title... Or are you"?

"No. I am simply Murdoch Stewart of Cumloden. That is my strength. I am one of you. After the coronation, who knows...? The King is a very wise man. He wishes to maintain as close an association with all his subjects as possible. That's my job and I like it!

I continued.

"To reach as many people as possible I would like to meet your friends who can spread the good word about King

Robert and join with him in promoting a United Scotland. The army that he is gathering is not to subdue ordinary Scots but to put down any opposition forces that His enemies may mount. The King's motto is *'A United Scotland;* **Not** *a Subdued Scotland'*. He comes not as a conqueror but as a Saviour."

"Holy Mary!" shouted Angus out very loud. Several people who were passing by at the time looked questioningly at him before passing on.

"It is not our intention to beat the Scottish people into submission" I added, "but to get them to understand what the King wants to do. He is sure that the people want unification of the country after so many years of strife and mayhem. I have been given the task of leading the plan to approach as many of the people as possible and have designed a tactic to approach as many public singers, mummers, poets, balladeers and message-minstrels as possible to get the good message out that the King is on the side of the people. Your assistance, Angus, will be of tremendous help!

"The vast majority of the Scottish folk must have a chance to glimpse the King's good heart and benevolence. We have started in the Doon Valley, and it has proved that such an approach can be achieved where the King's good name is well-established as the Earl of Carrick."

Angus was impressed by our goal. He said that he would introduce me to some of his friends who were well talented and who would assist me bringing the name of the good King Robert to the local populace. This sort of news would be a welcome antidote to the English slander that was everywhere. He would have to go back to Whitletts before he was missed but he wished me well.

He was as good as his word. The people he introduced me to at the Old Church readily caught on to what I was trying to achieve and arranged for a roundtable that very evening to discuss detail and to set up a clandestine organization of itinerant entertainers to carry the message to the people. The priest of the kirk was also at the meeting and told the assembly that he had had instructions from the Bishop of Glasgow to include the very same messages which he would incorporate in his sermons every Sunday from now on.

I rose to speak to a much larger group which had gathered in the kirk in the evening.

I started:

"Good evening, friends. I am here by the Grace of God who has delivered me from the hands of the English garrison at Ayr. I also had a near-encounter with some Scotsmen who had apparently sold their soul to the English for the sake of commerce. And they were citizens of what I call Wallacetown and they now refer to as Newton-upon-Ayr forgetting all reference to Scotland's patriot and now martyr, Sir William Wallace. These are your neighbours to the South of you. So be warned that Ayr is not a centre of support for our appointed King who is to be crowned at Easter. I should like at this time to counteract the terrible lies that the English are spreading throughout the entire nation. The cruel murder that was perpetrated in London on our elected Guardian of Scotland, William Wallace, was never betrayed by King Robert the Bruce and such a slander is in no way associated with this present activity.

"As to the killing of Lord Cormyn in front of the altar in a Dumfries church the King takes full responsibility for the unfortunate event. He only stated that he did not know if he had killed the Red Cormyn over a private matter, but he suspected not, and one of the King's knights went to find out and finish Cormyn off, thinking he was just doing his King's wishes. The King has accepted the Pope's condemnation and excommunication as a punishment he will have to bear for the rest of his life.

"This present quest lead by me on the King's behalf," I continued, "is an effort to resurrect the King's previous popularity. As the Laird of Annandale and Carrick he has protected the Western Scottish Borders from the depredations of the Percy's and his thieving associates from Carlisle. He has granted smallholdings to deserving vassals and set them free of bondage Those bonded men who have joined our small army will be rewarded with land of their own in their own parish.

"The present campaign with a small but talented group of volunteers is designed to assist as many people as possible to know and understand King Robert's good intentions and good heart as he moves towards Perth and Scone. It will be beneficial to all to not speak badly of him but to acclaim the unity of Scotland at every opportunity so that our country can take her place in the Community of States where the citizens and all subjects have a life that is free from all political strife, servitude, and conscription.

"As evidence, the many situations within His estates of such programmes being enacted speak to the honesty and truthfulness of His intentions for our entire country. His Majesty has tasked me with contacting good people like you to consider adjusting your public messages when entertaining others to insert any positive remarks about out Sovereign King and his upcoming coronation.

"For example: Jokes or anecdotes that place the Sovereign in a bad light should be eschewed. His Highness's all political actions should be supported if you truly feel they are right and if you do not, then omit any reference to them. This is not meant to be a listing of dos and don'ts. We would like you to be honest just as you normally are, but not to say anything that is likely to reflect badly on His Majesty. On the other hand, do not draw opprobrium on yourself by adding obsequious or lickspittle interpretations to any of your utterances. This kind of slanted message is not persuasive nor productive and, I am sure, is not something in which you would indulge in any case.

"I hope my message strikes a chord with you all." I said with a smile on my lips and a sincere look in my bright blue eyes that even in the gloom of the Kirk were very noticeable. "I do not have a lot of time, but I shall be available to talk with any of you on a one-to-one basis to answer any questions you may have. I must leave this evening to catch up with the King and the Troops at Cushats before they get too far away from me and I cannot catch up!

Remember, I am not encouraging any of you to put your hard-won career and reputation or life on the line. If you cannot find anything nice to say about King Robert, may I ask you to say nothing at all? Most of all, do not argue against or repeat the scurrilous lies being told by the English."

"In conclusion I would like to tell you of a situation that occurred in Dalrymple. The soldiers were marching away and singing one of these indecent songs that lampoon the gentry and their ladies. You probably know it. Seeing the King's displeasure, the leaders halted the parade and warned them that the song was not appropriate for the King's Troops. Several of the long-term soldiers said that there was another version of the song, and they would sing that to keep up their spirits. The new version of the song replaced all references to the Ruling Classes and substituted the male army ranks for ridicule which was a lot more amusing than the original and produced a smile on the King's face."

There was a round of gentle laughter followed by enthusiastic applause. When this had died down and people started to go, several of the audience came up and wanted to shake my hand or to ask questions.

One short young man of dark complexion explained he was glad that Murdoch had selected Prestwick for this message because this town was somewhat of a residential centre for and of local entertainers. It was more obvious in the Winter months when travelling was difficult in that the town hosted many literary and debating societies and comic reviews. These were enthusiastically supported by the local artistic community as were dramas, busking, and morality plays. He felt sure that my message had struck home I thanked him for his enthusiasm which he clearly displayed.

On departing the young man threw his arms around me and gave me an unexpected embrace.

An older man with tears in his eyes shook Murdoch's hand most warmly saying that he had not been so motivated for many years thinking that any Scottish initiative was useless, He now felt that his new ballads would be more like those of the historical balladeers whose sagas of derring-do, of bold knights, and intrepid battles to stir the listener's heart. All that was needed now was '*fair maidens in distress*' to be saved by handsome knights on horseback!

Lastly, Angus Davidson came up. He said: "I could not leave without staying to hear your stirring words. Thank you. Thank you. God save the King." And he went out to greet some of his more intimate friends before departing for Auchencruive.

I was invited to sup with what I reconised as the leaders of the Prestwick 'artistic' group. This turned out to be a very stimulating meeting over a largely vegetarian meal which was just as well, as I afterwards stepped out along the Kilmarnock Road towards my rendezvous with the King and his troops, now reported to be nearing Bogend Toll on the outskirts of Kilmarnock.

CHAPTER XII

CUSHATS ARGUMENT AND ARRIVAL DUNDONALD

The troops had progressed across Kyle maintaining their schedule and the King had caught up with them at Stair Bridge without any problem. They were now in the business of setting up camp on the grounds of Cushats Priory and the King had been invited to stay in the Priory buildings where an empty cell was available for his occupation. I caught up with them all at Bogend Toll where the priory was situated. This was a good place in which to make a halt before marching on Dundonald which was only a couple of hours away.

Scott was busy with the camp arrangements for the troops. I came across the King sitting outside the Abbey's dormitory building where the brothers had their individual cells. A good fire in a brazier was burning. He greeted me warmly and asked me to join him and tell him all about my adventures in Ayr. It was late in the afternoon and there were plenty of rugs to put around our shoulders as the temperature was going down with the setting of the sun. A servant from the Priory brought out a large flagon of the Priory's famous mead with which to augment the heat derived from the brazier and the blankets. A little later, Scott joined us fresh from his drills.

I started with the disappointing news. "We should not look to big towns like Ayr with its twin town north of the river Ayr, called after Scotland's Great Hero, Wallacetown, for supporters of Your Majesty. Nowadays it is called Newton-upon-Ayr."

"And why is that?" enquired the King.

"Because the English garrison at Ayr Castle has intimidated the middle-class tradesmen. That the Baliol party has the perceived better cause and because the English king will ensure its legitimacy. Fancy that? They are actually praising English domination. They are accusing you, Your Majesty, of all sorts of foul deeds and every villainous action that they initiate and perform are laid at your feet. You should hear what you and your rogue military have done to the people and the countryside between Dalrymple and here at Bogend Toll.

"I'd rather not, if you don't mind" exclaimed His Majesty.

"My troops were perfectly behaved!" added Scott, with some heat in his voice.

"But that's not what many of the citizens of Ayr have been told. Scorched earth and wholesale rape have been the order of the day."

"Damn!" expostulated the King. How can we combat lies like that?

"Well, proceeding onwards to Whitletts which is a small village practically attached to Ayr, I did come across a couple of Your Majesty's stalwart supporters who directed me to the artistic community in Prestwick who are responsible for spreading good news and entertainment around the whole district of Kyle.

"It seems that once the weather closes down for the winter, these people make Prestwick their base from which to make daytrips rather than to perform in circuit which is a good weather style of their operation. That way they can reach more country people when the weather is good."

"And…?"

"Almost to a man, they are on your side, Majesty!" I made this concluding remark, keeping the best for the end.

"That is certainly good news." The King vehemently agreed.

"Huh! A small community of anti-social gossipers and purveyors of nonsense to entertain the bumpkins is thin gruel, indeed." was Scott's reaction.

"I consider this is good news." I countered. "I was very impressed by the width of cover even in the winter, and of the sincerity of the group.

"By the way, Sire, Bishop Robert Wishart has instructed all priests in his diocese to emphasize your candidature from the pulpit every Sunday and this priest was also with the crowd, and we were in his church." I felt this might be a telling statement.

I was correct!

The King congratulated me and thanked me for my efforts in keeping our project hot by pressing forward even when the situation looked hopeless. But to keep the conversation running on a level footing despite Scott's pessimistic assessment of my efforts, he then asked Scott how his troops were doing?

Scott was ready with his reply. They had been responding well to discipline and to drills. He still needed some fresh officers, but he had been unable to recruit or promote any since the three Cornets in Dalmellington. Did the King notice that rude marching songs had been done away with and that singing in the ranks now favoured jocular anti-military Dittys?

King Robert interjected that he had not noticed but thanked Scott for his intervention.

This afternoon Scott had rehearsed the troops on the order and discipline that he required for entry into Dundonald and the castle. He was positive that they would make a good impression on the villagers and the castle guard.

The brazier had been recharged twice and even so, the night was getting colder when the King concluded the meeting with the instructions that we should get on the road to Dundonald no later than ten in the morning to make a regal arrival at the Dundonald Castle gates between 12 and one o'clock. Scott and I accompanied the King to his cell within the Brother House and he suggested that we should use the passageway that served the cells as our own sleeping quarters.

Not wishing to refuse Majesty, we agreed. He shut the door to his cell and left us standing in the draughty hallway which reminded me a lot like the nights I had spent at Rathlin Castle outside the door of the reception room as a first-alarm boy. Then I had looked for things to make me as comfortable as possible. This again I did, and I was pleased to find some old dusty velvet curtains which made tolerable cover from the wind. Scott closed the door to the outside and we settled down to get some sleep before tomorrow's parade.

Like a lot of ecclesiastical buildings, the ceiling was high and structured in stone and plaster, exaggerating even whispers. Scott was wanting to talk, and I had to hush him down lest his customary booming voice would awaken any others.

"What did you and the King talk about after I had gone to organize the troops? He asked.

"I don't remember. Honestly! I think we had discussed the Kings solitary journey across Kyle. He said that the folks at Drongan House, the Rowans, had asked to be remembered to me but that was about all." I said in a nonchalant way.

"You know the Rowans?" was Scott's doubtful question.

"Why, yes!" I replied. "They are second cousins through marriage. My mother's niece married their only son and heir who unfortunately died at a young age."

"You seem to be connected to everything and everybody" remarked Scott sourly.

"Well. That's the point about living in the same spot and having large collateral families in the same district."

"But you said your father was a stranger from Norway?"

"That's true. But my mother is well connected. She comes from a long line of yeoman farmers in the district."

"Sometimes you make me sick with your snobbery!" exclaimed Scott. "Here I am, having to suffer a new name which does not connect me with anybody whilst you can hob nob with everyone as an equal!"

"Scott." I was barely restraining my anger. "You have a great name. 'Scott' represents your country and 'Boyd' is a glorious name and one you can be proud of".

"A lot of good the Boyd name has brought me" He petulantly complained. "Thank goodness the King has allowed me to show my talents by permitting me to demonstrate my skills at training and leading the King's Force.

"Is that not enough for you?" I questioned.

"It may be the way to achieve honours for some folks, but here I am left to *'just get on with it'*! When you were gone, the King relied on me, so I was virtually doing two jobs, mine and yours!"

"Bully for you!" Well, you cannot duplicate my role as Royal Boatmaster!"

"Huh! Who cares for that half-a-groat title and job."

"That's a bit harsh. Even coming from you!" I exclaimed. "And what do you do? The King's 'Toy Soldier'"?

"At least He relies on me to do a good job!" Scott's voice was rising.

"Who was he relying upon scoping out the important Ayr region?

"Swanning about in Pubs and chatting up stupid citizens who can catch every free beer that's offered for any message tailored to the demands of the stupid enquirer!"

"I bet you made up more than half of your story!" He added for good measure.

Oh! For Heaven's Sake! Go and boil your head in a pail of pig's swill!" But before Scott could answer. An angry voice emanated from the King's cell.

"There will be no heads available for boiling at least any that are attached to a body.! Quiet down! I am deeply disappointed in both of you. Shut up! You are both easily replaceable and I shall start the ball rolling tomorrow morning when you are ordered to face me with your silly argument before breakfast!"

"My apology, Majesty….." But this was cut short by the King shutting me off with a curt retort.

"Now, I command you both to shut up. Don't you know what that order means?" The King was really angry now.

Scott and I looked at each other.

"Yes, Majesty." "Yes Majesty" Both voices were quite contrite sounding.

I do not know about Scott, but I had a very troubled sleep. All at once I was in a court proceeding; condemned to die by beheading; and marching to the scaffold in front of a jeering crowd. I woke up in a sweat and could not get back to sleep. Being close to the winter solstice, daylight did not come soon enough but seemed to linger well past the breakfast hour.

Even getting up from my temporary bed in the draughty hall did not go well. In the first place, Scott was already awake and shaving in the only lavatory space that served this part of the Priory. What's more. There were several brothers in the queue before me so by the time I was able to perform my ablutions, I was already running late. Scott and I had exchanged curt words and arranged that we would present ourselves together before the King.

The dreaded interview had at last arrived.

Saluting the King in his small sleeping cell, there was hardly any space in which to bow let along stand in a dignified manner. Scott, I noticed, was in full armour and ready for combat whereas I had nothing to wear except my woollen travelling suit. The King was unusually dark of face with a scowl that was deeply furrowed into his forehead.

"You young scamps. Loudly arguing with each other within the King's hearing and doing no good at all for your present temporary positions? How dare you!"

If there had been space to grovel, we would have gone down in our knees, at least I would have, I do not know about Scott. I hung my head in shame, and I saw that Scott had done the same.

"It is too late now to do anything about your disgraceful behaviour, but you are not forgiven, and I shall deal with you both when we get settled in Dundonald. Now, Go Away! I want to see as little as possible of you both. You are dismissed."

Scott said:" Does that mean I am dismissed from the army?"

"Don't be impertinent, Boy. You will continue to perform your military duties until I expressly say otherwise." And with a dismissal wave of his hand, the interview was over.

As we were on our way out, the King said to me "Ask my Lord Darnconner to attend on me!" No 'please' No 'thank you'. Darnconner was one of the attending baron's sons. He had studied at Leyden University and spoke three European languages. He was only 24.

If I had wanted to feel threatened in my job, Darnconner would be the one I would be most worried about.

I felt threatened.

Scott and I went our separate ways. It was going to be a long day and the pleasure that had been anticipated of settling in for several weeks was now as dust.

Anyway, the show must go on and once the troops were inspected and lined up in the proper formation as required by Scott, the King of Scotland's Royal Brigade moved off, marching along the well-paved country lanes towards the end of our Great March across Kyle, Ayrshire from Dalmellington to Dundonald.

It was a lovely bright winter's day. First the King with Scott at his side, followed by me and the principal courtiers of cabinet rank. Thereafter came the knights and their personal squadrons and lastly the troops own special brigades, the Loch Doon Archers; the Dalmellington Yeomen, the Coylton Cavaliers, and the new Tarbolton Battalion. All we needed was a band to keep us all in step instead of the solitary drummer whose job it was to set the pace and to regulate it on his instrument.

The passage was between dry stane dykes and hedges of woven thorn and beech. The enclosed fields now bare of crops were either in pasture for upland sheep, wintering in the more equitable coastal plain, or freshly ploughed and ready for sowing when the last of the frost had passed. Dotted here and there were tidy whitewashed farm steadings with substantial farmhouses of two-storeys signifying the levels of prosperity as well as the great manor houses of the landowners hidden behind their tree screens and revealing their towers or spires over the surrounding seasonal leafless branches but with avenues leading up to the house from the roads on which we were traveling lined with evergreen bushes. Some fields were in winter crops like turnips or kale which provided a variation on the landscape.

Every so often we would pass a farm labourer's roadside cottage. The man of the house was off at work somewhere, but his young, pretty wife would come outside with their babies and young children to clap and wave as our men passed by. There were lots of shouts and whistles emanating from both marchers and spectators with the rosy cheeks of the toddlers all wreathed in big smiles with gurgles of pure pleasure produced from rosy sweet lips.

Soon, the kirk steeple of Dundonald Church was seen surrounded by closely built, squat cottages. The grey stone of the dwellings with their thatched roofs contrasted with the several colourfully painted two-storey houses with dark slate roofs. The Main Street was quite straight but was hilly going up to the north-west, the direction in which we were marching, and fairly steeply down beyond the half-way point to reach the outer castle wall and gate at the end off to the left.

The castle consisted of a central keep towards the back with lower stone stables, kitchens, and barracks to the left and front encasing a large open concourse area. The keep was built on an ancient volcanic granite plug which made its four-storeys even higher and there was a second plug immediately but separately behind the first on which the new heavy guns were placed. The entire castle was surrounded by a tall, thick protection wall and was continuous even rising up to the fortifications for the big guns at the back. Immediately behind the castle was a thick forest growing right up to the castle's outer walls but separated from the castle wall itself by a deep gully with a natural stream flowing through.

Entering through the only gate at the front just off the Main Street of the village, our troops formed up in regimental manner. The King and I went over to be greeted by the waiting castle dignitaries which included Lord Montgomerie, Lord Stewart, Lord Dundonald and several Castle functionaries. Lords Montgomerie and Stewart were uncle and nephew whereas Lord Dundonald was a grandson of the Montgomerie whose father of the same rank had been killed in battle as a young man. The Montgomerie line also had the distinction and the lands as the Earls of Eglinton, one of Scotland's ancient titles.

Under the normal conditions that prevailed at the time, Dundonald Castle had been built by the Stewards (now Stewarts) to be gifted to the King who, however, had leased it on a *'Grace and Favour'* basis to Montgomerie. With the recent death of Lord Stewart's father and the bestowal of his father's official position as Lord High Steward of Scotland, the King had decreed that Dundonald Castle should be re-leased to the Stewarts and that Montgomerie should flit to his new modern mansion house nearby called Auchans. In other words, there was an ongoing question about who was tenant of what? I only mention this because a further change was soon to take place and the reader will benefit from knowing what has gone before.

The small royal party had been allocated to the third floor of the keep tower where we made ourselves comfortable. The King was allocated a private chamber at the front end whereas the other members of the King's Court were each to use a private sleeping alcove curtained off the main third floor hall. Having spruced up as best we could after the march, we went downstairs to meet Lord Montgomerie and his family, other guests and staff and to partake of the evening meal. The ladies were present at mealtime, and it was at this time that I came across my long-standing impossible love for my Lady Stewart whom when I first set eyes on her all those years ago was the daughter of the Earl of Galloway now King Robert Bruce and his first wife Lady Elizabeth of Mar. This daughter had been born Lady Marjorie Bruce and I had fallen in love with this lovely lady. At the time, I was merely a boatwright apprentice and she a Princess of the Royal Blood, so I had pined away in hopelessness. In time she had married Walter Stewart who was the heir to his father's rank of Lord High Steward of Scotland to which he had recently ascended following his father's death.

Lady Marjorie's marriage to Sir Walter had been of dynastic importance, but it did look like a really romantic union as well, so I could but stand and watch the two lovers and their, by now, two children. You may recall that I had given myself the surname of 'Stewart' which I had selected because of my love for Marjory.

To be 'thrown together' now at Dundonald was the cruelty of fate!

This was the start of our lengthy stay in Dundonald Castle where the planning of the final part of our expedition was to be done. Several intense meetings were scheduled by King Robert which lasted for hours as the various points of view were discussed and studied.

King Robert's second wife, Elizabeth de Burgh was married in 1302 and came to Dundonald whilst we were there. They had had a daughter Margaret then a son, David along with his twin brother named John. She was getting over John's early death and came to be with her husband. The result of this family reunion was a daughter, Matilda. As David was now the male heir to the Earldom (and the Crown), his elder sister, Marjorie, was no longer the heir apparent, but the Princess Royal which seemed to worry her not at all. Being the wife of Scotland's Steward (the English equivalent is Chancellor) was not an insignificant role to play.

But this overall social and domestic environment was getting to be a bit of a bore and I could see that King Robert was getting irritated with such a home-like situation as occasioned by the Queen and her lady attendants. As a veritable man-of-action he was simply not used to the constant witterings of women and the clamour of babies.

After a very short time, he prevailed on My Lord Montgomerie to find an apartment where he could be with his men rather than on the third floor of the castle which we had discovered was normally the abode of His Lordship when he had no royal guests. It seemed that on most nights he repaired to his newly built mansion which he called Auchans House until the following day so that freed up his study and library room on the second floor to which our Sovereign could find solace from time to time. It would be used also by Lord Stewart, however, when he had business to perform.

It was in one of these *'escape'* sessions that the King brought up the topic of Scott's and my falling out with each other. Lord Stewart who was at the time sitting at a corner desk and was only taking a casual and friendly interest in our business while we were all relaxing and smoking in the Montgomerie room. The King suddenly broke the amiable silence saying:

"What is all this nonsense about where you both do not get along with each other?"

I was somewhat taken aback for I saw Stewart suddenly taking an interest in this exchange just when I was beginning to think of the incident at Coodham to be by now a dead issue. Before I could speak, and reassure the Monarch that the situation was nothing to be worried about, Scott spoke up:

"Your Majesty" He began, "I am afraid that I do not get along with Murdoch. He is insufferably superior in his tone and is always prattling on about his good work at spreading his propagandist theory. I cannot stand him. He is a two-faced, devious bastard and does not understand the value of military force."

"It is more than a 'theory', son" said the King in a mild tone. And the absence of a marriage between his mother and father is none of our business. As a matter of fact, his mother told me all about the impossibility of obtaining a church blessing at short notice which satisfied me."

"I think it is a complete nonsense" replied Scott. "We all know that a strong, punishing force will bring all the peasants to heel, at least as many as we shall need, anyway!" Scott was getting onto his topic now and was not to be stopped.

"To follow your advice then, when we go to take on Kilmarnock, you will have no trouble in killing your Boyd friends who have vouched for you?"

"You are not going to do that?" protested Scott.

"Oh? And why not?"

"It is entirely unnecessary for your campaign to pick a fight with Kilmarnock and the Boyd family!"

"I do not like your tone of voice, Scott. Kindly remember to whom you are speaking!" The King was now showing his irritation.

"I do remember that I am discussing military affairs with my King. But my King must surely listen to advice that is offered by the most successful commander of his troops!"

"Really? I was always led to believe that '*self-praise*' was no praise at all and in your case, I heartily agree with the proverb."

"If you include Kilmarnock in your military plan then I shall resign!" Scott was now on his 'high horse'.

There was no stopping Scott by this time. He was going to commit a serious offense against the King.

"Then your departure is accepted!" Robert was just as angry now as Scott. "Just remember, Boy, that you were never appointed to your role as commander in the first place. You have only attained command through your own efforts and by this King's approval. I find it not difficult to withdraw my support. You cannot resign; you were never appointed!"

Scott lunged at the King with his hand suddenly at his dagger's hilt. I sprang forward to fend off this attack on the Monarch, and it was as if Scott had suddenly changed his target to me. We fought like deranged men. By now, Scott had his dagger in his hand and was lunging at me. The King was shouting:

"Guards! …Guards!"

I was twisting Scott's wrist as I had never done such a thing before. I am not a fighting man, but I realised that this was a contest to the death. I put all my strength into a punch on Scott's face and he reeled back. I drew my own dagger that had never been drawn in anger before and grabbed Scott's chin. His throat was exposed to my blade, and I was not sure whether I had the will to sever it.

Suddenly, I felt myself being drawn back from Scott. A couple of castle guards had responded to the King's shout and had come into the apartment to break up the fight. Lord Stewart was helping the King back to his seat from where he had fallen at Scott's attack. The King had his dagger drawn and for a minute or so, it looked like he was going to take my place and finish Scott off. I could see Stewart laying a restraining hand on the King's reaction.

"Wait!" I yelled and the King hesitated.

"Put him in irons and lock him in the dungeon!" he instructed the Guards referring to Scott who was dragged out screaming foul epithets at the King and me.

He was all bloody so I must have cut him somewhere. I was afterwards to learn that I had slit his tunic and ruptured his stomach.

The wound was not life threatening.

Once calm had been restored and additional whisky had been brought in by the castle steward, the King and I began to review the evening's dramas. I was effusively apologetic, but the King would have none of it.

"You saved my life, son!" he kept saying repeatedly, but the dynastic implications of the entire incident had not yet fully sunk into my brain: I was still more surprised at my reaction, the speed by which I had acted, and the courage which I did not know I possessed?

Robert was babbling a bit. At one stage he was announcing that he would take charge at the head of his army. He was only 33 and young and fit enough to do so. On another tack he was talking about creating a Royal Dukedom which would confer honour and status to the appointee. It would have a generous stipend but no land or vassals except for his abode All of this was churning around in my mind and getting hazier by the minute as my heart had stopped beating at a furious pace.

I eventually fell into sleep and when I awoke, I was still in Lord Montgomerie's study Fully dressed, alone, and lying on his daybed.

CHAPTER XIII

THE CLAN BOYD OF KILMARNOCK

On the following morning, I presented myself to the King. I had carefully brushed down my best suit and shaved as I half expected some kind of reprimand for having been the cause of trouble on the night before. Scott was in the dungeon. Good! That was where he needed to be after being such a bother to me and attacking Robert in a way that could only be construed as treason. I wondered about his future. It was my fault that he had come into our small circle.

I had introduced him to the King and spoken well of him as if I knew his fine qualities. On balance, however, it was the fact that he was of Norwegian origin like me that had persuaded me to bring him to the King's notice and nothing else. What had I been thinking of? Age had something to do with it too; he was within a year or two of my own age whilst most of the others in the King's court were of the Old School. Darn! There was not a great deal I could say in my defence that made sense!

218

The King was in a very blue mood when I entered his chamber on the third floor. He was accompanied by his son-in-law, Walter Stewart. He seemed listless and unwilling to speak any more than was necessary to respond to my observations and questions.

I said, "This will be the occasion when our propaganda effort before an attack will be beneficial. The more the citizens feel that our incursion is not belligerent and deadly, the more difficult it will be for the gentry to call up an army unless made up of the rogues and rascals and ne'er-do wells who will always want a fight anyway."

"Scott is an unruly rascal, and he needs his wings clipped." The King was still nursing his anger. "Many another young man has felt my sword for saying less, I do not want him near me. When we let him go there must be a clear understanding that he is to go where he can do no harm to me or my reign. I think Norway is not far enough away... perhaps even the New World that the Icelanders have discovered?"

"I have direct communications to His Excellency the Danish Ambassador in Edinburgh who controls the Icelandic business." offered my Lord Walter Stewart who was sitting with the King. "I shall request of him to accede to your Royal request." I was left with a vision of Scott trying to impose his discipline on Chinese men without knowing any of each other's languages! Aloud, I said:

"It must be on the way to the Far East. Perhaps it's just an offshore island off China where there is a more civilized community?" I pondered to keep the conversation going and get the King off the subject of Scott. "It's many days sailing west from Greenland, so it cannot be too far from China."

Looking back, the King was still on his Boyd-tirade, but by now, he was beginning to moderate his determination to send him to an unknown land.

"But the young man has been irritating me for some time now, and I must admit to breaking on this occasion Even so, Murdoch, sending him to this totally unknown land does seem a little harsh."

King Robert was in a deep pensive mood. I saw there was no point in avoiding the *'elephant in the room.'*

"If we are going to take Kilmarnock," I repeated, "then it will be necessary to scope out the level of general public approval of the Boyd's. Kilmarnock is like Ayr, it is a fairly large community. We will have to know whether the citizens in general favour a Boyd leadership or cannot wait to get out from under a medieval yoke of oppression. After all, it is somewhat unusual to have a Lowland town dominated by a single Clan.

The King looked up at me with a glint of interest in his eyes.

I felt confident to continue:

"We shall have to persuade the people of the town that our incursion is not belligerent and deadly, then the more difficult it will be for the gentry to call up an army unless made up of the rogues and rascals and ne'er-do wells who will always want a fight anyway.

"We are not going to fight the Boyds" the King muttered as if the thought had just entered his head.

"I am sorry, Sire, I thought last night you were planning such a move."

"It was on my mind, that's all" he said and after a long pause, he continued. "It was in my mind to see what Scott would have to say when I announced such an action."

I was beginning to see that the King was looking for a 'face saving' position to cover the incident.

"Given the time factor, it seems to me that the better strategy will be for you to work your wonders with the Boyds and tell them that we are going to bypass their town and proceed up the Irvine Valley via Riccarton. That way, they can be calm about our nearby presence and even join us if the feeling strikes them." The King was getting back to his old ebullient self. He was at his best when he had a plan that would work and that he would be in charge.

"What a magnificent strategy!" I was not toadying but realised that this could be seen as a test of my ability and if I did well, the King would forgive me for last night's drama and the Cushats argument. Now, if only I was not to be by-passed and pushed aside like Scott then the door was open. A vision of Lord Darnconner came unbidden into my mind.

I thought of my long-term goal to be the best I could be. Not that I was expecting promotion exclusively through this extraordinary circumstance that had placed Scott and me in the King's favoured position, but because I was genuinely working and learning to be recogised for my merits as the only person who would be able to satisfy the King in his quest for the best men in his cabinet. Scott's downfall showed me how fragile was the position of *a 'favourite'*. I did not want to end my career as the *'former Royal Boatman'* and as a footnote to history!

"You will want to spend today reading up on the Boyd's and Clan Boyd. I am sure books of this sort will be in Montgomerie's room if they have not gone to Auchans already. They have a history of being mere vassals of the de Morvilles who were given estates around Largs and Irvine.

"The Clan Boyd was involved in the successful Battle of Largs against King Haakon of Norway in 1263 and are known to be kin of our hosts here, the Montgomeries of Eglinton. One of their Clan was second-in-command to William Wallace so their credentials as supporters for the War of Scottish Independence, and presumably Scottish Unification, are sound.

Their seat is at Dean Castle in Kilmarnock and they are anxious to become gentry. It is my wish that they join us rather than oppose us and I want you to go and arrange for this. The present head of the family is Sir Robert Boyd."

"As the King commands" was my reply. I had been given this incredibly important task and not rusticated as I had feared.

But I felt there was something more I had to say concerning last night, if only to clear the air!

"Is there anything I can do with regards to last night's problem with Scott, My Lord?" I delicately ventured to raise the topic.

"No. There is nothing to be done!" The King replied. "I suppose I should thank you for your intervention. Do you think he would have struck me down?"

"It is my view that Scott was certainly very angry. He had drawn his dagger. He was at that moment capable of regicide!" I carefully replied.

"I thought so, too" was the King's reply. "I had given him more scope than I have ever endowed except for your good self, and I was extremely proud of you two young boys who occupied important positions in my suite. It has hurt me immeasurably to be betrayed in this manner. Do you think he was working alone or is he part of a plot?"

Robert peered at me with lowered brows. Surely, he did not think of me in the same light as Scott. After all, he had thanked me and mentioned how proud he was to have me especially in his inside cabinet. I couched my reply in neutral terms.

"After all, Sire, Scott's disapproval was with me and not you. It was strange to see his reaction to the mention of the Boyd's and Kilmarnock. I did not think he was particularly impressed by his connection with this up-and-coming family and was just using the connection for his own ends, but clearly, we hit a nerve when you said, 'you were thinking of removing the Boyd's as they stood in the way of our progress up the Irvine Valley.'

"Perhaps he has been in contact with them that we know not. They did lose a couple of aspiring younger family members at the Battle of Largs so perhaps he saw a future in succeeding to the chieftainship and leading the Clan into the nobility through his association with me?"

"He has never mentioned such a plan, Sire."

"I *hate* to be used!" He said with strong conviction.

I ventured an idea that had just occurred to me:

"I could always make discrete enquiries when I am at Dean Castle. We only know Scott's side of the situation. Let me try to discover any background information that might shed a different light or at least an explanatory light, on the situation,"

"Yes! That will do for the moment." The King was thinking out loud. "I shall write an introductory letter to Chieftain Boyd which you can take with you. We were once companions-in-arms. He is a good fellow." And with that I was dismissed on the assumption that I should journey to Kilmarnock on the morrow. I was to dress my best and a good gelding from the King's personal horses would be available for me for the ride.

For the rest of the day, I closeted myself in Lord Montgomerie's library which was quite extensive and quite took my breath away when I discovered its scope and range. Some of the information raised more questions than it answered but His Lordship was away on a hunt, and I could not seek his opinion on several dynastic matters concerning the Norwegian hegemony in the Western Islands and the Clyde Estuary which had been leased to the Scottish King Alexander after the Battle of Largs.

Unfortunately, King Haakon had died in Orkney before any political agreement had been confirmed so the leasing of Man, Arran, Bute, the Cumbraes, the Inner Hebrides, and most of Argyll, had only been a personal deal between King Haakon and King Alexander all those years ago. So too, an arrangement for rent or feu duty had never been paid by Scotland to the Norwegian Exchequer. Other former Norwegian holdings on the Scottish mainland had been obtained by Scotland in conquest and were not involved with any payments.

I was up before dawn on the next day and absolutely in top form. I had slept deeply albeit with numerous dreams alternating between excitement and disappointment. The King's letter to Chief Robert Boyd was on my dresser top propped up against the mirror where I could not forget it. Perhaps the contents revealed my future and perhaps not.

In any case I would not interfere with the seal that closed the message. Yet despite all this anticipation, it never occurred to me to disobey my instructions and carry them out to the best of my ability. Perhaps it was this determination that permitted me to sleep deeply. I did not, however, attribute this valuable insight until much later so I only offer it to you as a possibility.

My servant called me at six o'clock, but I was already up and half-prepared. He told me that a horse was waiting for me on the parade ground in front of the family entrance to the keep, when would I be down?

I answered that in less than a quarter of an hour, I would be ready to get on my way to Kilmarnock and that was exactly how long it took.

The turnpike that ran near Dundonald Castle went between Troon and Kilmarnock. It was a major highway and had been built by the English Duke of Portland to enable the coal from his mines near Kilmarnock to reach the coast at Troon then via coastal shipping to Northern Ireland. For this reason, it was well-paved and maintained so riding from Dundonald to Kilmarnock was a comfortable and easy journey.

The day was bright and sunny in spite of a chill in the air. I was well, wrapped up against the weather although standing around at Gatehead while my horse was watered and fed proved to be a bit chilly. A visit to the tavern at the stable soon fortified my insides so that by the time I reached the main parts of Kilmarnock in under one hour, I was warm and comfortable and looking forward to my task.

Kilmarnock town seemed to be a fairly substantial and prosperous place. On the Dundonald side, the outskirts displayed a number of large mansions that seemed to denote some citizens at least were doing well. In the main streets, the pavements were busy with pedestrians of a lower rank and the traffic on the wide thoroughfares was somewhat heavy with tradesmen's and delivery wagons.

What continued to please me was the number of strangers who wished me '*good day*' or '*good morning*' as I passed them by. It did not matter whether they were mounted or walking, the general attitude seemed to be welcoming. The throngs of country-dressed pedestrians seemed to indicate that it was possibly Market Day.

I passed through the main part of the town to get to the other side where Dean Castle was situated. Eschewing the main entrance gates, I looked for the postern gate which I thought would be a more likely locality to gain entrance to Sir Robert.

I was wrong.

The kilted guard on the Postern Gate seemed uninterested in my request to visit with Sir Robert. I had the inspiration of suggesting that I was a messenger from the Duke of Albany but the only reaction I received was that he would pass the message back to the '*Laird*'' when a staff member happened to come by.

This opportunity never materialized until a comely kitchen maid came to the gate from the town with her marketing basket nearly one hour later. The Guard gave her a message and I hoped it had to be mine, although it looked as if some flirting was going on. The maid, however, glanced quickly at me when she was sure I was not observing the exchange, so on that slender thread, I had to be content with my quest.

Imagine my surprise when a professionally dressed, young man with a haughty air came out from the main castle to escort me and my horse to what amounted to the stable where I was subject to a thorough yet seemingly friendly inquisition to ascertain why I was seeking an audience with the '*Chief*'. Meanwhile, my horse was being very-well looked after and within another half-hour, another functionary came to take me inside the main part of this fine, well-built castle keep. There was an inside stone staircase that either bypassed a very tall floor or even two floors before ending on a landing outside a business-office where a most industrious older man was busy with his ledgers and barely noticed my arrival.

It was only when I slipped the envelope in front of him with the Royal Seal uppermost, that he chose to address me. "Your name, Sir?" He enquired.

"I am Murdoch of Cumloden and I come as the messenger of King Robert the Bruce now resident at Dundonald Castle as the guest of Lord Montgomerie."I explained.

With that statement, the gentleman immediately stood up and saying: "My Lord, I go at once to advise Sir Robert that you are here and that you desire a meeting with him. I am sure that if he is available, he will see you at once!"

Off he went and in a very short time, a large man dressed in a subdued tartan suit over a white shirt unbuttoned at the neck, burst into the room and full of welcoming phrases. This was Sir Robert.

We were talking over each other. I was telling Sir Robert who I was. What my mission was, all the while and at the same time, he was ushering me to another staircase that led to the floor above and telling me all about his family who were about to quit the room we were going to but perhaps not clearing away their toys and sewing paraphernalia before our arrival.

When we reached this magnificent and large living room which had a merrily burning fire at the end, there were still odd family traces lying about but no sign of the occupants who must have quickly fled on hearing us climb the stairs from below. It was now clear to me that Sir Robert had been talking loudly to warn his family of our approach.

Pulling up a couple of well-embroidered chairs before the fire Robert Boyd bid me sit down. He still had the King's unopened letter in his hand. He indicated to a decanter and glass on a side table and asked me to pour my own whisky while he read the King's letter which he proceeded to do.

When he had finished reading the communication, he looked at me and said:

"You really should have announced yourself as the Duke of Albany. It would have passed you through the security measures much more quickly. I am most humbled to meet with you, Your Grace. You honour our house with your presence."

I was taken aback at this sudden and unexpected salutation from a Knight of the Realm.

"Please, Sir Robert, I am just plain Murdoch of Cumloden and a humble but grateful messenger of His Majesty, King Robert Bruce. The King's statement that I am Albany is a trifle premature. The investiture has not yet happened."

"What do I call you? You seem to have no end to your ranks and distinctions."

"Please call me Murdoch. My ducal role is still in the making."

"Congratulations are still due, Your Grace. It is my honour to receive you. You bring prestige to the family of Boyd of which I am the head. At your suggestion I shall be honoured to call you Murdoch. Please call me Robert and we shall get along famously. Now let us discuss the reason for your visit."

I had to state my admiration for the comforts of the room which my host accepted with evident pleasure. Robert and I then settled down with a whisky refreshment and the discussion began.

"As you can read from the King's letter," I began, "His Majesty wants you to know that he is on his way to Scone for the Coronation Ceremony. Our projected route is up the Irvine Valley and into a part of

Scotland which is not yet particularly hospitable to His Majesty but may be more likely to support one or more of the King's rivals who are out to kill the King's chances of ever completing his journey to Scone.

"We shall be by-passing your lands and I shall be obliged if you will kindly outline your boundaries on the eastern side so that we shall not stray onto your Domaine in error. In other words, we propose to by-pass Kilmarnock at some point near Riccarton if that reaches with your agreement?" Boyd nodded his head but said nothing.

I continued: "Our army is small enough that we can keep the common soldiers in line." We are on our way through Galston, and Darvel to rest at Loudon Castle before venturing further east. It has been spoken of that Lord Aymer de Valence is anxious to confront our progress to keep King Robert from ever arriving at Scone and leaving the coronation open for one of the usurpers. De Valence soundly beat His Majesty at the Battle of Methven and our Monarch is looking forward to extirpating that unfortunate occurrence. Notices have been exchanged by knight-messengers and the battle site is confirmed.

"It occurred to me that the bold warriors of the Boyd Clan might be interested in joining the King in this expedition. We have noted your fine relationship with the late Sir William Wallace and your reputation for fielding brave and disciplined forces, whose reputation goes before them! Having the support of the Boyd's would make the King's plans even more likely of success!"

"Do you know Scott Boyd?" I added just to change the subject a little. "When he joined us, the King christened him Scott Boyd as he had wished to be associated with Clan Boyd and his forenames were Robert Stewart which seemed at the time to be too many Roberts and Stewarts!"

Replied Sir Robert: "Between you and me, I do not think he is a very dependable person. Not only was he disliked by his family equals but on a couple of occasions he was attacked by a group of angry soldiers of his own cohort." Robert was obviously neither hesitant nor sparing in his words about Scott!

He added: "What really happened? I can tell there is more to your story than is covered by your simple question?"

"It is not for me to relate the story that perhaps disfavours a particular person, but since you are a family connection and the leader of your Clan, I can tell you that Scott alias Robert has been accused of regicide, a capital offence!"

"Good Lord!" Exclaimed Boyd whose reaction to my revelation was as angry as it was genuine.

I continued: "Between us, the situation was originally between Scott and me.

"Although I was instrumental in him getting the King's tacit approval to bring him aboard. For several reasons he always resented me as I was not as belligerent towards mankind as he apparently was."

"Dear. Dear! But how did the King come into the picture?"

"The King has changed his mind about becoming an old-fashioned warrior-king to ruling in a Christian way and remembering that the people want progress too."

"And that was your influence?" Observed Sir Robert shrewdly.

"I...I guess so" I admitted. "My main theme was that King Robert was going to unite and rule Scotland in a benevolent manner, He was not wanting to conquer her. The people would view Him as an Enlightened and Fair King and his enemies would view him as a Relentless Opponent who would not hesitate to kill them when caught. Scott was not in favour of the first but was behind the King in the second case."

"No wonder that Scott was irritated by you and the King's new philosophy. Up until now, Robert the Bruce has had a very violent and ruthless disposition. His paths have been strewn with the bodies of his opponents and those people he just did not like!" revealed Sir Robert.

"Had Robert er Scott acquitted himself as a leader of men within the King's army?" Added the Chief.

"He had indeed. That was why it was so unexpected that he would break in the way he did."

I explained: "He was the real Captain of the King's Force and the King let him organize and train the troops, which he did very well."

"Looks like there very well could be some mitigating circumstances." Commented Chief Boyd looking somewhat severely at Murdoch.

I was tempted to lower my eyes in response to the searching look from Robert, but I did not as I realized that a Duke would never have done so. Instead, I returned Robert's gaze which gave the impression of steadfastness, I hoped.

After a pause that lasted a minute or two, Robert said:

"Come downstairs and have the midday meal with my wife. I want you to meet her."

This we did. Lady Boyd was a charming matron in her middle 40s I should reckon. She was tall and slim and had a winning smile which she used often particularly towards her husband whom she obviously adored. She laughed at his jokes and set her face with deep interest when he talked about the Clan and the heroes that had been part of it and contributed to its fine military reputation.

Towards the end of the meal, their four children came in to meet me and to either bow or curtsey before shaking my hand as well. Two boys who were already showing signs of steadfastness, and two girls, The Chief called them 'lassies' were at that 'sweet' age when all small girls are adorable.

Something I had not expected then transpired.

"I shall need some time to discuss your suggestions with my military leaders. This I shall do this evening. Might I suggest that you take up lodgings in the Inn, which is just outside the Castle, and return tomorrow mid-morning when we can conclude our discussions before you return to Dundonald."

I could see that Sir Robert was intent on doing what he had said, and I could do nothing but graciously accede to his directions.

This time, however, I left the castle via the front gates and was directed to the inn by the same dapper gentleman who had barely given me a second look on the first occasion.

"At what time may I call upon **Your Grace** to escort you to the Castle tomorrow morning?, he asked.

"I have no need of an escort, thank you very much." I replied.

"Approaching the castle gates in my company will gain you immediate access, My Lord. I am sure you will not want to be held up as you were today, and it will be my honour to assist you in all ways possible." And with that, my dapper gentleman's task was completed.

CHAPTER XIV

LORD KILMARNOCK; SURPRISE BANQUET; SCOTT BANISHMENT

The Inn was quite comfortable, and I had a pleasant drink in the Tap Room, a satisfying meal in the Dining Room and a restful overnight sleep in a cheery warm bedroom. What is more, my horse was well catered for in a clean and dry stable with plenty of fodder.

After a leisurely breakfast, I repaired to the castle to present myself to Sir Robert Boyd to continue our conversation of yesterday.

Sir Robert was in his previous jovial mood, and we soon settled down to resolve the remaining issues.

"Is young Boyd behaving himself and is not being maltreated?" asked Sir Robert.

"I regret I cannot reply truthfully to your question because I left Dundonald to come here on the morning following his outbreak and not much had happened by the time I left. Scott was, however, in the dungeon and I suspect that the sooner I return to the King with your answer, the better it will be for your protégé". This was a truthful answer, and I could say no more.

"He is no protégé of mine." Countered Sir Robert. "But I am interested in his case and would like to put myself forward as an interested party since I have known the rascal for many years.

"May I propose that we shall accompany Your Grace along with some of my Clansmen to Dundonald and also send a messenger ahead to explain to His Majesty that we come in peace?"

"That would be most appropriate, I replied. "So, it is settled, then? I must say I am delighted at your decision. I know it will go well for Scott as well" I added for good measure.

"I want to be in service for the King, if asked." The Clan Chief's excitement was showing.

"Great! I thoroughly believe that the King will be delighted at your offer and will be able to appoint you and your men to suitable positions in his standing army. How kind of you to acquiesce to my suggestion. My personal thanks are hereby extended. May I shake your hand?"

I was just as excited as the Chief.

Not only did we shake hands, but I received what I can only describe as the embrace of a bear as Robert drew me to his chest and gave me a tremendous hug. I could anticipate that we were going to be firm friends.

We went down to the castle courtyard where Boyd's *entire* military brigade was patiently standing and waiting for their Chief's instructions. There was a huge cheer went up from the waiting troops as we emerged from the castle keep.

I involuntarily drew in my breath at the passion the joyful noise represented. My rapid breath intake was noted by Chief Boyd.

"What is the matter, Albany? Did you not expect such a crowd of men anxious to join their King?"

"I must admit, I did not" I replied. "I am overwhelmed. Here are your followers cheering you to the heavens and anxious to march with you to wherever you want to take these valiant troops."

Giving a hearty laugh, "That's **LEADERSHIP**" Boyd answered. "When you add leadership to your undoubted talents you will be a formidable courtier. Now watch!"

Chief Boyd was very popular with his Clansmen. I was introduced as the future Duke of Albany which flattered me no end!

Boyd of Boyd, was a tall man. He was head and shoulders above his troops when standing on the level parade ground.

Their Chief made a very impressive leader and even more so, when he made one of the most relevant and historic speeches, I had ever heard. I am unable to report it in full, but the highlights remain forever in my memory.

Boyd spoke of the King and his quest and how it was the correct direction for our country. It was in each man's interest that this venture be successful. His entire address was of a power that would be totally acceptable in a best-selling book of military instructions.

Robert Boyd only spoke for twenty minutes or so. In that time, he talked about Family, Clan, Scottishness, Kinships, Personal Pride, Loyalty to his Regiment and Fellow Soldiers, Loyalty to the King and Country, Loyalty in general, Confidence, and Obedience to their Leadership, Healthy Living, and Remembering the Women and Children left behind at home.

It was a masterpiece of motivation and exhortation, and I was most impressed. At the end of the speech there was a roar of approval from the men who were immediately formed into marching order lead by musicians on drums and something called bagpipes

"The aim of this present campaign is to Unite Scotland and the King and your Clan Leaders have vowed to achieve this goal. With God's Blessing, we shall overcome those who would oppose our quest. These former leaders are just seeking personal glory whereas we, on the other hand, are seeking Scotland's Glory," Boyd thanked all the men standing before him who were all volunteers. They were

'*The Flower of Scotland*' and he was so proud of them all and their positive commitment. Holding up his right hand as a defiant gesture he shouted:

'*Confido*' !

His family's and his Clan's motto.

The Troops returned their Chiefs exhortation with a rousing repeat of their Leader's declamation that rang off the stern gray walls of the castle.

The beginning of our march towards Dundonald took us down the wide, main streets of Kilmarnock so we soon attracted attention from the people who were on the streets. This had a lot to do with the stirring music that heralded our progress that was cheerfully performed by the Boyd's own Pipes and Drums marching band.

I had never seen or heard the bagpipes before. Their origination was from the Middle East or the Steppes of Central Russia. The bagpipe was made up from a small animal skin set up with a mouthpiece at the former neck and a flute-like finger tube at the tail with three legs standing up and finished off at their ends to create a tuned drone effect. The player blew into the mouthpiece to inflate the body bag and the air was partly let out through the fingering of the flute when the musician squeezed the bag with his elbow allowing the remaining trapped air to exit through the drones.

A tune was created by the fingering of the flute or chanter as it is called and provided the player kept the bag filled with his breath. I was later told that the sound of the bagpipes in overseas military situations often raised complete alarm on the part of native opponents who ran away rather than fight the approaching fiend.

Very effective!

Boyd and I led the parade on horseback followed by the pipers who were in front of the troops and who maintained good marching order especially when passing a group of girls in the street or outside a country cottage on the route to Dundonald. Boyd sent a messenger on ahead to herald our coming and that it was a friendly visit.

It was easy to imagine as I allowed myself to daydream of my future life as a Duke. But there were no Dukes in Scotland. The senior honour was Earl and that came from antiquity, from the rulers of districts and areas of Scotland where they and their families had held sway over the years, not to say centuries. Duke was a Continental and English rank which was the equivalent to Earl in Scotland.

I was in a strange ebullient mood as we rode along. Thinking of my new rank as a *Royal Duke* no less! It had to be a royal duke as it came with no property and was supported by a stipend directly from the King. How unusual could it be that a liaison between a Norwegian seaman and a Scottish peasant woman could have resulted in such a successful outcome!

It was true that I served and continued to serve the Sovereign King and that I was very proud and thankful that my inherent sailoring, archery, and diplomatic skills had apparently added up to a reward, but what a reward! A Duke, no less!

Then to select the Stewart name to be attached to mine. That had been a decision only made when I was emotionally and hopelessly in love with Princess Marjorie (King Robert's only child with his first wife) and before her marriage to the heir to the very important title and position of The High Steward of Scotland, Walter Stewart, recently elevated to his deceased father's role and title as the sixth Grand Steward of Scotland and Justiciar of Scotland which were the enhanced Scottish parallel to the English Chancellor of the Exchequer.

Ah Ha!

That..... is another all-Scotland title that covered the entire country! Marjorie certainly did well in her marriage to Walter the High Steward but if my elevated position had come earlier, she would have been no worse off with me, as a Murdoch!

And there was the prevention of Scott's drastic action and display of animus towards his King as an extension of his dislike of me. Had that really been regicide? Or simply bad manners that had overwhelmed his reasoning for a moment? Certainly, Sir Robert's intervention would bring this matter to a head, and it would be settled one way or the other. Poor Scott! He was in a terrible mess!

It was glorious sunny weather and progressing along the good road between the hedgerows was a real pleasure. Soon it got Murdoch into thinking again about his Dukedom issues. 'I would have to act as the conduit to the King as petitions and petitioners would have to pass through me. How would that work? I would have to be readily available for all Scotsmen. Did that mean travelling around the country or by staying in one place, where these petitioners would have to come to me.'

'That left out Loch Doon Castle. Dundonald Castle was already leased to the Stewarts and although my name was now Stewart it would be inconvenient to have two Stewarts in the one place of the same rank. Even although one Stewart would be dealing in financial matters and the other...? What? Well, just about everything else from feu boundaries to fishing rights? How about the Scottish Navy? Would that come under my ducal role as well? This last thought was pleasing to me.'

'And just supposing this was a ruse to create a problem appointment where I would be bound to upset a lot of people with the King's decisions relayed by me. Perhaps, after Scott, the King had grown tired of his young men? A way of getting rid of me would be to set me up in order for me to fail at my job. Or by creating my own enemies I might be assassinated! What then? The King's hands would be clean even although he had set up the means to an end: End of Murdoch! End of my dream! This thought did not please me, but it had to be a possibility.'

We had reached Dundonald Castle by this time while I was mulling over the pros and cons of these new thoughts.

Once inside the castle walls Robert and I demounted our horses and went inside to the second-floor library where we had been told the King would receive us. I wondered what the King's reaction to what he had started and practically promised Boyd, would be. It was all very well for me, Murdoch, to say that Boyd might get the leadership of the King's troops and gain a title by so doing. But that was perhaps not how the King saw it.

I was somewhat surprised when the King then dismissed me after greeting Sir Robert, so I withdrew politely and left the two magnates to get on with their business. Clearly, the Albany business was not going to be on the agenda, and I would have to wait a little longer for clarification. Had the King forgotten his utterances? What about the letter to Sir Robert? Did it not say that I was going to be the Duke of Albany?

What was life like as a Duke? I had just had a taste of it with Sir Robert and I liked it!

But there was Scott's drastic action and display of animus towards his King to think about and eventually, I would be the one person to attend to it. Scott disliked me intensely and I had already made my *Ducal Enemy Number One* no matter what might happen in the future? Certainly, Sir Robert's intervention would bring this matter to a head, and it would be settled one way or the other. Poor Scott! He was in a terrible mess! After all, it might have been simply bad manners that had overwhelmed his reasoning for a moment. Or even childish petulance! Listen to me talking as if I were the wise old courtier! My job might descend to adjudicating feu divestitures or fishing rights, but I doubted it.

Late in the afternoon, the King and Sir Robert went down to the dungeon and stayed there for at least an hour. When they at last came up again, the King announced that he would have a banquet with the entire Boyd Guards and the officers and senior men of his own regiment. This would have to start much later than the usual time for the evening meal as there was much more preparation required than if just the family had been involved. Again, I was not invited to participate but to oversee the arrangements in the castle banqueting room. In normal circumstances I would have relished something like this to demonstrate my organisational abilities but to apply my personal touch when I was about to become a Duke was perhaps no longer in the King's mind. Anyway, the castle butler and I completed the task in short order and as the butler made his way to the kitchens to see how that side of the preparation was going, I went to my room to lie down.

There it was, I ruefully thought: a regimental banquet going on below me and a family dinner going on just above me, and I had been invited to neither! Not that I was hungry, but it would have been nice to have been asked to one of the meals instead of none at all. I dismissed the idea that it was inappropriate for me to be included in either function. I was not a military man and truthfully, I was not family after all. But it seemed that I had never been so neglected before.

Obviously, the King's new pal was Sir Robert and I, would just have to get used to the situation.

Was I feeling sorry for myself? Yes, I was! It was not a good feeling and one which I had not experienced many times before. Let's face it, I was used to being the 'golden boy'. To be treated pleasantly but nonchalantly distressed me as I had no right to be.

Imagine my surprise and alarm when at around an hour before midnight, my chamber room curtains were torn open and three of the Boyd fellows along with the two young men that we had promoted to junior officer status when we were in Dalmellington came in with a whoop and a holler and dragged me from my couch. I was just reaching for my dagger when I recognised my assailants but there was no use asking any questions for, they were quite merrily drunk and intent on their mission. But what mission? This I could not fathom so remained a little scared inwardly although I managed to outwardly demonstrate equanimity with a calm face and a demand that they would let me dress in my day clothes to which they agreed.

They frog-marched me down the stairs and into the banqueting room. There was a loud drunken cheer when they brought me into the room and dragged me to the head table where King Robert and Queen Elizabeth; Lord and Lady Montgomerie of Eglinton; Lord Walter and Lady Stewart, and Sir Robert Boyd with another gentleman whom I did not immediately recognise as the Bishop of Armagh whom I had met at Rathlin Castle, these many months ago.

The King stood up to speak. The room at once became quiet.

"We are all here tonight for a serious purpose although there is no reason not to enjoy good fellowship with your fellow warriors. My Lord Montgomerie has excelled himself with the hospitality and I thank him on your behalf and especially from me for he has made my quest all that bit easier by his ready support, especially in making sure that the ladies of my court are taken care of and made comfortable in this fine castle. The Chief of Clan Boyd is also with us. He has committed his **entire clan** to our endeavour. (*Cheers!*)

"At this time in the proceedings, there is one important activity yet to perform. Some of you, the young bucks who have yet to learn the virtue of patience have anticipated this activity and forcibly and I hope not too violently have left this hall and dragged one of my suite to appear before us.

"There he is, a pitiful creature standing to my right and wondering what his fate is going to be (*laughing and clapping*) I see no sign of the head jailer or the fellow who is good at chopping heads off, so perhaps the offense is not too egregious, but it is as final and for life. (*This said in a jocular vein. The audience chuckled in anticipation.*)

"He is Muireadhach the Sailor and sometimes Muireadhach the Page having joined me at Loch Ryan to guide us safely to Rathin Island off the northern coast of Ireland. Although his mother had called him Muireadhach we found that his name translated into Murdoch and so we now know him as such. (*shouts of welcome*) I have met the distinguished lady who calls herself Murdoch's mother. She is a formidable woman with a store of knowledge that belies her humble station. In fact, she wheedled out a sizeable plot of land from me to create three holdings one each for her sons in the barony of Minigaff which when added to her own freehold land had made her family one of the largest freehold landowners in Wigtownshire. I trust that the new feu duties will be forthcoming (*groans*) to assuage my crazy acts of generosity. (*laughter*)

"Murdoch has been with us through the many travails that have beset the genesis and initial trials and tribulations of our venture. In fact, it would not be amiss to state that he has been the conceptualist of the entire project from the whole route we have followed to the two-pronged presence in the Scottish community of the military might of our determination, (*cheers*) to the approach to all citizenry along the way that emphasize**s** our intent to persuade rather than to conquer our own countrymen whether they be supporters of other men or existing under another overlord. Our only goal is a United Scotland! (*cheers).*

"At one time Murdoch so irritated this King that I was on the point of at least having to flog him myself as those of us with close family members in their lives are often driven to state if not to conduct drastic punishment on their siblings. In any case, he was saved by a sudden burst of enduring patience on my part.

"Time and time again he has made himself more than useful as when he was responsible of bringing certain Lords and gentry into our sphere of influence and attracting many of their followers to our banner. He has even singled out individual soldiers for promotion and time has proved the wisdom of his selection.

"You are all here as a result of Murdoch's careful analysis and advice. Give yourselves a cheer! *(cheers)*. Especially Coronets MacLaren, Newell and Waugh who have distinguished themselves since their promotion. *(loud cheers)*. But all these golden attributes do not amount to much if his existing and yet-to-come countrymen are unaware of his history and his value to this Monarch. I therefore request all of you to be my witness as I confer the honors of the **Duke of Albany** on my faithful servant. *(Oh! Ah!)* This is a new honour created by your King and it will be solemnized by the Bishop of Armagh who, as the Queen's brother-in Law, is also here tonight. *(clapping)*.

"There is also a great family secret that I am about to reveal to you. The incident occurred twenty years ago, and although it would have been a scandal then had it been generally known, it slipped into our lives and was never talked about until now. Mesdames, cover your ears. I am going to talk scandal"

The ladies pretended to cover their ears, and with a great deal of pantomiming they effected compliance with the King's request.

"Gentlemen! Murdoch is none other than my stepbrother! We share the same mother, and his father was a visitor from Norway! *(Ladies affect shocked looks!)* A stranger: A handsome rogue of a man, devastating to many ladies, but I forgive him as I forgive my late mother, Marjorie, the Countess of Carrick of sainted memory. *(cheers and clapping)*.”

“Our duty now calls for such an endorsement and he will represent all of you, the people of Albany, Scotia, Caledonia, or Scotland the Great! *(cheers and shouts: God Save the Duke of Albany!)*”

The ceremonial of conferring the new title upon me was then conducted by the King and thc Bishop with the entire audience of Scotsmen as witnesses. I was speechless with happiness and at the same time absolutely stupefied at the revelation that I was the King's stepbrother! How could it be?

I was afterwards told that when my father went back to Turnberry after losing his way in the wilds of Galloway, he and the Countess had a very brief liaison before he left to return to Norway. She managed to keep her pregnancy secret and, although she was approaching 30 years of age, she wanted to keep the child. When the baby was due, she joined a trip into the Galloway wilderness arranged by her husband for the ladies of the Turnberry Court which ended up at Craigencallie where my 'mother' took the baby in and brought him up as her first son. My 'mother' was chosen because she was often spoken of most affectionately by my father when he returned to Turnberry from Craigencallie.

The King-to-be learned all about the deception and the plans to protect his mother's reputation but he did not know of my whereabouts when we first met at Loch Ryan. It was at that time that recognising the strong family resemblance he had enquiries made and by the time we were resident at

Loch Doon Castle he had the proof of our relationship that he needed. Even then he kept the matter to himself.

The concept of the dukedom was a creation of His Majesty so that the historic and regional Scottish Earls did not feel too badly that they were being usurped. But a Royal Duke title is a very high one, in fact second only to the King. It is in the King's gift; carries no land or serfs; is supported by a stipend from the King's purse; and it is heritable, only subject to the King's approval. In fact, The Duke of Albany is very much a political position rather than a dynastic one. In many respects, it represents the King's presence when it is not possible or *unsafe* for the Monarch to be present, yet it requires the highest attention.

Afterwards, I was welcomed to the top table to receive the personal regards and congratulations from the ladies and gentlemen who were present. There was a special and sensitive moment when My Lady Marjorie Stewart held out her delicate white hand and permitted me to kiss it. I looked into her golden-brown eyes which were moist with emotion. She curtsied fully and murmured something that ended

"…Your Grace." I was almost overcome by the sudden surge of my own long-suppressed ardour but managed to outwardly control my internal feelings.

The troops were just as welcoming and full of congratulations so by the time I returned upstairs to my couch, I was merrily drunk, not so much with whisky which seemingly everybody had thrust upon me, but by the internal working of my brain and body which had provided the mental and physical uplift that one can ever hope to achieve even once in a lifetime.

On the following morning, the Master of Montgomerie, and Lord Walter Stewart, 6th High Stewart of Scotland, who had moved out of Dundonald Castle with my arrival and who was staying with Montgomerie at Auchans, joined me in the small library room which I was now to be using as my habitation and reception space. With a dash of whisky for it was very cold outside, served by the castle butler we quickly got down to business. The King had given me instructions to arrange the details. Sir Robert Boyd's future was being discussed.

Did I accept the 200 or so Boyd Clansmen to augment the King's troops and Robert Boyd, suitably elevated to a title to be determined as overall grand marshal of the King's army?

With Lord Montgomerie's and Stewart's kind support, I did so accept subject to the King's ultimate approval. Boyd accepted these terms. Would I augment any arms or armour from the castle's old supplies for the Boyd contingent? Again, my response was in the affirmative. Lastly, when are the troops required to join the King's force? My answer was imprecise, and I begged absence from the negotiations while I consulted the Monarch.

King Robert who had been listening to the discussion through a concealed ingenious listening device that ran between the library and the Montgomerie study where he was located was in full agreement with my handling of the negotiations. He advised me that the first formal battle would be held near Loudon Castle which was the gathering point for our troops against the opposition lead by Lord Aymer de Valence who had routed the King's troops at the Battle of Methven several years ago.

Robert was determined for a victory this time as de Valence was rumoured to have a strong contingent of English troops at his disposal. His defeat would surely send the appropriate signal to Edward I that this time, there would be a real battle on his hands. Time for the English to get their own way in Scotland had passed and it was important to get that message out!

"The Boyd contingent should be ready to move out along with me, their King on the day after tomorrow and Lord Kilmarnock will be grand marshal of the troops answerable only to me." the King was quite precise with his orders.

"Lord Kilmarnock?" I queried.

"Send Boyd up here to meet with me and return yourself with Montgomery and Stewart" were the King's orders. This was duly done and over another whisky, King Robert I of Scotland honoured Robert Boyd, Chief of Clan Boyd, with the title and estate of **Baron Kilmarnock of Dean, in the County of Ayr**.

Next day, the King addressed the re-assembled troops and when he mentioned the need to defeat de Valence there was a loud cheer but when he came to the part that told of Chief Boyd's elevation to Lord Kilmarnock there was such a pandemonium of rejoicing and jubilation that I am sure passers-by in Troon and Symington five miles away, must have wondered what the noise was! I had never heard such a volume of public approbation before, and it quite moved me.

The rest of the day was spent in preparing for the King's departure and getting the troops kitted-out for the following day. I was quite interested in viewing the victualing arrangements which largely depleted the castle pantry. I noted that there were butchers, bakers, and candlestick makers (yes!) appointed to perform their respective duties while conscripted and when required. On enquiry, I was introduced to tailors, metalworkers, and leatherworkers to keep soldiers and horses in good working order as well as barbers with their other services of attending to the wounded and the dead.

Truly, it made our preparations at far-off Dalmellington look like very amateur efforts. To think we were planning at that stage an entire Scottish pacification seems ridiculous now. I am very glad that Scott is not in charge as surely, he would have been found wanting in experience and training not to mention leadership in the full panoply of waging war. Thank God for Lord Kilmarnock!

That evening, I made a visit to the castle dungeons to see how Scott was faring. He was not particularly happy to see me, unshaven and dirty of body, but his desire to receive more information was driving his curiosity so he subdued his antagonism towards me to receive any information I would reveal.

He accepted the latest events of the day until I came to the elevation of Baron Kilmarnock. At hearing this Scott went into paroxysms of invective against Robert Boyd and the King. I would have left at that moment except that he calmed down when I told him that Lord Kilmarnock had spoken in his defense to the King who might subsequently free him.

I added that I would follow up with His Majesty to ensure his plight might not be forgotten as I was now the nominated patron of Dundonald Castle as the Duke of Albany.

At this last piece of information, Scott completely broke down, throwing himself on the floor and crying, clasping me by the legs in despair. I explained that the King had not been so upset by the threat on his life as he was completely enraged by Scott's betrayal of the King's trust. There was nothing more I could do so I left him sitting on the edge of the stone ledge which constituted his only seating place in this stark dark dungeon place. On the way back upstairs to the living quarters I encountered the jailer with the order to ensure that the prisoner was afforded a goodly supply of fresh straw for his comfort and heat.

It was only afterwards that I learned that my visit was followed by Lord Boyd who had promised Scott that he would appeal to King Robert for clemency although regicide was a capital offence met only with death. Scott had told his side of the story by which he correctly revealed that it was only because the King had said that he would have to destroy the Boyds who were standing in his way of marching his troops up the Irvine Valley. Scott had opposed this strategy and said so to which the King had responded that it was none of Scott's business to oppose the King's policy decisions. He had then removed Scott from his position of military adviser and leader and Scott had vehemently objected to the unfairness of the action and many hot comments were interchanged resulting in Scott's drawing his dagger and lunging at Robert. Scott said that his physical anger was more addressed towards me than at the King. He could not stand me. I was a two-faced, devious bastard and did not understand the value of military force.

Boyd quietly remarked that it was the King who had felt attacked. Scott replied that he was angry at the King for being continuously taken-in by my suggestions. Boyd then suggested that this transfer of anger was unfortunate because an attack on the life of the Monarch inevitably lead to a death sentence.

"But I was protecting you and the Clan Boyd!" wailed Scott.

"Well, you cannot have your head chopped off twice for two anger transfers!"

Scott wailed and repeated: "I wanted to protect the Clan Boyd!"

"You were under the impression that we could not look after ourselves? It is my view that you were just thinking about yourself!" Boyd emphatically accused Scott who, on hearing this accusation from someone whom he thought would be an ally, sunk to the ground in despair.

I know about this exchange from Lord Kilmarnock himself who told it to the King in my presence on the following morning. Boyd was laughing as he related the incident although I detected an undercurrent of disapproval as Scott's version was discussed. It was not my imagination that Boyd's air of reservation included the actions and statements of all three of us including the King and me.

The feeling of great apprehension was wafting in the air as I looked worriedly at the King who was busy consuming his porridge and seemingly letting all this knowledge pass over his head. His comments when they came were a surprise.

"Looking back, it does appear as if the whole affair was entirely unnecessary and could have been prevented if cooler heads had prevailed. But the young man has been irritating me for some time now, and I must admit to breaking on this occasion. Scott is an unruly rascal, and he needs his wings clipped. Many another young man has felt my sword for saying less. Nevertheless, I do not want him near me. When we let him go there must be a clear understanding that he is to go where he can do no harm to me or my reign. I think Norway is not far enough away... perhaps even the New World that the Icelanders have discovered?"

My Lord Kilmarnock gave a huge laugh at the King's suggestion.

"Why I believe my King has a sense of humour but I concur with my Monarch's sentiments precisely. The New World! What a fitting destination!"

The apprehensive air was instantly dispelled, and the King was being jocular!

"Shall we send *Albany* down to have him released?" Kilmarnock was all for keeping the joke going.

"Why not?" replied the King. "It will be a kind of *Poetic Justice*! After all he is partially responsible for the situation in that he behaved like a pompous ass to Scott, and he merits some penalty. But I think we had better leave Scott's freedom until tomorrow after we have worked out how to get him on his way from here."

"I have direct communications to His Excellency the Danish Ambassador in Edinburgh who controls the Icelandic business." Offered my Lord Stewart. "I shall request of him to accede to King Robert's request."

This suggestion being most agreeable to all parties, our group broke up and we all went on our separate ways.

But It did not please me that I would be the bearer of banishment to Scott. At least it had been delayed by the promise of Stewart volunteering to involve the Danish who controlled Iceland and to make the sentence official.

Then I thought *'could not the Duke of Albany have the same authority?'* It was a question I was asking of myself. I would have to watch Walter Stewart and the effortless way he exercised his authority as Grand Steward of Scotland not to mention Justiciar of Scotia. I would always have a Steward or Stewart to contend with. The larger problem was Walter's rank, and it was hereditary! I would always have a rival and competitor.

As Murdoch Stewart then, I was created Duke of Albany although it could easily have been Craigencalie, my mother's house, or Cumloden, my own piece of land in Wigtownshire awarded by King Robert when he recognized my brothers and me. But Murdoch Stewart it now officially was and for good or bad, I was stuck with this full name. It did carry prestige. I hoped the name of Stewart never went out of popularity.

CHAPTER XV

THE BATTLE OF LOUDON HILL; CORONATION OF KING ROBERT I, THE BRUCE.

But the more pressing action now was the departure of the troops from Dundonald on their way to do battle at Loudon Hill against those who were in opposition to King Robert's crowning at Scone. We had been told by a Knight Messenger that an opposing force lead by the Norman-English Lord Aymer de Valence had challenged our force to do battle at the border of Strathclyde at a place and time of our choosing.

King Robert and Sir Robert Boyd had consulted private maps which were only in the Clan Boyd possession and a location was selected which Lord Boyd assured us was a favourable spot and would suit us very well. The Knight was sent back to his leader with the notice that we would meet in battle south of Loundon Hill.

I was to stay behind at Dundonald along with Stewart and Montgomerie so my report on the glorious victory over a predominantly English army is only repeated here from third parties.

In the first place, our army under Lord Kilmarnock was well disciplined and ready for battle. The ground adjacent to Loudon Castle had been well surveyed and all physical topography well noted. This pre-knowledge was to prove most valuable to the execution of ***The Battle of Loudon Hill*** and came from the Clan Boyd archives.

It seemed that the actual battleground selected by King Robert to the south of the hill was only about 500 yards wide and margined by soft marshy ground on both sides. These marshes were the result of small streams meandering across the flat meadows creating what were called deep morasses. Such impediments to mounted attack from left and right were prevented over this soft land unsuited for any attack by horsemen who would be expected to bypass the frontal advance of the King's spearmen and attack the weaker flanks of our army.

The battleground that was selected was the one recommended by Boyd. It was just half a mile south of Loudon Hill on a meadow bordered on both sides by marshy ground. Boyd caused three ditches to be excavated so that the English cavalry on the day of the battle had a very restricted movement which funnelled them towards the waiting King's spearmen where they were easily slaughtered The English began to panic at the ease by which they were ambushed that those at the rear did not venture forward but turned and withdrew from the battlefield, along with de Valence. The battle is memorialised in a narrative poem by Barbour, extracts of which appear in Chapter XVIII. The King and his men were victorious. The Battle of Loudon Hill was the first big battle win for King Robert and his cause.

In the end, the future King of England, Lord Pembroke (later Edward II) who was leading the battle on the English side, was struck down by a Scottish arrow and had to be rescued and removed from the field of battle just before the complete victory of our King's men. It was a great and total victory for Scotland although Pembroke survived. Of de Valence, we saw not a hair. Neither was it necessary for the King or Kilmarnock to get involved with the affray. I understand that the King was on the battlefield along with Chieftain Boyd but never had an opportunity to face de Valence as he had so dearly wished in order to avenge his personal defeat at Methvyn where he had been wounded.

I was not involved with Loudon Hill although I had been in attendance at the planning stage when the King and Lord Boyd had developed the winning strategy.

King Robert I now had a clear and commanding progress through the middle of Scotland with his formidable army. He was met with rapture in Perth and his march towards Scone was conducted by great rejoicing and acclamation. Indeed, Scotland had been without a true Monarch for over twenty years. Now here was a noble and brave King to rule and guide the Kingdom of Scotland.

MURDOCH'S SCRIBE TAKES OVER THE NARRATIVE.

Since The Duke of Albany has a great deal to think about and act on, I shall continue to contribute to this history for the Duke as I have done in some of the previous chapters. Murdoch has given me full leave to record his actions from his daily diary and my versions of the internal musings of the Duke are based on my conversations with him.

I note that we have yet to record the formal crowning of the King at Scone during Eastertide of the year 1306. it was a brilliant affair. King Robert who had spent his younger years in reading all about historic monarchs and world leaders and their coronations, had definite ideas about the ceremony. it seems to me that King Robert has taken a page out of historic books from such accounts as Charlemagne and even Alexander the Great to form his own ideas of just how a King should be crowned.

He had told me of these significant occasions many times with his eyes sparkling at the majesty of these occasions and how they inspired their people at the time, and the world since, of their significance.

On a more practical note, the King had instructed Murdoch and Bishop Wishart of his requirements and they both worked on the ceremony to reach a form of service that would be acceptable to him and yet conform to the historic and traditional structure of the simplistic and uplifting ancient Pictish style.

I could almost say that there was to be a touch of pagan in the ritual but then King Robert the Norwegian, and then Norman was nothing if he wanted to be more than descended from the ancient blood of old Scotia; the land of the Picts. This stream of his heredity although stemming from his blood relationship to King David I but more recently through his wife's genuine and recorded Pictish heritage provided the ancient authenticity the King desired and which Scotland needed.

Fortunately, the royal robes and vestments had eluded English plunder although the historic stone relic called Jacob's pillow, and sometimes 'The Stone of Scone' was lost to English thievery and carted off to London to become part of the English coronation chair just as it had been in Scotland.

———————————————

3 *The 'Stone of Scone' which Edward I had taken and taken to England as a souvenir and indicator of his de facto overlordship of Scotland and placed under the seat of the English Coronation Chair in Westminster Abbey was 'stolen back' in 1950 by four Glasgow University students who were members of the Scottish Nationalist political movement at the time. Originally declared a national crime, the incident was downgraded to a 'student prank' to forestall any political advantage to the Nationalists. The stone was ultimately recovered in Arbroath Abbey. It was damaged when being handled at that time and repaired in Glasgow before being restored to London in time for the late Queen Elizabeth's coronation in 1953. It has since (1996) been returned to Scotland in care of Edinburgh Castle but will be available for all British coronations in London. It is an ancient sandstone relic and may not be the 'original' if indeed there ever was one to support the many existing legends.*

Visitors to the Isle of Skye may be shown another 'stone' which has an altogether different provenance.

Many Scottish and Scots-Irish bishops and earls took part in the solemn and formal crowning of King Robert I the Bruce in Scone. The ceremony was held on Moot Hill the traditional Pict location for ancient coronations. The Hill is located on the grounds of Scone Palace, the abode of the Murray family, the Earl of Mansfield and his Countess. The Great Banner of Scottish Kings flew over the ceremony when a circlet of gold was placed on King Robert's head as signifying the Earl of Carrick, Lord of Annandale, King of Scots, and his Countess, now Consort Queen Elizabeth.

At the King's direction, My Lord Montgomerie had graciously endowed Dundonald Castle to Murdoch in his capacity as Lord Murdoch, Duke of Albany and has stationed a platoon of his personal guard at Albany's disposal. This has been an opportune solution, as the Stewarts never really wanted to come to Dundonald and leave their house in Edinburgh to which they will happily return. Also, The Duke of Albany is much more accessible to the Scottish subjects in his intercessionary role. Loch Doon Castle is considered too remote and too inaccessible for this purpose.

The position and responsibilities of the Grand Steward, of course, are an inheritable position and the current family are the Stewarts of which Montgomerie is a member.having been at one time Grand Steward himself.

At the time of the transfer of tenancy, Montgomerie was heard to say: *"Rather the comforts of my nearby newly- built Auchans mansion house than the drafty old stone pile that is Dundonald Castle."* Over this past winter, everyone would heartily agree! The residence of Royal Castles is in the hands of the Monarch and tenants are customarily endowed with a lifetime residency that may be passed on to a succeeding son.

But it must be mentioned that such leases are at the King's Pleasure which all depends on the recipient's continuity of being in the King's good graces and not being superseded by some other favourite or more diplomatically honoured. In this case at Dundonald Castle which had been built by and for the Stewart family, but gifted to the King, had Montgomerie then briefly Stewart tenancy and was ceded to Albany. It is almost like *musical chairs*, a parlour amusement of women and children

There is quite a full portfolio of recent and pending issues to be resolved or neutralized as Albany moved ahead with his duties. The on-again, off-again war with England continues and the King's recent successes in the field first at Loudon Hill and ending with a hopeful triumphal victory to seal King Robert's coronation yet to come with the removal of most significant threats, and the chronic English opposition, based on the alternative Baliol faction here in Scotland.

In the meantime, most of the Earls who had already pledged loyalty to King Robert have called on the Duke of Albany to enquire just what the King meant when he said that most of the hereditary earls' land holdings will be reviewed. They were anxious to assure him not only of their loyalty to King Robert the Bruce but also to himself as the Duke of Albany. This was very reassuring as Albany then took their presence to point out what the King was planning to require of them in the years ahead.

He is working on a gathering of nobles like to that the late King William of England instituted when he was on the throne. But there will be a major difference. The Scottish version will have the King dictating the terms of the lords' duties to the Crown rather than the other way in England when the Barons told the King what his duties were and what they would accept as their own commitment to the Throne.

It was a judgement matter based on the division of Power between the King and the Gentry. The basis for this is that while King William of England was a conqueror, our King Robert is not. He is in fact a uniter. It is true that he is a great warrior, but his necessary military actions are those of a champion of the people's interests. It will be Albany's duty to craft a useful compromise of the outcome.

Albany outlined the gifts in the King's favour and told his visitors that they could look forward to a larger estate with their better-managed holdings expanded to incorporate the lands of poorer-managed neighbours. Such expansions would be accompanied by additional responsibilities such as the establishment of schools, for children, apprenticeships for teenagers, and land grants and freedom from vassalage as recognition for hard- working or military-drafted tenants All details of the King's Intentions will be worked out at the meeting of the Scottish Parliament.

Prosperous lords departed Dundonald with visions of an even grander future and magnates of lesser success were now worried about withdrawals of ancient privileges and inclined to draw Murdoch into clarification.

To those persons he assured them that their ancient titles and main abode were sacrosanct. The enhancement of their meagre income would be up to their own ingenuity, this was not normally accepted with calmness especially among the Highland chiefs but as Albany followed up, there would be plenty of time in which to consider all options. The Highland situation is complicated in that the clan chiefs owe their authority and position as both *Clan Chiefs*, that is, their elected position by their own familial people, and to the crown as *Area Leaders* like the traditional Earls. In the meantime, Albany's major problem is how we are to manage our assets at sea. After all, he was a sailor first and he was always to have a special regard for sailors and their profession. It is Albany's duty to establish Scottish authority on our deep sea and coastal seaboard as well as aboard our military and commercial boats and the seamen who man them. The King has particularly noted these points and the Duke is bound to carry out His instructions to the best of his ability. Our merchant ships frequently encounter pirates when in our waters. These are likely of Scottish origin. We must take steps to eradicate this scourge. One of the secondary titles granted to Murdoch is *Lord High Admiral* (a responsibility previously allocated to the Mar family!) for this purpose and it was his first action to enfranchise privateers for surveyance and protection until the Crown was able to build up the military fleet.

Then, there is the ongoing job of the rise of Scottish religious Reform. This schism is leading to much trouble in certain areas where Catholicism is being used to resist call for the First Scottish Parliament in 1309 at St. Andrews. The problem is the likely list of suggested participants and their representation status will be issued shortly by Lord Murdoch and aggressively challenged by well-educated ministers of the faith and a growing public of congregants. King Robert has been crowned as a Christian Monarch which the people must take to be a staunch Roman Catholic faith and Murdoch's duty is clear. Although he has his own opinion on religion, the official attitude on this situation suggests caution. Religion is apt to raise the strongest emotions taking logic with it.

Fortunately, Murdoch has the good Bishop of Glasgow to re-enforce his tepid Catholicism. His Eminence tells him that there is not much liking for the foreign power which is Rome. Indeed, the Pope has excommunicated our King which the Duke takes to be a political action associated with the erroneous facts of the murder of Cormyn. Our enemies are making doubts a product of Albany's immaturity and that the older he becomes, then his faith will strengthen towards the issues of Rome and the Pope.

But he is looking further ahead. I have already recorded the King's formal crowning at Scone this Easter. There is still a long way to travel. While Galloway and Ayrshire as well as the Scottish part of Northumberland and mainland Dalriada are somewhat reconciled to the new executive, the rest of Scotland has yet to be incorporated into the unified construction of our land. The Western Isles and perhaps Orkney and Shetland might be amenable, but this part of the equation is yet to be tested. Truly, there is a great deal of work to be done! Murdoch is thinking of invoking the

Treaty of Perth from 1266 when the Norwegians expressed their ancestral instincts to permit the original inhabitants of the Norwegian-controlled Scottish Western and Northern Outer Islands to manage their own affairs.

Also, there is the opportunity for some sort of understanding between Scotland and England which is an obvious opening which Murdoch shall explore. He is not too optimistic that some benefit may be reached through negotiations, as King Robert is seminally set on resolving many issues against England by force of arms. He is, of course, a typical man of action as befits his class and upbringing and any modifications on that particular cast of mind can only be attributable to Murdoch's own influences on our Monarch of which Murdoch is all too aware has its limitations. He did not agree with His Majesty's hard form of diplomacy but in this instance, the ongoing intransigence of the English may very well only be accomplished through decisive military action.

On the topic of the Scottish Navy, Murdoch tends to the philosophy that if the English Navy has a mechanism that works and we do not, we should work with the English to develop a Scottish version for our own use with their cooperation and acceptance. The other way around would also apply.

Albany was expected to take an interest in the development of the Scottish Navy through development of another important title and responsibility, that of Lord High Admiral that was originally granted to the Mar family in perpetuity. This role came by default to Murdoch as the shipping interest had waxed and waned for several reigns and eventually will reach an important role as an arm of Scottish international political influence and royal support during the reign of King James IV (1473-1513)

[Historic Fact not known at the time - Ed]

Concluding that Murdoch had done little with this additional responsibility before his death.

What he had done is to continue issuing Warrants to Privateers which have been issued from 1214 to owners of merchant galleys and birlinns initially for inshore maritime operation but eventually to become a significant instrument of Scottish in-shore authority and one could argue has been the genesis of the Scottish Coast Guard. On the occasions when the Scottish Navy seemed to be anti-French it was seen to be pro-Protestant. On the other hand, an anti-English bias on the part of the Scottish Navy was viewed as reflecting the pro-Catholic position of the gentry, perhaps a useful barometer of the country's current religious inclinations.

While His Grace's work schedule is filling up, he is still wearing the clothes he had always worn. Any clothes that he had left behind at his mother's house no longer fitted him or were hopelessly out of fashion. Being entirely on his own at Dundonald Castle with only Lord Montgomerie's library for comfort, he settled down to take his leisure, something he had been unable to do for what seemed like an exceptionally long time. His lordship was very solicitous and hospitable and invited him to eat at the family table either at the castle or occasionally at the sumptuous dining room at Auchans House, which he accepted.

One of the many topics of conversation was his wardrobe. It was no longer suitable for a duke, so a bespoke tailor was summoned from the nearby village of Troon to properly kit Murdoch out. Mister Radford was his name and he had garnered quite a good reputation among the local gentry He was up to date with the latest gentlemen styles in Edinburgh, London, and Paris. Not being at all familiar with this sort of thing, Murdoch left it to his advisers including the Duke and his sons to guide the tailor in his selection of fabrics and styles. When it was all over, there stood a tall redheaded gentleman of fashion in front of a full-length mirror to admire himself and his beautifully fitted dark blue silk suit and everything else that goes with such splendid attire. The rakish hat was his only problem. It was full-brimmed and adorned with an extravagant pheasant feather, the previous owner of which was now practically tail-less and no doubt the laughingstock of his communal flock.

It was shortly after the acquisition of a suitable wardrobe that Albany received an invitation to dine with a local gentleman who wanted to introduce His Grace to some local worthies. He was cautious enough to enquire of Lord Montgomerie if it were a suitable appointment that would not upset local precedents. Being assured that it was perfectly in order and that he would have a good time, he accepted the invitation and presented himself at the front door of his host, Mister Hall in the company of a young man named Thomas who had been assigned by Montgomerie to be his travel companion and protector, and who presented themselves at the front door of the Hall House which was at the mid-point of the village of Dundonald's one and only street. It was a substantial stone-built structure and lighted by a series of glowing braziers in front and magnificent candlelight chandeliers inside.

Lord Murdoch now takes over the narrative:

Mister Hall bade me welcome and introduced me to his wife and their guests. There were three other gentlemen. One was the priest of the parish, the second a local knight with substantial property holdings in the neighbourhood, and the third, a former steward and manager of the county. It appeared that our host, Mister Hall was a merchant of some standing and was the principal seller and distributor of locally produced farm products.

After a very good dinner following which, the ladies withdrew to the drawing room, we men relaxed with a delightful decanter of wine fortified by a fine whisky.

"Your Grace..." began the Priest, "Your presence in our midst is most welcome and I ask if any of us can be at your service? Do you have any business in this area? My Lord Bishop is anxious to know if the church interests are involved in any way?"

"As you have been told, I am under the instructions of King Robert who is presently on his way to Scone to be crowned King of all Scotland at Eastertide. His Majesty has appraised me of his high regard for this area and of his reliance on the good people of the parish who can set a good example to the rest of Scotland about the church, the loyalty, and the industry of the ordinary people, and leaders such as yourselves. The King, being a busy person, has stated that most promising ideas come from the working of God's good earth, and we count on you to communicate to the Crown all your clever ideas, and on grave political and state matters that have been delegated to me to be your conduit to him. You may be sure that the interests of Dundonald will always be close to my heart."

"Your statement is very inclusive and general, my Lord, but I fear that it is political in nature and designed to assure listeners that the Crown is on the people's side rather than with the Barons."

"Sir David, you have posed a perfectly sensible question." I replied, "What I have yet to reveal is that King Robert will convene a council of the Lords, the church, and the laity to create a Bill of Rights that will incorporate all the God-given rights to everyone that are the building blocks of immutable law and common law established by the people and for the people.

"It is the King's intention that as many serfs and tied servants as possible are freed from their bondage. Those who toil in the soil will be given land of their own. Lords within a parish will be responsible for schools along with the church, and businesses will be obliged to take apprentices for their trades.

"Our Lord Sovereign also recognizes that everyone should have an interest in how a united Scotland will be run".

"That's a good system. How will it affect the raising of an army if and when the occasion demands?" asked Mister Hall.

"We already have a professional army at our disposal, but we welcome new recruits who volunteer Our military is headed by the King and Lord Kilmarnock whom you will all recognise as Lord Boyd of Dean". I countered. "Remember, it is not just Galloway and Strathclyde we have to conquer but also the Highlands, Sutherland, Grampian, the Western and Northern Islands, Northumbria and Dalriada as well. It will be from those distant kingdoms that real opposition will come.

"What we are proposing to do is to subsume all these smaller kingdoms to recognise the one and only collective King. Our marching troop of warriors storming Strathclyde will not be a hindrance to contrary forces from elsewhere in the land unless our men do well and win all the way through to their destination."

"By the way where does our military campaign end? You never have said." The Priest was anxious to be assured that no war efforts would be coming to Dundonald.

I laughed. "You may be sure that this part of the country is quite safe from outside strife. Although I am a little worried about the attitude of the citizens of Ayr. But in response to your direct question, it is my belief that after the Coronation and the Battle of Loudon Hill, the rebel forces will have to move up the East Coast and cross over to the Highland Line which may be their last stand.

I would not be surprised if we encounter a fixed concluding battle somewhere north of the Forth."

"My goodness! You certainly have all the facts before you. I am impressed! Said Sir David.

Again, Murdoch's Scribe Adds:

The Duke told me afterwards that he was very pleased with his first real meeting with constituents. The evening drew to a close shortly after the conversation and young Thomas was assigned to accompany Albany to the castle gates and see him safely inside.

CHAPTER XVI

THE DUKE OF ALBANY, LORD MURDOCH STEWART

<u>*LORD MURDOCH STEWART WRITES;*</u>

What I liked about the title was that it made no difference to my job.

***I** was still beholden to the King and immediately* responsible to carry out his orders. I have always said that performing a job you like to do is not the same as 'work' which usually is something you do not really want to do but you do it anyway because of your training and condition of your hire.

But as time went on, the King was increasingly away from Dundonald and either in Edinburgh, St Andrews, Perth, or Stirling. I was always available for subjects requiring help or decisions but for important decisions of great national importance like King Robert's First Parliament in 1309 where I spent many hours struggling with who would represent the people of Scotland. The King had instructed me that the **"three estates"** were to be fully represented. This meant that the interests of the aristocracy, the church, and the ordinary subjects (laity) had to be brought into the equation.

The aristocrats presented problems. There were questions of seniority, net worth, multiplicity of titles, closeness to the King, and an interest in finance or legal matters. As far as the church was concerned, there were the cardinals of Scottish Sees, Administrators, Church Lawyers, and Parish Priests.

But the laity group were the most difficult of all. The individuals represented civic and rural groups, all the professions, all the trades, land holders, renters, wholesalers, retailers, military and civil peace officers, educators, medical practitioners, and so many other special interests that need to be represented. I had given myself 500 places and was getting up to and beyond that number when I realised there would have to be a smaller steering committee of say 20 leaders to help to create policies for debate by the entire parliament.

And what about the topics for debate?

First and foremost, the Common Law had to be codified. Then the rights and responsibilities of the three estates not to mention the rights and responsibilities of the King and his Court. Awards and Decorations, stipends and emoluments, expenses, accessibility, public works, public--private partnerships, penal laws land-holding regulations, employment regulations, the list goes on.

What good would come out of this parliament? It never occurred to me that the results would only **cover** about half of the total of work that was scheduled to be completed.

But the daily work has to go on. My biggest activity is acting as the go-between the citizens and the Crown. This is a three- way job. Getting the Cause to the also busy and peripatetic King, receiving His reply, and passing the decision back to the petitioner without delay. Also, there are the issues of the Scottish Navy and liaison with the English Navy, not to mention the arrangement of the public appearances of the King and His direct interaction with His subjects.

When the King was crowned at Scone in 1307, I had a lot of law to absorb, and my scribe was very helpful. He told me that our Common Law was based on what invaders had brought with them and was not original to Scotland. Many of the concepts came from the Bible and that means from God via His various Prophets. When Scotland first was acquainted with these Holy strictures was when the Romans came and reached as far as Antonine's Wall at Scotland's narrowest width. The result of this limitation was that the Highlands and Islands were not exposed to these civilizing precepts. But they were subsequently enlightened by the arrival from Ireland in 563 AD of our holy Saint Columba, an evangelic priest who made it his business to spread God's word throughout the area and convert all that heard him and his disciples, to Christianity from his Iona base off Mull Island.

Given then, these great influences have been melded into one Common Law and are the foundations of our jurisprudence. Any local laws that might cause resentment by the populace having been promulgated by their feudal lord. It may be of Norman-French or Scandinavian origin depending upon the gentleman's family origin, but unless there is a Scottish equivalent in Common Law it is unlikely to stand examination against the King's Law.

So too, the church's laws when in conflict with common law and the King's Law have no validity in Scotland and must need to be adjusted to comply with our system of governance. The church is strongly against any restrictions that put upon its long-standing rules and traditions, but I am quite strongly opposed to any of the church's strictures that conflict with the Common Law or the Laws of Scotland.

My Scribe and I have contributed to this chapter:

It is not that I am complaining of course, but I have to admit that getting away from it all or trying to, is become a more attractive thought as the months advance without end. I have now been Duke of Albany for seven years and I am pleased to say that I have escaped from my most accessible location at Dundonald Castle and moved to Loch Doon Castle. This move has been well advertised so it does not look as if I am shirking my duties. On the way up to Loch Doon, I stopped for two days at Lord Symington's mansion near Dalrymple and was pleased to recruit young John of Symington whom I had met on my last visit to Dalrymple in 1306. He had impressed me then and I was anxious to find a position for him in my suite. He joined us as my equerry but will be doing many activities more than looking after the horses. He is in fact, now my right-hand man. Also, when preparing to move, I told my scribe in Dundonald that I would write the last chapter in the book form he was planning to assemble with what he and I had written, and this will be the ultimate chapter which I shall send to him to complete any loose-ends that may have arisen. It is the least I can do for this dedicated man of letters who is also an authority on Common Law and Current Royal Regulations.

You will recall that Loch Doon Castle was raided and sacked not long after we embarked on our mission. The sad part of that story was that My Lord Seaton, all the women and children were put to the sword owing to a dastardly betrayal by one of the hired tradesmen, the locally hired Macnab, helping us with the boat building. Coming back to the castle after several years presented us with some problems as much of the castle remained in ruins and the work to restore parts of it had never been finished.

I would not like to be here in the cold weather of winter as many of the chimney heads have been broken open by the raiders looking perhaps for hiding people or their valuables. A good fire in a former fireplace quickly fills a room with smoke until it finds its way through a hole in the stone walls higher up and escapes to the outside. At the fire-setting hour it is best to be outside in the open air. A view of the castle from the shore reveals a shapeless stone wreck of a habitation still on fire with smoke billowing out from holes in the outer wall.

The English troops who had been responsible for the destruction and murders and the tradesmen have all been called away except for a handful of caretakers who were disposed of by one of my brothers leading a small team of specialized Royal soldiers. They were met with little resistance and our men set about restoring the ruins again for limited habitation. The English never have returned so far. Even the despoilers seem to regard Loch Doon Castle on its own island as a hopeless ruin and not worth restoration work.

The only other place I could retire to is Craigencallie, my mother's home. It is not far from here, but I shall keep that place unknown in detail as regards actual location. One never knows when one shall need a place of refuge. It is not that I have ever received a bodily threat because of my doing the King's wishes but given the material that I have handled and the class of petitioners, some who accept the King's word with good grace and others who rage at the apparent injustice that has been meted upon them by me speaking on behalf of the King. They leave my presence in high dudgeon vowing retribution but are never heard from again.

There is not much comfort from strangers here. I know most of the soldiers by name and, of course, am thoroughly familiar with my own suite. If it were not for John Symington, I would tend to get very lonely. Occasionally I take the one and only single-handed boat out and visit one or other of the nearby habitations incognito, sometimes with James and sometimes not.

ALBANY'S SCRIBE WRITES:

The Dukedom of Albany position has proved to be a 'poisoned chalice'. It has been revived six times and each time it had no continuance after the original person died or was removed. Our original Murdoch Stewart, of the first manifestation of the rank which lasted only nine years before his death which was natural in that he drowned whilst resident in Loch Doon Castle. He had been a regular visitor to the boat harbour under the castle and frequently took one of the smaller boats for a sailing voyage around Loch Doon. He had been alone on the boat which was discovered in an upside-down condition and adrift. There was speculation that he had gone to one of the lochside communities where he had often visited a farmer's daughter.

Murdoch Stewart was only a 'Stewart' in that he had selected the name when having more than a single name became fashionable. As he explained, he chose 'Stewart' as it was now the family name of Princess Marjorie Bruce whom he would have married had he, at the time, been of noble birth and powerful. He was neither when she married Walter Stewart who came from an influential family of stewards, the Scottish equivalent of a 'chancellor' in England who handled all the money of the estate (or country) and had access to the perquisites of the rank.

There should be no confusion concerning 'Murdoch' being a First name and or a Family name.

This is quite common even up to the present day. Whilst it is unlikely that parents would call a male offspring 'Murdoch

Murdoch', your scribe knows many Murdochs of both styles and is related on my mother's side to a vast army of Murdochs in Ayrshire and Galloway. I think an ancient castle in a Scottish Loch is not worth raiding for a third time in Ayrshire and beyond. Nothing is intentionally meant to suggest in this note that both Murdoch Stewarts (1 and 2) were related in any way. Both held the honorific, Duke of Albany, But nearly 40 years apart. They are not the same person although the second Murdoch admirer was probably named after the first which happens in families but there is no blood relation.

At this stage in the narrative, Murdoch's story is taken over by your scribe as from 1307 until his death in 1326. He was unmarried and died aged 29. during the nine years that he was the Duke of Albany on trial, He was a party to the establishment of the Scottish Nation from the event of King Robert's official coronation at Scone near Perth in 1307 with due pomp and ceremony supported by the clergy and loyal lords. The traditional Scottish coronation robes and paraphernalia had been secreted away by Bruce supporters in Glasgow and were available and used for the occasion. The only item missing was the Pope's unction as Bruce was still under excommunication for the murder of John Cormyn.

Whilst Murdoch (1) Duke of Albany was alive, he lived either at Dundonald Castle or Loch Doon Castle. He would have lost daily contact with his Sovereign but would doubtless have had a hand in preparing King Robert I for his First Parliament in 1309. It is speculated that he would have been a useful Ambassador to Norway given his Norwegian ancestry, but this is unknown. It may well be a fact that after the creation of the Dukedom, Murdoch (1) had very little to do as he was left behind as the King's action moved away towards Scone and communications were very rudimentary.

In today's (2024) limited state of the duties of Royalty the function of Albany would naturally fall to the government in parliament. With the initial responsibilities remaining the same as when conceived, the Duke of Albany's role would now be a Cabinet position and raises several questions.

A limited conduit between government and the people with certain attention to the Prime Minister outwith the usual red-tape channel or *'slow walking'* as it is now called, would surely be an attractive functionality that could be a useful political mechanism. ***Minister of Public Access?***

Given, however, the job description has been removed from the title which is now only a sinecure of the ruling King or Queen to favour a close member of the family, some totally fresh thinking will be required to resurrect such a potent management tool. One can readily understand how there would be a great deal of caution in bringing about such an obvious and hazardous public relations tool.

Perhaps, one day Murdoch would have exercised his duties at Court. Then there would be plenty of company and as a Royal Duke, he would have had an adequate position to hobnob with the good and the great.

But with all the jealousy and strife among the courtiers and all their political ideas he would be swamped with in-house activities to the loss of universal access which is so necessary. As someone said (l think it was Scott whom you all know) being good looking and the King's stepbrother he would probably have raised resentment by his very presence.

Anyway, his lordship did a lot of writing and correcting my contributions as scribe to this book's chapters. One of Lord Murdoch's enthusiasms was old Scottish poetry, ballads, and sagas. I have collected a few notes to add to this chapter which might give you a flavour of this very old branch of literature coming to us from the middle and dark ages.

When at Dundonald, Albany's middleman duties expanded from one or two a week at the beginning to three or four petitioners every day. Problems that the supplicants brought in the belief that only the King could solve the issue range from the very personal such as encroachment on an individual's land by a neighbour to the application of a title inheritance brought by an illegitimate offspring of a randy old earl who had sown his oats far and wide.

Petitions came from all classes ranging from the humble serf looking for a return of his errant wife with a King's order, to wild and bombastic declarations from a member of the gentry who grandly disclosed the strength of his position and doubted that the King would rule otherwise. Most petitioners came personally to him but there also were some letters delivered that sought the King's ruling on more complicated issues of business or ownership. These latter items came from further away where it was not always feasible to make a personal appeal owing to the distance involved. Interestingly, one of the faraway petitioner's problems was about his right to travel whenever the supplicant desired which was opposed by his overlord.

Any Subject whose cause was unresolved in the course of first inspection, had to be reviewed by Albany again in six months time. On no account had 'false promises' ever to be given.

HIS LORDSHIP'S FINAL WORDS;

I love the lonely splendour that is Loch Doon. The loch lies in the north-east edge of the great Merrick Upland. I was brought up somewhat south of this loch but on the banks of another loch, not nearly as large as Doon called Loch Dee where my mother and two other brothers reside at the freehold land of Craigencallie. The family property lies south of Loch Dee and stretches further south towards Minigaff. It is divided among the three sons of Craigencallie from north to south, Sir Mackie, Sir Maclurg and me, the Duke of Albany (Lord Murdoch).

My brothers like me are not often at home as they have trained for a military career and are available for various government missions. My grand uncle is the retired factor of Berbeth Estate but is the honorary Steward and lives at Dalpharson Lodge as a *'grace and favour'* tenant during his lifetime.

The Loch Doon Castle on its island off the western shore of the loch has been ravaged by English soldiers since I was last here, but the damage has been partially restored except for the lowest section which was the boat harbour. The boats are long gone and there is no sign of the extensive boatbuilding that we developed. There is an eerie and desolate appearance to this sector of the castle which was once full of labouring men with bustling and noise. The residential apartments have been restored to a spartan degree which pleases me although I miss the extensive library that used to be a part of the Laird's quarters.

The King's Law is the basis of all law in Scotland. There is no other. It has been formed as including the interrelationship among the King, the Church, the laity or people, and the Barons. All sides have ancient laws and privileges to which they refer as proof of their position. There will be a Grand Charter discussion with all relevant parties to work out any differences with a view to inclusion in the living Scottish Regulations that will be turned into immutable law to which, lead by the King, all shall give respect. The King and Barons must recognise the rising Middle Class who have contributed greatly to the improving economy of Scotland.

The following nuggets are samplings of things I have learned in the six years I have had the honour of managing access to the King:

- There is a need for the Monarchy to be regarded by its citizenry with reverence, obedience, and loyalty and for the Crown to be seen as the servant and not the master of the state. Whenever the Monarch may lose the reverence of the people it is the responsibility of the King and his Council to recognize that that loss may lead to further losses or widespread disobedience and above all, to the loss of **prestige**.

- The King has a responsibility to His people to rule without individual favour or being observed to disregard his own and his Country's Promulgated and Common Laws. Creating laws to cover reverence, obedience, loyalty, and prestige to the Crown cannot be legislated for or against, therefore, these attributes must be earned and once earned, not needlessly disregarded

- *Prestige constitutes vital capital in international affairs and the fear of losing it has always been an authentic one.*

- The way that capitalism, when allied to the right to own secure property, and the rule of law, have unleashed the energy and ingenuity of Mankind that has been remarkable and forms the basis for the English-speaking peoples' global hegemony. So long as they retain the technological edge in the military field and the **PRESTIGE** that goes with it The only way they can be replaced as the world-hegemon is through another great power adopting an even more effective form of capitalism.

- The first law of ruling: *"No good deed goes unpunished."* Therefore, it is wise to attend to the small problems first since the larger problems usually take care of themselves or develop into a host of small problems in time.

***"Render unto Caesar the things that are Caesar's
And unto God the things that are God's."***

- Provided the national community obey all laws there will be a loyal nobility, a dutiful gentry and an honesty of all. Should this agreeable situation fester then the community might disregard all laws
- There was a general impression that the only people to trust were a man's brother, his wife's brother, or his son (But not his heir or 'second son!)
- If the King should be curbed in any way then so should the Barons. Common interest should be respected and the Middle Class should be recognized as they had done so much to enrich the the King, the barons and, the country
- A development beyond feudalism is the growth of knightly and bourgeois classes.
- Bannockburn: It is the nature of supreme executive power to withdraw itself into the smallest compass and without such contraction there is no executive power.
- For all Scots whether Lowland or Highland, the royal house has a sanctity which commanded reverence through periods when obedience and loyalty were lacking, and much was excused those in whom royal blood ran. But **reverence** is not an effective instrument of government or religion.
- The Scottish peasant farmer and the thrifty burgesses throughout these 200 years of political strife pursued their traditional ways and built up the country's real strength in spite of the numerous disputes among their lords and masters.
- The long bow handled by a well-trained archer class brought into the battlefield a yeoman type of soldier

with whom there was nothing on the Continent to compare. Arrows were the weapon of choice before gunpowder came on the scene. It is said that Welshmen from the Marches were the finest archers in the known world at this time.

- One of the main functions of the representatives of the shires and boroughs was to petition for the redress of grievances, local and national, and to draw the attention of the king and his council to urgent matters. The Duke of Albany was designated as *the ombudsman. (to use a 20th century word)*

CHAPTER XVII

SIGNIFICANT TREATIES DURING THE 14TH CENTURY

1312: Treaty of Inverness

The treaty between Scotland and Norway that ended all Norwegian interests over the Scottish Western Isles and the Isle of Man (in the Irish Sea) and promotes Scottish maritime interests and control of maritime trade routes.

1320: Declaration of Arbroath,"

"For as long as but a hundred of us remain alive, never will we on any conditions be brought under English rule, it is in truth not for glory, not for riches nor honors that we are fighting but for freedom -for that alone, which no honest man gives up but with life itself."

<u>1328: Treaty of Edinburgh-Northampton;</u>

- ✓ England recognises Scotland as a free and independent Kingdom;
- ✓ Marriage between King David II and Joan (English King's sister);
- ✓ Scottish and French alliance to continue;
- ✓ Non-Intervention in Ireland.

[In May 1328, the 'Shameful' treaty of Northampton recognized Bruce as king north of the Tweed and implied the abandonment of all the claims of Edward I in Scotland. Edward, the son of John Baliol the nominee of Edward I had become a refugee at the English court.]

CHAPTER XVIII

'SCOTTISH' POEMS, BALLADS, SAGAS, AND 'BALLAD POETRY'.

We conclude the main story to give some thought to the Songs and Ballads in Scottish History from the book by William Gunnyon published by Hamilton Adams in London and Menzies and Company in Edinburgh in 1897. All rights were reserved and permission was granted to publish a review of the book in as much as there was reference to the 13th. And 14th' Centuries. Most of the quotations from the book are anachronistic to the contents of the Murdoch story but refer, more or less, to the epoch.

Many poetic lines come down to us from the times of '*The Bruce*' and the '*Gude Wallace*' which are often satirical in nature. The butt of the satire is usually England and England's Kings, the Plantagenet Edwards. For example: David, son of the Bruce married Princess Joan, a daughter of King Edward I, himself lampooned as '*Edward Longshanks*'. Joan was called in popular Scottish songs as '*Joan Makepeace*' for the obvious reason that the marriage was anticipated to bring to an end the enmity between Scotland and England which it did.

"It is to be inferred that these songs were for the most part of lowly origin-the expression of overpowering passion inspired in a rustic bosom by the charms of some Hebe of the farm or fold or the embodiment in humorous pathetic exuhant or wailing strains of an incident, personal or national that had struck the fancy or the heart of some untaught bard."

Surprisingly, it was the ladies of the court and castle that kept these songs alive, the more malicious and references to '*rumbelowe*' the better*!*

> *'Young women when they will play,*
> *Sing it among them ilk o day.'*
> *'With hey and how, rumbelow,*
> *The young folks were full and bold'*

"The remains of ancient song are extremely scanty but what beyond question the early prevalence of song in Scotland and the popular delight in it"

"After the Restoration, the songs of Scotland became so popular that they were manufactured in England and afterwards accepted in Scotland as genuine."

"The situation is similar to Scottish song in that Scottish Ballads were likewise constructed in England and passed off as the genuine article These spurious ballads, often referred to as 'ballad poetry' attained a high degree of excellence among the educated class in that they seem to follow the examples of Livy and his history of an early Rome and of Macaulay in his *'Lays of Ancient Rome.'* In fact, taking into consideration Sir Walter Scott and Robert Burns we are quite familiar with this type of artistic expression right down to the present day."

"But there were others which had come to be regarded with peculiar pride and affection and were pointed to as proofs that Scotland had a tradition ballad lore not only rivaling but in many respects transcending that of any other nationality'. The only problem with this was its non-Scottish origin. This 'artificial school of rhymesters' was sympathetic to and knowledgeable in Scottish history and its bloody past and there were adequate fragments of genuine Scottish ballads to draw style, language and spelling from which to seek inspiration within an English heart. One example should suffice:

"In 1719 there appeared in a folio sheet in Edinburgh a heroic poem styled 'Hardyknute' written in affectedly old spelling as if it had been a contemporary description of events connected with the invasion of Scotland by Haco, King of Norway in 1263" (Battle of Largs). Later, it was admitted that Hardyknute's saga had been penned by an English lady who was alive in 1719 and did not die until 1727, four-hundred years later than the battle in the story that was passed off as contemporaneous.

So even as some Scottish songs and ballads were or may have been written elsewhere, the history depicted in them can be taken as based on truth leavened by the passage of time and possibly more accurate than contemporary reports."

As an example of what King Robert I faced after his coronation it is informative to note that the Lord of the Isles had taken a long time in recognising Irish or Dalriadian people who had moved into his territory as Scottish for as far as he was concerned, he was the King of Scotland despite anything that supported King Robert Bruce who had broader claims on the whole of Scotland and was gradually encroaching on his Western Islands kingdom. In fact, as the Lord of the Isles, King Donald's pride and power enabled him to proceed as a feudal king and to have feudatories under him despite the widely divergent code of law or rather of custom between Celt and Viking (the previous administration) which he called Teutons.

Confirmation of Murdoch, however, is enshrouded in the ballad that refers to several battles between the 'Lord of the Isles and Robert I as supremacy was challenged. In one ballad, our hero Murdoch's two brothers collectively called 'the Knights of Panmure':

> *"The Knights of Panmure as was seen,*
> *Were mortal men in armour bright.*
> *Sir Thomas Murray stout and keen;*
> *Left to the world their last good-night."*

We assume that Kie and Lurg who were not 'knights' when we last saw them at Craigencallie, were not the knights the ballad was identifying but perhaps their offspring who might reasonably identify themselves as 'Panmure' to indicate that they should be identified as a group and not singly. In any case, their 'last goodnight' would seem to be the end of these original gifts from King Robert. No doubt the inheritance rules played an important step in their disposal. Murdoch of course, was elsewhere when the battle in the ballad was recorded.

An important distinction is highlighted in the book and is explained thus:

"God has made of one blood all the nations of men for to dwell upon the face of the earth"

This is a quotation from the Bible that is very powerful.

"But however bitter the strife may be between nationalities, that between races is infinitely more so."

The Saxon solidity have been super added to the Celtic grace and self-respect; the Norman and Northmen have settled with the 'savage' Scots; and all the people of Great Britain are the better for it.

It should be noted that the Scot is a martial and not a military person, having no delight in the pomp and circumstance of glorious war. The Scottish motto if there is one is "Defence; not Offence" and although many wild and undisciplined warlike forays have been recorded throughout history, it is *Bruce* and *Albany* not the Scots who are looking for annexing a territory and abiding there. A Scot will fight and fight hard in a manner that brings fear and respect to Scottish regiments. It has been recorded that the Scottish mercenaries attached to the French Army were more ferocious than their paymasters. This would seem to reflect payment for the job well done rather than patriotism for pay.

"The Scottish Guard of French Kings were the foremost individual soldiers in superiority. The Scottish battalions that fought with great Gustavus **"found no Continental superior"** But the Scots were credited with having something dangerous in their blood that might impel them to the greatest and most unexpected atrocities. This was the general feeling of other forces who would oppose them.

Wallace is said have a military style that was cramped and easily thwarted while Bruce's military capacity was pre-eminent and his action un-controlled, his troops had to be highly disciplined and wisely handled whereby they performed wonders. Scottish troops could be difficult to handle:

"They ne'er saw a horse but they made it their ain."

In short, an internecine battle in Scotland might be a bloodbath. It was the Highland Scots who had the fiercest reputation which the Lowlanders feared most. Racial antagonism.

SCOTTISH SAGA:

There was not, sin' King Kenneth's days,
Sic strange intestine cruel strife
In Scotlande seen, as ilk man says,
Where monie likelie lost their life;

Whilk made divorce tween man and wife,
And monie children fatherless,
Whilk in this realm has been full rife;
Lord help these lands! our wrangs redress!
In July, on Saint James his evin,
That four-and-twenty dismal day,
Twelve hundred, ten score, and eleven
Of years sin' Christ, the soothe to say;
Men will remember, as they may,
When thus the veritie they knaw;
And monie a ane will mourne for aye
The brim battle of the Harlaw.goes unpunished'

17/18th CENTURY SCOTTISH POETRY:

The following stirring poetry fragment is not the Scottish National Anthem but some say it should be.

The Robert Burns' poem that follows refers to the Scottish King's exhortation of his troops on the eve of battle with the English at Bannockburn (1314). Robert Burns, (1759-1796) born at Alloway in Ayrshire. He was a Scottish patriot.

Robert Burns is revered as Scotland's National Poet.

'Scots, wha hae wi' Wallace bled
Scots, wham Bruce has aften led,
Welcome to your gory bed
Or to Victorie!

"Now's the day, and now's the hour:
See the front o' battle lour,

See approach proud Edward's power-
Chains and slaverie!".

Burns clearly was in his patriotic style while the following extract from **Scott** was in a romantic mood - both moods essentially Scottish.

Then, there was the romantic narrative ballad by Sir Walter Scott (1771-1832) who wrote of 'Young Lochinvar' a Scottish Border knight whose dramatic actions were the very epitome of knightly valour in the wooing of his 'fair Ellen' despite her father's and her mother's disapproval until…

"O young Lochinvar is come out of the west
Through all the wide Border his steed was the best
And save his good broadsword, he weapons had none,
He rode all unarm'd and he rode all alone.

"So faithful in love, and so dauntless in war,
There never was knight like the young Lochinvar"

When he and the fair Ellen escaped…

"She is won!
We are gone over bank, bush, and scaur;
They'll have fleet steeds that follow:
quoth young Lochinvar."

And finally, a word from a Scottish Observer, Andrew Fletcher (1655-1716) who was opposed to the Union of the English and the Scottish parliaments in 1703.

"I knew a very wise man who believed that… **_if a man were permitted to make all the ballads, he need not care who should make the laws of a nation._** *And we would find that most of the ancient legislators thought they could not well reform the manners of any city without the help of a lyric and sometimes of a dramatic poet."*

Here we have the Celtic romantic inclination. And even with a dash of Viking aggression the result was a bold and dramatic rhyme rather than a worldwide 'Scottish Empire' but an English hegemony under the new name of the British Empire.

*It will be noticed that the style and lexicon have changed over the 13th to 17th centuries but it should be noted that by the latter part of the 17th century, the authors were assisted by editors and publishers who often restrained writing in the vernacular Scots in favour of the British standard style and spelling. Scott and Burns would write fluently in both forms but the standard of literature for the middle and educated classes had become the same in all of Britain **and in many other parts of the world.*** But in the English Language.

Unfortunately for Scotland, Wales and Ireland, the use of the phrase 'British Empire' and the 'British People' somehow became the 'English Empire' and the 'English People' in foreign lands, and for that confusion we must blame the world-wide use of the English Language.

English is the language of diplomacy, commerce, transport, science, education, entertainment and a host of many international means of communication, and it has become the major language of our time. But then so was Latin in its day and we must not forget Spanish is spoken and understood by so many people.

Since this book has been about Scotland, her people and her language within the diaspora of the Anglo-Saxon language, the Scottish people, must, nevertheless, take some ownership of the *Lingua Franca* that does not bear her name but significantly has been moulded and shaped by the important Scottish contribution to its growth and usage.

Perhaps, we should use the words that describe 'Britishness' a bit more and let 'Englishness' line up for attention along with the rest of the world seeking just recognition. What is wrong or parochial about Anglo-American, or Anglo-anything when what is obviously meant is British-American or British-Anything? We of the Celtic Line (and its dilution by the hundreds of its collateral streams) would like to see some recognition before, in turn, England and English slip away to be subsumed by the latest future hegemony. This final paragraph will conclude the book. with this amendment. But within the British Language that. Winston **Churchill** paid much attention to, as the key to the survival of our World being dependent upon the "English Speaking Peoples" by which he meant the Anglo-American Special Relationship, he was revealing the prejudice of his class when what he really meant to say was the 'British-American Special Relationship'?

Churchill takes six volumes of magnificent readable prose to posit the theory that the world will depend absolutely on its survival by speakers of the English/British language, I feel that his enthusiasm for an English language-based world sustained by one particular language alone may, unfortunately be all that is going to remain (like Latin in High Schools and churches) and that all who speak with the same English (British) tongue are destined to find themselves in the back seats as the world moves on.

Churchill's Books: *"A History of the English-Speaking Peoples"* and its follow up: *"History of the English-Speaking Peoples Since 1900"* by **Andrew Roberts**, should be required reading. As my own high school's motto enjoined: *'Respice Prospice'* We can but take that instruction "Look Back-Look Forward!" whether in Latin, English, British, Anglo-American or British-American, the phrase demands careful consideration. It is comforting to think that things will never change but somehow in these turbulent times such positive thinking needs more reinforcement than a platitude.

Was it ever thus?

THE END